CASTLE EPPSTEIN

CASTLE EPPSTEIN

Alexandre Dumas

Translated from the French by
NORMA LORRE GOODRICH

FRANKLIN WATTS
New York • Toronto
1989

Library of Congress Cataloging-in-Publication Data

Dumas, Alexandre, 1802-1870.
    Castle Eppstein.

    Translation of: Le Château d'Eppstein.
    I. Title.
PQ2225.C46E5   1989   843'.7   88-36267
ISBN 0-531-15102-6

Contents

Afterword

Alexandre Dumas

Castle Eppstein and Gothic Fiction

VOLUME
I

Introduction

It happened during one of those prolonged and delightful evening parties we attended in the winter of 1841 at the palace of Princess Galitzin in Florence. By general consent, during the course of the evening, each guest would tell a story. His story was supposed to be imaginary, however, and each person had already told one, except Count Elim.

Count Elim was a tall, handsome young man, blond, slender, and pale, but of a melancholy temperament characterized by bursts of crazy laughter that came over him like hot blushes and passed off just as fast. Several times already the conversation had sounded him out; every time the question of ghosts had come up and we asked for his opinion, he had replied with such a positive tone of voice that nobody could doubt him:

"I believe in them."

Why did he believe in them? Nobody ever asked him; but when it comes to a question like that, either you believe or you don't, and any one of us would be really hard put to give a solid reason for belief or disbelief.

Certainly Hoffmann believed in the reality of his characters; he had seen Master Floh and had known Coppelius.*

So much so that when Count Elim was asked about the

---

*Master Floh (Flea) and Coppelius are characters in the *Tales* of Hoffmann. E.T.A. Hoffmann (1776–1882) invented the modern tale, one of his most famous being *The Sandman* (1817), in which the evil alchemist Coppelius appears. The heroine turns out to be a mechanical doll with glass eyes. After her maddened lover sees her sprawl broken on the floor, he commits suicide. The story of a girl being a mere doll was transformed by Délibes into the ballet *Coppélia* (1870).

wildest tales of phantoms, manifestations, and ghosts and told us, "I believe in them," no one doubted but that he truly believed.

When Count Elim's turn came to tell a story, everybody naturally looked at him with great curiosity, already determined in the event that he refused to honor his debt to insist he do so and convinced that the story he would tell would have that degree of realism that makes such an account so spellbinding; but our last narrator did not even make us beg him to begin, and the Princess had hardly invited him to abide by his promise when he bowed in token of his assent but begged our pardon for telling us about an adventure *that had really happened to him personally.*

As you will easily understand, this preamble only added to our desire to hear his story, and as we fell silent, he began abruptly:

"Three years ago I was traveling in Germany; I had letters of introduction to a wealthy businessman in Frankfort who owned a very fine domain in that area and, knowing I was a great sportsman, invited me to hunt with him (I should say he himself detested that sport), or rather with his oldest son, whose tastes were rather different from those of the father.

"On the appointed day we assembled at the rendezvous, which was one of the city gates; there horses and carriages awaited us; we each either took a seat in the buckboard or mounted up, and we all set off in high spirits.

"After riding for an hour and a half, we arrived at the farm on our host's estate; there a lavish luncheon awaited us, and I had to admit that if our host was not a sportsman himself, he knew admirably well how to serve up the game from his lands.

"We were eight in all: our host's son, his university tutor, five friends, and myself. I found myself placed at table next to the tutor. We talked about our travels, as he had been in Egypt and I had just come from there. This experience set up an instant bond between us, the sort of ties one thinks are lasting at the moment they form but which break one fine morning as one sets off again and are never renewed.

"As we rose from table, we agreed to hunt side by side. He advised me to pivot and fan out toward the Taunus Mountains,* given that hares and partridges tend to escape towards the woods which cover these mountains, so that in this way I would have a chance to bring down not only the game I would raise but also what the others raised, too.

"I followed his advice with so much more warmth since it was after noon when we began to hunt and since in the month of October the days are already short. It is true that we soon saw, from the abundance of wildlife, that we would easily make up for lost time.

"I was not slow to grasp the excellence of the advice my fine professor had given me. Not only did hares and partridges rise up before me minute by minute, but I could see, moreover, minute by minute whole companies of them scattering into the woods ahead of my fellow sportsmen. I easily picked them off from the underbrush; and the upshot was that after two hours of hunting, as I had an excellent retriever, I decided to push on deeper up into the mountain, telling myself that I would keep to the higher ground so as not to lose sight of my fellows.

"But it is especially for hunters that the proverb was coined: 'Man proposes and God disposes.' For some time, as a matter of fact, I did keep the lowlands in sight. But then a flock of red partridges took flight towards the valley; they were the first reds I had seen that day.

"But two shots brought down two: eager as the hunter in La Fontaine,* I took off in pursuit. . . .

*The Taunus Mountains, near the Rhineland Castles, are just north of Frankfort, and Wiesbaden, and rise to a height of 880 meters, approximately 3,000 feet.
*The reference is to Fable (III, XXVII), "The Wolf and the Hunter" of Jean de La Fontaine (1621–95), where, after three kills, the hunter is himself killed.

"Excuse me," Count Elim said to our ladies as he inter-rupted his narrative. "Excuse all these details concerning venery; they are necessary in order for me to explain how I came to be isolated from the hunting party and the strange adventure which I experienced as the result."

Each listener assured Count Elim that she was following the story with the greatest of interest, and so our narrator continued:

"Furiously I followed my flock of partridges, which, from one covert to another, from slope to slope and valley to valley, ended by drawing me deeper and deeper onto the mountain. I had expended such passion tracking them along that I had failed to notice the clouds that by that time had obscured the sky or to see that a thunderstorm was about to strike; a rumble of thunder drew me away from my false sense of security. I gazed around me in a circle; there I was at the bottom of a valley, in the middle of a small clearing which allowed a view on all sides of wooded sum-mits; up on the plateau of one peak I could make out the ruins of an old castle; but there was not the trace of a road! I had come out there, hunting as I went, consequently through thorns and briars; if I wanted a road cut through the trees, I would have to search for one, but where? I had no idea.

"Meanwhile, the sky grew darker and darker; the thunder roared about me faster and faster, at shorter and shorter intervals; and a few large raindrops fell noisily upon the yellow leaves which each gust of wind swirled up by the hundreds like flights of birds leaving a tree all of a sudden.

"I had no time to lose: I took my bearings as well as I could under the circumstances, and when I felt that I had a good grasp of my position, I walked straight ahead, re-solved not to stray from a straight line. Surely after a dis-tance of one or two kilometers I would end up finding some path, some road, and this path, this road, would of necessity lead me somewhere. Moreover, I had nothing to fear in these mountains, neither from animals nor from men; nothing around but fearful wild creatures or some poor peasants, that's all. The worst misfortune which could befall me would be to have to sleep the night under a tree, which would have been no hardship at all if the sky was not taking on minute by minute a more and more threatening color. Therefore, I resolved to make an effort to reach some sort of a refuge, and I redoubled my pace.

"Unfortunately, I was walking, as I have said, along a swath cut up and down the slope of the mountain; as a result, I kept being stopped by obstacles I had to climb over. Sometimes it was the regrowth which squeezed me out and even made my dog himself sink back on his haunches; sometimes it was one of these tangles of uprooted trees which occur so commonly in high mountainous terrain and which forced me into a long detour. Then, for the height of misery, darkness was dropping fast down the sky, and the rain began to fall in amounts that would disturb anybody who has not the slightest idea of what shelter awaits him. Add to that the fact that our host's luncheon began to be rather long ago and that the exercise I had taken since six had astonishingly speeded up my digestion.

"However, as I continued up it, the swath widened and became more like a cleared woodland. I was walking, therefore, with greater ease; and yet, according to my calculations, I probably had deviated, because of the circles and detours I had been obliged to make, from the straight line I had projected. All that worried me not a little, just the same. As I advanced, the woodland took on a more grandiose appearance as it became a real forest. I stepped on into the darker depths and found, hardly more than a kilometer ahead of me, just as I had anticipated, a forest path.

"Now, as to this path, in which direction should I follow it? Was it to the right? Was it to the left? To this question nothing appeared to give me an answer; I therefore had to leave it to chance. I went to the right, or rather, I followed my dog, who chose that direction.

"If I had been then in the shelter of some shed, inside some cave, in some ruined structure, I would have marveled at the magnificent spectacle unfolding before me. The flashes of lightning followed each other without interruption, lighting up the whole forest in the most fantastic explosions imaginable. The thunder growled in redoubled bellowing that rose from one extremity of the valley, which it seemed to follow as it dwindled off into the other end; then, from time to time, great blasts of wind swept over the treetops, bending the massive beeches, the gigantic spruces, the centenary oaks, as the breezes of May bend the sheaths of wheat. However, their resistance was powerful, the struggle was vigorous, and the trees did not bend without a groan. To the hurricane's anger as it whipped the forest with wind, rain, and lightning, the forest answered in sad and solemn moans, as if it were an unfortunate man whom adversity pursues unjustly.

"But I was myself too directly involved in this grand cataclysm, feeling its assault too much to notice all its poetry. Water now fell in torrents until not a thread in my clothing but was soaked, and meanwhile, I grew more and more hungry. As for my path, which obstinately I kept following, I sensed that it was widening and that it looked more used. It was therefore evident that it would lead me to some sort of a dwelling.

"And actually, after another half hour of walking in the midst of this horrible, natural disaster, I caught a glimpse, once when the lightning flashed, of a little thatched cottage to which the path I followed led directly and where it came to an end. I quickened my steps, forgetting that very instant how tired I was at the thought of the hospitality hopefully awaiting me. A few seconds later, there I was face-to-face with this refuge I so much desired. But, to my great disappointment, I could not see even a flicker of light. Although it was not yet late enough for the residents of the little cottage to be in bed, both doors and window shutters were as if hermetically sealed and seemed to me to reflect such desolation from within that I sensed it from without. As far as the rest of the house was concerned, that is, the area around the cottage, aside from such damage as the thunderstorm had caused, I could easily recognize the day-by-day attention of some caretaker. There was a vine, that had already lost a good bit of its leaves, running along a low wall; there were some great pillars of roses where several late blooms still tossed in the wind, adorning the paths of a little garden one entered through a wooden trellis. I knocked on the door despite my conviction that nobody would hear me.

"Truly, the sound of my fingers rapping died away without having roused any movements from within; I called out, but nobody answered.

"I will admit that if there had been any way to enter this little dwelling, even in the absence of the proprietor, I would have employed that way in. But the doors and the shutters appeared not only hermetically but even more solidly sealed than that, and no matter what confidence in German hospitality I might have felt, still I admit that this confidence did not include housebreaking.

"However, one thing consoled me; this was that evidently this little house could not be totally isolated and had to lie in the neighborhood of some village or castle. So I rapped some more, less hard than before, but as a kind of last appeal. When this effort also remained fruitless, I made my decision and moved forward again on my quest.

"After about two or three hundred steps forward, just as I had suspected, I came up against the stone wall surrounding some vast domain. I followed it along, hunting for a wrought-iron portal; a breach in the wall came to hand instead, which spared me the pains of a longer search. I stepped over the crumbling stones of the wall and found myself in a nobleman's demesnial forest.

"These woodlands must once have been, in bygone days, one of these princely promenades such as one still views occasionally inside Germany but such as one will no longer be able to discover inside France fifty years from now. The place was of a magnitude of Chambord, Mortefontaine, or Chantilly; only, as much as the little thatched cottage I had just seen, with its surrounding grounds that I had appraised at a glance seemed to be objects of a particularly meticulous care, to that same degree the lordly woodland appeared desolate, derelict, and overgrown.

"Actually, as clearly as I could judge during occasional rifts in the clouds and infrequent pauses in the downpour, when the moon tried to shine through the gloom and nature struggled for calm, this demesnial forest, which in bygone days had been so splendid, now wore the air of a pitiable wasteland: High bushes had grown up under the timber, and trees, uprooted by the ragings of hurricanes or broken by old age, lay crosswise to the avenues of the promenade, so that I had to peer up through a tangle of branches in order to see where I was walking or had to straddle fallen trunks as stripped and as laid bare as cadavers on the ground. Such an appearance gave me the shudders and warned me of how little chance I had to find the castle inhabited, for towards that castle these somber, littered avenues could hardly fail to lead me.

"However, when I got to a crossroads where of five gateposts four were lying flat on the forest floor, I did catch a quick glimpse of a light that passed, I thought, behind a window and as quickly vanished. Rapid as this other flash of lightning had been, it had sufficed to guide my steps. I stepped off again in the direction of the light, and after about ten minutes or so, I came out of the surrounding woodland ride and saw, across a lawn from me, a black mass which seemed to me to be wrapped around in trees. I presumed this was the castle.

"Going closer, I saw that I had not been mistaken; only, that flicker of light I had seen swift as a shooting star, had totally vanished; more than that, as I drew closer and closer towards the weird foundation, it appeared to me to be utterly uninhabited.

"It was one of those ancient castles which are so common to Germany, upon which architectural conglomeration such as had survived successive remodelings which the necessity of age and the caprices of heirs had had executed was stamped the date of the fourteenth century; but which conglomeration gave remarkably to its massy stones an air of indefinable mournfulness, because for one thing not a one of its ten or twelve windows along its facade showed any glimmer of light. The only thing was that three of these windows were closed off with shutters on the outside; but as one of these shutters was broken halfway up, thus offering to my view a wide window space, I could see that this chamber was no more illuminated than were all the other rooms, considering that if it had been lighted, I would have been able easily to see light shining through such a wide aperture. As for the other windows, they also must once upon a time have been protected by heavy storm blinds, like the three still so provided; but these blinds had by this time either been completely torn off or hung unrepaired, held on by a single hinge, more resembling the broken wing of a bird.

"I walked down the length of this facade, hunting for a way to penetrate into one of the inner courtyards, where I hoped finally to come again across that light in search of which I had set out, and at one of the corners of the pile, between two round towers, I finally found a door which at first appeared to be closed but which, because it lacked both lock and bolt, yielded to the first push I gave it and swung open.

"I crossed the threshold, I plunged under a dark vault, and next finally arrived into an inner precinct overgrown with grasses and thistles, far on the opposite side of which, behind an opaque pane of glass, I saw, as if through a dense fog, that blessed light shining which I had begun to attribute to a figment of my imagination.

"In the glow of lamplight, two old people were warming themselves, a husband and wife, no doubt. I searched for the door; it was beside the window, and since in my anxiety my hand dropped down on the latch so hard, the door flew ajar; the woman screamed. I hastened to calm the fears, which in spite of myself I had caused these good folk.

" 'Have no fear, my good people,' I told them; 'I am a hunter who has lost his way; I am weary, hungry, and thirsty; I shall ask you for a glass of water, a crust of bread, and a bed.'

" 'Pardon my wife's start,' replied the old man as he rose to his feet. 'This castle is so isolated that only an accident could by chance conduct any traveler here; it is therefore not surprising that seeing an armed man appear before her, my poor Bertha should have been somewhat startled, although, God be praised!, we should have nothing to fear from bandits, neither for our part nor for our master's.

" 'In any event, my good friends, be reassured upon that score,' I told them; 'I am Count Elim M. You are not acquainted with me, I know that; but you should not be unacquainted with M. de R. . . . , to whom I have been recommended at Frankfort and with whose hunting party I was riding when, as occasioned by a flight of red partridges, I lost my way in the Taunus Mountains.'

" 'Oh! Sir,' the man replied again while his wife continued to gaze inquiringly at me, 'we are no longer acquainted with anybody in town, considering that pretty close to twenty years, I believe, have passed since my wife and I have set foot there; but we have need of no more information than what you give us. You are hungry, thirsty, and you need your rest; we are going to prepare a supper for you. As far as a bed is concerned' (and here the two oldsters exchanged a glance), 'that will perhaps be a little more difficult, but, well, we shall see.'

" 'Merely a portion of your supper, my friends, and an armchair in a corner of the castle, that's all I ask of you.'

" 'Let us set about it, sir,' replied the woman; 'dry yourself and get warm. By that time we will have arranged things as best we can.'

"Her recommendation that I dry myself off and warm myself was not inappropriate; I was wet straight through to the bone, so much so that my teeth chattered from the cold; my dog, in addition, set me a good example, for he had already lain down right across the hearth, enduring a degree of heat sufficient to have roasted the game he had worn himself out pursuing.

"As I presumed that their larder was only modestly provisioned and that, according to all probability, the supper of these fine folks was probably limited to the stew simmering at the front of the fireplace and to the kettle which sang on the hot plate, I put my game pouch at their disposition.

" 'My word,' the husband said as he chose a few partridges and a hare, 'these couldn't come at a better time, sir, for you would have been reduced to sharing our meager supper so that, considering the hunger you told us about, that would otherwise have caused us no little embarrassment.'

"No sooner had the husband and wife exchanged a few whispered words between them than she began to pluck the partridges and to gut the hare, and he left the room.

"Ten minutes more or less went by during which, by

turning myself around this way and that before the fire, I began to dry out. However, when the husband reentered the room, I was still steaming from foot to head.

" 'Sir,' he said to me, 'if you will be so kind as to pass into the dining room, there is a great fire blazing there, and you will be much more comfortable there than here. We will serve you there shortly.'

"I scolded him for the trouble he had taken on my behalf, telling him that I was marvelously comfortable right where I was and that I should have been delighted to have supped at the same table as they themselves. But to this he replied, as he bowed to me, that he knew perfectly well what he owed to a nobleman to accept such an honor. Then, as he still stood at the doorway, hat in hand, I rose from my seat and signed to him that I was ready to pass into the apartments which he had prepared for my entertainment. He preceded me, and I followed. My dog let out a loud groan, struggled to hoist himself up on his four paws, and followed me in his turn.

"I desired most of all to approach as soon as possible the equal of the warm fire I had just deserted, so that I hardly noticed the halls and chambers which we crossed on our way; and yet my impression was that all these lay apparently in a state of total dilapidation.

"A door opened; I saw an immense fire lit inside a hearth of gigantic size; I virtually threw myself up towards the blaze; but notwithstanding all the speed I put forth in getting closer, and thanks to his four legs, which had recovered all their spring, my dog Fido captured a spot ahead of his master.

"Heat was my prime concern. But hardly had I set myself down before the fireplace than my eyes darted towards the table that had been laid for me. It had been covered with one of those superb linen tablecloths that are imported from Hungary and set with a superb china service.

"Such an unexpected magnificence aroused my curiosity.

I rose to examine the place settings and the plates; all that represented the finest workmanship at an unbelievable cost. Each piece was engraved with the proprietor's coat of arms, surmounted with the golden crown signifying the title of Count.

"I was still deep in my investigation when the door was again opened, permitting the entry of a servant formally attired in the most elegant livery, carrying the soup course in a silver tureen worked similarly to the rest of the table service.

"Raising my eyes from the tureen to its bearer, I recognized the same old man who had received me into the castle.

" 'But my friend,' I said to him, 'I must repeat, you treat me with far too much ceremony; and truly, you will rob me of all my pleasure in your hospitality because of all the pains you are taking on my account.'

" 'We are only too aware of the respect we owe to a visiting Count,' the old man repeated with a low bow to me, and he set the tureen upon the table, 'not to receive him as suitable as it is in our power to do. Moreover, were it to be otherwise, Count Everard would not forgive me.'

"I had to let him do as he pleased. I was going to sit down on a nearby chair, but my strange majordomo drew up for me a grand armchair, which was that of the master himself. The chair back was carved with the same cognizance and the same coat of arms as those I had already observed on the table service, which, just like them, were also surmounted by the crown of a Count.

"I took the place he had drawn up for me. As I have said, I was dying of hunger, so that all I could do at first was gulp my food. And to tell you the truth, everything that was dished out for me, even and including the share of supper I gobbled away from the two servants, was excellent; the wine especially was from the best vineyards in Bordeaux, in Burgundy, and in the Rhineland.

"During this meal the old servant continually apologized for the meager reception he was obliged to offer me.

"In order to divert him from his embarrassment, which so upset him, but out of pure curiosity on my part, too, I asked him who his master was and if he did not reside anymore in some part of this domicile.

" 'My master,' he said, 'is Count Everard von Eppstein, the last of the Counts of this lineage. Not only does he still inhabit this castle, but close to twenty-five years went by during which he never once set foot outside it. The illness of a person for whom he feels a particular affection has called him to Vienna. He left six days ago, and we do not know when he will return.'

" 'But,' I continued, 'what is this little thatched cottage that is so neatly tended, so charming, so garlanded with flowers, which I glimpsed about a kilometer away from here and which makes such a striking contrast to this castle itself?'

" 'That is the real residence of Count Everard,' the old man replied. 'Its former occupants have all died, and since the death of the last one, that is to say, the death of our forester Jonathas, His Highness the Count has reserved it for his personal use. He spends his daytime hours there, not returning to the castle proper until his bedtime. So the poor castle, as you have just observed this evening and as you will see more clearly tomorrow, is fast falling into ruins, so much so that with the exception of the Red Chamber, there remains not a single bedchamber habitable in the entire castle.'

" 'And what is this Red Chamber?'

" 'It is the bedchamber which has inhabited from father to son all the Counts von Eppstein; this is the chamber where each of them was born, from the Countess Eleonore all the way down to Count Maximilian.'

"I noticed that as he articulated these names, the old man lowered his voice and seemed, with a perceptible air of uneasiness, to look about him. However, I said nothing to him about this and made no further request for information. I sat there musing about this poetical and peculiar situation, that of the last living Count von Eppstein living his solitary life inside his ancient castle, which probably some little time after his death would crumble into dust above his tomb.

"I had no sooner finished dining, once my hunger and thirst were appeased, than the immediate necessity of sleep began to weigh upon me. I arose from table therefore and begged the majordomo, who had so well done the honors of the castle, if he would be so kind as to escort me to my room.

"At my request, he seemed again to feel a considerable degree of embarrassment, stammering excuses that were virtually inaudible, but then he seemed to have come to a decision: 'All right, Sir Count,' he said, 'please follow me.'

"I followed him. Fido, who for his part had regaled in the supper as much as his master, before again sprawling out in front of the fire, got to his feet, grumbling, and brought up the rear.

"The old man led me back into the first room, that is to say, into the one I had first entered on my arrival. The cupboard bed there was now made up and covered with fine linen sheets.

" 'But,' I told him, 'this is your room that you are offering me.'

" 'I must ask you to pardon me for doing so, Sir Count,' replied the old man, who misunderstood my protest, 'for in all this castle there is not another single bedroom that is livable.'

" 'Where, then, will you and your wife sleep?'

" 'In the dining room, in the large armchairs.'

" 'I will not allow it!' I cried. 'I am the one who will sleep in one of the armchairs. Keep your bed or assign me another room.'

" 'I have the honor to assure His Highness the Count that there is not, in this entire castle, another chamber that is livable, with the exception of the one—'

" 'With the exception of the one . . . ?' I repeated.

" 'With the exception of the one occupied by Count Everard, of the Red Chamber.'

" 'And you know that it is impossible for His Highness the Count to sleep in that one!' his wife cried sharply.

"I stared at the two of them. They lowered their eyes again with expressions of great embarrassment. Already aroused by everything that had happened to me up to that point, my curiosity once more got the better of me.

" 'And why impossible?' I asked them. 'Has your master forbidden it?'

" 'No, Your Highness.'

" 'If Count Everard were to learn that a stranger slept in his bedchamber, would he as a result reproach you personally for it?'

" 'I believe not.'

" 'Well, then, why this impossibility? And what is there, then, inside this Red Chamber that I hear you speak of it with such terror?'

" 'The fact is, sir . . .'

"He stopped and looked at his wife, who by a shrug of her shoulders seemed to say to him, 'By our Lady, tell him if you want to.'

" 'The fact is . . . ?' I repeated. 'Come on. Speak.'

" 'The fact is that it is *haunted,* Sir Count.'

"I thought I had not caught his meaning, since the old fellow always spoke German to me.

" 'What was that you said, my friend?' I asked him.

" 'The fact is,' his wife told me, 'that ghosts appear in there. And that's a fact.'

" 'Ghosts!' I cried. 'Oh, my God! If that's all it is, my dear fellow, I have always had the greatest desire to see a ghost. In that case, far from finding your excuse of excluding me from the terrible chamber valid, I declare to you that this gives me an even greater desire to spend the night there.'

" 'Let the Count reflect carefully before insisting upon this.'

" 'Oh! All my reflections are quickly made. Moreover, I repeat it for your benefit: I have the greatest desire to find myself in close relationship with a specter.'

" 'That relationship served Count Maximilian very ill,' murmured the old woman.

" 'Count Maximilian may have had his own reasons for fearing the dead; as far as I am concerned, I have none, and I am persuaded that if they came back out of the earth where they lie buried, it is either to protect or to punish. Now, then, it cannot be to punish me that these dead would rise out of the ground, for I cannot recollect having, in all my life, knowingly committed one evil act for which I reproach myself. If, on the contrary, it is to protect me, then I would have no motive for fearing a shade who would come to me with such a charitable intent.'

" 'Oh! it's impossible,' the wife said.

" 'If the gentleman still wills it without reservations,' her husband added.

" 'I absolutely do not will it,' I said, 'for I have no right to assert my will in this place. If I had that right, I would enforce it, believe me. However, not having it, I can only request your assent.'

" 'Well?' the wife said.

" 'Well, let us do as His Highness desires. You know what our Count always says: "The host is the master of the master." '

" 'I agree,' the wife told her husband; 'but on one condition, which is that you will come up to make the bed with me. For all the gold in the world, I would not go in there alone.'

" 'Of course, her husband assured her. 'His Highness will wait here or in the dining room until we have finished.'

" 'Go, my friends, and I will wait.'

"The two aged servants took a candle apiece and left the room, the husband walking first and his wife close after him. I stayed there pensively beside the hearth.

"A thousand times in my youth I had heard tell of such adventures which befell lost travelers in oldtime castles, and I had always smiled at such improbable accounts, which I always considered pure fantasy; so I was absolutely astounded to be upon the threshold of becoming in my turn the hero of a similar story. I ran my fingers along my body to see if I was not asleep and dreaming. I looked all around me to assure myself that it was really me in this extraordinary situation. I even stepped outside to convince myself that I actually was there inside this ancient castle, the same pile of stone whose dark and massive cadaver I had glimpsed off and on through the dark of the night. The sky overhead by that time had cleared, so that the moonlight silvered the cornices along the rooftops. All was dead still—everything seemed dead, in fact—and the silence of the night was broken only by the sharp cry of a screech owl hidden in the limbs of a tree which I could just make out as a black shape in one angle of the courtyard.

"I really was there in one of these castles shrouded in ages-old traditions and wonderful legends. And certainly, if the promised apparition passed me by, the phantom would not be putting all his heart into his act that night. The castle where Wilhelm led Lenore* bore no less fantastic an air than the one where I was about to spend the night.

"Perfectly convinced that I was not dreaming but that I walked in full command of my faculties, I stepped back into the old persons' room; the wife had already returned there, so anxious was she to perform her duties, but her husband had remained behind her to light the fire.

"Suddenly, a bell rang. I jumped despite myself.

*In the macabre German folk ballad of G. A. Bürger (1744), the dead soldier returns to abduct his beloved Lenore. They are wed in a graveyard.

" 'What's that?' I asked her.

"Oh! that's nothing,' the woman told me. 'It's just my husband ringing to notify me that everything is ready. I will escort the gentleman to the bottom of the staircase, and my husband will be waiting at the top.'

" 'Let's go, then,' I urged her, 'for I am in a hurry, I confess, to view your infamous Red Chamber.'

"The good woman lighted a candle and led the way. I followed her, and Fido, who understood nothing about all these peregrinations, for the third time left his warm fire and accompanied us both. Just in case, I took my gun.

"We followed the same hallway through which we had already passed to go to the dining room. Only, instead of turning toward the left, now we bore to the right and found ourselves then near one of these gigantic balustraded stone staircases such as one no longer sees in France except in royal castles or public monuments. At the top of this staircase the old servant waited.

"I climbed the wide steps, which seemed to have been chiseled out for giants; then, in his turn, the old fellow served as my guide, and we arrived at last at the infamous Red Chamber. I followed him inside.

"A bright fire burned in the fireplace—two candelabra with three branches each had been lighted and placed on the mantelpiece—but nevertheless, I still could not clearly see or estimate the vast dimensions of the chamber.

"The oldster asked me if I needed anything else, and at my reply in the negative, he withdrew. I saw the door close upon him. I heard then the sound of his footsteps retreating and finally found myself not only in solitude but, more than that, in dead silence.

"My eyes, which had till then been fixed upon the door, swept next across the chamber; being still unable, as I have explained, to encompass it all in one glance, I resolved to examine it in its details. I therefore grasped one of the candelabra and commenced an inspection.

"Its name of Red Chamber came from enormous tapestries dating from the sixteenth century and in which the color red predominated. Handled in the manner of the Renaissance, they depicted the wars of Alexander the Great and were stretched on large panels of wood, probably last regilded in the eighteenth century. Only certain strips of wood remained brilliant enough to sparkle and reflect the rays of the candles.

"In the corner to the left of the door was a grandiose old bed raised upon a dais bearing the coat of arms of the Counts von Eppstein; it was furnished with very ample curtains of red damask. The bed curtains and the gilding on the platform looked as if they had been redone not less than twenty-five years ago.

"Between the windows were two gilded metal console tables from the period of Louis XIV, both topped with mirrors, their frames ornate with golden flowers and birds; from the ceiling hung a great copper chandelier with crystal prisms, but it was easy to see that it had not been used for a long while.

"Slowly I made the circle of the perimeter, followed by Fido, who stopped every time I stopped and couldn't fathom the craze that possessed me to creep around like that. Between the head of the bed and the window, that is to say, as he walked along close to that wall which faced the fireplace, Fido stopped suddenly, sniffed the paneling, drew himself up to full height, then lay down with his nose close to the base of the wall, smelling loudly and giving visible signs of anxiety. I searched for what could have caused this unease on his part, but I found nothing which could have disturbed him so much; the paneling appeared all of a piece. I could see no crack that broke its solid surface; I pressed my thumb down on various spots, searching for a hidden spring, but nothing moved, and after ten minutes of unsuccessful prodding, I continued my tour around the Red Chamber. Fido followed me, but he kept turning just the same to look back at the place to which he had tried and was still trying to direct my attention.

"I came back close to the fireplace, and everything relapsed into soundlessness, only momentarily disturbed by the sound of my feet; however, in the dead quiet, I could hear one other sound, which was the monotonous, funereal scream of the owl. I looked at my watch; it was ten o'clock. Despite fatigue, which crushed me with its weight, I seemed to have lost my longing for sleep. This immense chamber, so evocative of a bygone era, the events which must have occurred there over the centuries, what the old people had told me of the supernatural guests who frequented that room—all that inspired in me an emotion which I shall not even attempt to name. It was not fear; no, it rather resembled uneasiness, a kind of dread mixed with curiosity. I did not know what would befall me in that chamber, but I sensed that something was about to happen.

"I stayed for about another half an hour in the easy chair with my legs stretched out to the heat; then, hearing nothing, seeing nothing, I decided to go to bed and leave one candelabrum burning on the mantel.

"Once in the huge bed of the Counts von Eppstein, I called Fido, and Fido came to lie down beside me.

"Not a soul in such a situation, expecting such a manifestation of sorts, but tries not to fall asleep. Everybody knows how the eyes gradually close, only to reopen suddenly at the slightest noise, how the glance enfolds the entire room where one lies in bed, then, seeing it deserted and mute, how the eyelids close, only to pop open again. That's how it was with me; already two or three times fallen almost quite asleep, I awoke with a start; then, little by little, despite the light from the candles burning on the candelabrum, the objects in the room began to swim in upon each other. The tall personages in the tapestry seemed to move, the hearth appeared to spew out fantastic, unusual flares of light, my thoughts revolved about each other like a twisted ball of thread impossible to untangle, and I fell asleep.

"How long my slumber lasted, I have no idea; the only thing I know is that I was reawakened by an indefinable sense of terror. I opened my eyes again, but the candles had burned out, and the fire was extinguished. A single brand had rolled out and was smoldering on the marble; I looked all about me. I saw absolutely nothing that moved.

"I should add that the chamber was illumined, but only by a ray of moonlight that passed through the broken storm blind.

"The only thing I felt inside myself, as I have said, was something that was extraordinary, unidentifiable, and weird.

"I raised myself up on one elbow. At that moment, Fido, who had been lying beside me on the floor mat, let out a mournful howl.

"His prolonged, lugubrious howl made me shudder despite myself.

" 'Fido,' I told him, 'Fido. Well, dog, what is it?'

"But instead of answering me, I then felt my quivering dog had wormed his way under the bed, where he next proceeded to howl a second time, from far underneath it.

"At that same instant I heard a slight noise, which was that of a door squeaking on its hinges.

"Then a section of the paneling separated and turned outwards upon itself. It was the same section of paneling where Fido had stopped to sniff.

"Projected against the dark square which it had just created as the panel swung open, I saw, cut out, a shape white, airy, transparent, which, without seeming to touch the parquet floor, without giving off any sound whatsoever, advanced floating through the distance towards my bed.

"I felt my hair stand up on my head and a cold sweat break out on my forehead.

"I retreated in my own turn back almost into the space between the bed and the wall; the shadow approached closer and closer to the bed, mounted the dais where it was set, looked me in the face for an instant, and shook its head as if to say: 'It's not he.'

"Then she gave a sigh, went back down the platform that she had stepped up upon, passed back though the ray of moonlight, which permitted me once more to be sure of her singular transparence, and then returned back again in my direction, sighed a second time, shook her head once more, and reentered the darkness through the open panel, the door swinging closed behind her, squeaking as it had done when she had opened it.

"I stayed there, I admit it, speechless, powerless, feeling alive only because of the quickened beating of my heart. A moment later, I heard Fido leaving his refuge and resuming his former place upon the rug. I called him; he stood up on his hind legs and put his front paws over on my side of the bed. The poor animal was still shaking all over.

"What I had seen was therefore real enough; it was not an error of my faculties or a dream of my imagination. It really had been an apparition, a shade, a phantom. I myself really was under the weight of some supernatural occurrence. This chamber must have been the theater where some terrible and mysterious act had taken place. What could have happened in this bedroom? That's what vague investigation my brain launched itself upon during the wee hours of the morning, for, as one can well understand, I slept no more.

"At the first glimmer of dawn, I jumped out of the bed and got dressed.

"Just as I was finishing dressing, I heard footsteps in the corridor outside. This time it was human footsteps. I made no mistake about that.

"The steps stopped before my door.

" 'Come,' I said.

"The old servant appeared.

" 'Sir,' he said, 'I have been worried about how you passed the night, and I have come to inquire about your state.'

" 'As you can see,' I replied, 'it is excellent.'

" 'Did you sleep well?'

" 'Perfectly.'

"He hesitated for a moment.

" 'And nothing disturbed your sleep . . . ?' he added.

" 'Nothing.'

" 'So much the better. Now, if the gentleman will give his orders for the hour when he intends to leave?'

" 'But as soon as I have breakfasted.'

" 'Then we shall prepare it at this very minute, and when the gentleman shall have come downstairs, if he will then allow us merely a quarter of an hour, he will find everything ready.'

" 'Very well, then, in a quarter of an hour.'

"The old man bowed and withdrew.

"I remained alone for that quarter of an hour, which seemed precisely the time I needed to get to the bottom of what I burned to know.

"As soon as the sound of his steps had died away, I went to the door and shot home the bolt. Then I rushed over to the section of wall which I had seen pivot open.

"I counted upon Fido to guide me in my search; but this time, although I used threats and even the whip to make him leave the spot he had chosen, he would not go towards the paneling.

"I searched through all the moldings in the woodwork, but I could not find a single crack or joint that was visible to the eye. I pressed upon all the carvings that protruded, but not a one yielded under the nudgings of my fingers.

"I saw that there must be some spring mechanism, the workings of which I did not understand, and that without knowing the secret it was impossible to make it work.

"After twenty minutes of fruitless experimentation, I was therefore obliged to abandon my undertaking. Moreover, I heard the footsteps of the old fellow approaching. I didn't want him to find me shut up in the room, so I ran to the door and pulled back the bolt just as he was about to knock.

" 'The breakfast of His Highness the Count is served,' he said.

"I took my gun and followed him after having one last look at the mysterious panel.

"I entered the dining room; my breakfast was served from the same luxurious silver bowls as the dinner the night before.

"Although very preoccupied with my adventure of the night, I did not breathe a word of it; I had realized that it was not servants born into service in that house, and grown old in their trust, who should be interrogated about their master's secrets. I breakfasted, therefore, in haste; then, once finished, I thanked my hosts once again for the kind hospitality they had extended to me and begged the old man to point out the road that would take me back to town.

"He offered to escort me as far as the track that would lead me out of the Taunus Mountains; as I did not relish becoming lost all over again, I accepted.

"We walked about a kilometer before coming into a track well enough rutted to guarantee that I need have no more fear of straying off the road. Half an hour later I was entirely out of the woods; three hours after that and I was back in Frankfort.

"I barely took the time to change clothes before I hastened to meet my friend, the German tutor. In fact, I ran to his lodging. I found him extremely worried about my absence; he had already sent the two beaters and three or four farmhands in search of me.

" 'At last,' he cried. 'Where did you spend the night?'

" 'In Castle Eppstein,' I told him.

" 'Castle Eppstein!' he cried. 'In what part of Castle Eppstein?'

" 'In the bedchamber of Count Everard, who was off in Vienna.'

" 'Inside the Red Chamber?'

" 'Inside the Red Chamber.'

" 'And you didn't see anything?' the tutor asked me with an obvious curiosity tinged with some hesitation.

" 'In fact, I did,' I replied. 'I saw a ghost.'

" 'Yes,' he murmured. 'That was the ghost of Countess Albina.'

" 'Who is this Countess Albina?' I asked him.

" 'Oh!' he replied. 'That's a long story, a terrible story, too, unbelievable, unearthly; it's the sort of tale you only come across in one of our own, old Rhineland castles, in our own Taunus Mountains, such a story as . . . you would never believe if you had not yourself slept in the Red Chamber.'

" 'Yes, but I will believe it now that I have slept there, I promise. So go ahead and tell it to me, my dear professor, and I certify here and now that you will never have a more attentive listener.'

" 'Well,' my former hunting companion told me, 'the account is rather lengthy. Why not give me the pleasure of joining me for dinner, after which, with the dessert, some first-rate cigars between our teeth, and our feet on the andirons, I will recount this terrible legend, which our own Hoffmann, who was such a master of fantastic mysteries, would have turned into the most terrifying of all his *Tales,* if he had known it.'

"As you can well believe, I needed no further urging. I therefore presented myself at the appointed hour, at the professor's lodging, where, after we had dined together, he told me the long story, just as he had promised to do, of the Red Chamber . . . "

"Well, then, where is it?" we asked Count Elim.

"Out of his tale, I have made a kind of big, fat, quite tiresome book, which I will lend you tomorrow, if you absolutely insist, or which I will read you just as fast as my lips can go."

"And why not tonight?" I asked him, for I was burning with impatience.

"Because it's three in the morning," Count Elim replied, "which seems to me to be a reasonable hour for getting to bed."

Everybody else was of his prior opinion. We agreed to meet next day at ten in the evening. At a quarter to ten all the listeners were assembled; at the stroke of ten, Count Elim arrived, with his manuscript under his arm. We hardly gave him time to sit down, so keen was our desire to hear all about the events he had promised to speak of. We all took seats around the reader, and in the midst of the deepest hush, Count Elim began the tale we so impatiently expected.

CHAPTER

I

We are in September of 1789; the ground of Europe is still shaking from the fall of the Bastille, and Frankfort, which is an independent city, but a city where Caesars are being created, feels at the same time both hope and fear of this seething Revolution. Castle Eppstein feels fear only, for its Lord, old Count Rudolph, is entirely devoted to the Austrian Emperor, who is now steeling himself to declare war on France.

However, it is not only political anxieties that, beyond a doubt, were bowing down his head and withering away the heart of him on that day when our story commences.

He was seated that day in the great hall of his castle, his head bowed low and his wife by his side. Huge tears rolled silently down the gaunt cheeks of the Countess. The Count, too, wept, but only inside his heart.

The two were both handsome, aristocratic old persons; their every gesture bore witness at once to a profound dignity and yet to a tender gentleness also, and their white heads seemed, in the words of Schiller, as if crowned with deeds of sainted benevolence.

They deliberated together gravely and sadly.

"We must forgive him," the mother said.

"But how can I do it?" the father asked her. "If nobody were to see us, I would privately open my arms to Conrad and to his wife; but, alas, nobility obligates, and there are

so many eyes fixed upon us! We owe the world unimpeach-
able examples of conduct, and had we death stopping our
very hearts, we should have to die also standing fast. I have
driven Conrad from our midst, and Conrad shall never
again appear in my presence; my dear Gertrude, we shall
never hold him in our arms again."

"I would better understand your stern commands," the
mother ventured timidly to say, "if Conrad were the eldest son of our lineage; but the one who will be heir and
head of our house after yourself will be our son Maximilian."

"No matter," the Count replied. "Conrad is nonetheless
an Eppstein."

"Will he survive your anger?" the Countess dared protest.

"If not, then he will rejoin us all the sooner there where
fathers can always receive their children in their arms."

And he fell silent, for he feared greatly, if he uttered a
single word more, that he, too, would, like his wife, burst
into tears.

After a moment's silence, one of the old servants named
Daniel rapped discreetly on the door and was allowed by
his master to enter the hall.

"It is His Highness Maximilian who requests the honor
of a short interview with his father," Daniel told them.

"Conduct my son to me," replied the Count.

"That one," the old Count Rudolph said bitterly as soon
as Daniel had withdrawn, "that one is dishonored in my
heart of hearts, but at least he does not dishonor us in the
eyes of the world by making a misalliance in marriage; as
a man, he is depraved, but he holds rank up in society; he
forgets to be a good man, but he remembers that he is a
German nobleman. Therefore, he maintains his position in
aristocratic society, noble in name if not in fact, and at least
noble in appearances. Thus, Maximilian is worthy of being
my heir and successor."

"And Conrad," his wife added, "is worthy only of being your son."

And yet, as soon as Maximilian entered the hall, he bent his every most powerful effort to soften the otherwise severe and telltale lines of his harsh face, not completely able to erase them at will but setting himself the task of veiling them. He knelt before the Count, kissed his hand and his mother's hand, then arose and awaited in silence for the older man to acknowledge his presence and invite him to speak.

At that time, Count Maximilian was a man of about thirty years of age, with a face that was both somber and haughty, tall in stature, vigorous in appearance. Generally, his gestures were peremptory and decisive. In the ordinary course of a day his facial expressions showed more audacity on his part than intelligence. When a person came before him, he felt himself to be in the presence of a man of an implacable will, and this is precisely how, by means of a haughty, determined spirit, he knew how to impose his will on other men whose intelligence was frequently superior to his. In such a man as this Count Maximilian, his every desire had to be translated instantaneously into deeds. Others could only with difficulty sustain the attention of his glaring, staring eyes; they said among themselves that very few obstacles could long withstand his anger and that he, too, could probably not manage to contain the violence of his own nature, even when he should do it.

Count Maximilian, as we have stated, was probably about thirty years old at this time; but already premature age lines rutted his face, where the passions of ambition had already left their devouring imprint. The Count had one of these broad German foreheads that ring hollow to the touch, full as they are of pride rather than of ability. His hawk nose and thin lips contributed not a little toward giving him this overbearing presence that so struck everybody at first glance. The fold of his upper eyelid, which he wrinkled frequently, was awesome; and at the same time, his smile, and yet he barely smiled if at all, was the fawning, false, greedy smile of the courtisan. His tall, straight back knew how effective it was when bent low before the master. In short, in his private heart, as in his external presence, there was audacity but no real grandeur, coldness rather than serenity, disdain rather than mercy. He was ambitious rather in the manner of "Father Joseph" than in that of Wallenstein,* and a man could see at first sight of him that he would avenge his enforced humiliation before the powerful by his haughtiness toward little people.

"Before hearing your words, my son," Count Rudolph told him gravely, "I have to reproach you for a new source of grief you have brought upon us. As long as you were young, we treated your misdeeds with indulgence, attributing them to your time of life, but you are already well advanced along the path of the years, Maximilian. If God has seen fit to withdraw your wife from you, he has left you your son. Maximilian, you are a father; on top of that, within a few days, I feel, due to my weakness, that I will leave you lord and master of all our domains and sole representative of all our ancestors. Is it not high time for you to prepare seriously for your destiny and henceforth to watch over your conduct, which has caused so much scandal in the country hereabouts and so much sorrow here in the castle?"

"Father," Maximilian replied, "your own goodness has always caused you to pay a little too much attention, it seems to me, to the complaints of the villagers. I am a gentleman, and therefore I love to take my pleasures. The games of the lion are not those of the lamb, but I have never

*The man (1577–1638) called "Father Joseph," or "His Gray Eminence," was the confidant and counselor of Cardinal Richelieu upon whom his influence was considered unduly overpowering. General Wallenstein (1583–1634), about whom Schiller wrote his trilogy, was a highly ambitious warrior during the Thirty Years' War, but he was denounced to the Emperor as a traitor and was executed by three of his own officers.

forgotten my station, that I can recall. I have fought three
duels for the honor of my name; as for the rest, my conscience has allowed it to me, in truth. What new infraction
have I committed, pray tell? Have my beaters laid waste
another wheat field? Have my dogs allowed themselves the
privilege of choking the neighbor's sow? Has my horse
through carelessness trampled a peasant?"

"My son, you have dishonored the daughter of the bailiff
of Alpoenig."

"Alas! it's true," began Maximilian with a sigh, "but my
noble father really should not look upon such things. Does
he not know perfectly well that, like my brother Conrad, I
shall never degrade myself so low as to wed a commoner's
daughter?"

"Oh, doubtless, I have no such fear," interrupted the old
Count with a sad attempt at irony.

"Well, then," continued Maximilian, "what does Your
Excellency dread on my part? Only scandal, as he objected
a short while ago. Alas! Let him be reassured upon that
point also. An awful misfortune has occurred. Poor
Gretchen was walking alone yesterday on the banks of the
Main, probably intending, at least this is what I suppose, to
pick some wild rose or some periwinkle or some baby's
breath. Her feet must have slipped, because the river has
swept her away. In short, they only found her body this
morning. I am really in despair over this so unexpected
death. I loved Gretchen very much, and, please pardon this
in me, Father, I have shed tears for her. But Your Excellency can see that it may be without fears as to the consequences of my latest folly."

"Indeed," said the Count, who was staggered by the
obviously careless grief he saw, by such a selfish frivolity
that could pretend that what had been a crime was merely
an accident, and by a man who could perceive in all that
catastrophe only blind chance to blame.

His mother raised both her eyes and her hands to high

heaven, doubtless begging pardon from God and from Gretchen, too, on behalf of her older son, who knew not what wrong he was doing. After a pause, the Count spoke again:

"You had something to say to me, son?"

"Yes, Father, I have a favor to ask of you, not for myself, who have tried never to incur your wrath, but for my brother Conrad, who, if he is guilty, is also very unhappy. Come, my lord."

"That is good of you! Now you are acting truly like a good brother, Maximilian!" the Countess cried, overcome with tenderness, happy to find her older son inspired with some generosity, for once.

"Yes, Mother," pursued Maximilian. "As you know, I love Conrad. He is a weak spirited but an excellent person nevertheless who has from birth never failed to defer to me as to his master, and I have never once had occasion to be jealous of his soft, innocuous nature, which has uncontestably recognized my own superiority. It is not his fault that he was born to be a professor of philosophy rather than to wear the proud nobleman's sword at his side. I clearly understand that his blunder is a little hard to bear: to have secretly married because he loved her, a girl who is a nobody; to introduce into our family the legitimate offspring of a middle-class mother instead of enriching us, in the perfectly simple way of handling it, with a bastard child is to have committed an awfully silly sort of mistake, I concur with you here; but such a mistake is only an error on his part and not a crime. His little Naomi is very pretty, and she simply bewitched our innocent Conrad, for she was his first experience. After all, Father, the affair is less serious than as if I had myself committed it, as if I, the eldest son and head of the Eppstein family, had committed the same foolishness. I realize perfectly well that the Emperor will be furious if he sees you accept the paternity of such a misalliance, but I will go to Vienna myself and somehow manage to calm him. What we will do is give out that Naomi's father was not our forester but some old soldier, and in good time everybody will forget the whole business. You would only have withheld your forgiveness from me in such an affair, is that not true, Father? From me who am to succeed you in all your titles as well as in the favor of the imperial court? Well, out of friendship for this simpleminded Conrad, I stand ready to bear the consequences of his error. Through my own good zeal in Vienna, should I not repair this blot which now smears our reputation, and shall I not earn again for us all the Emperor's good graces? Rest assured on that score. Thus, I beg of you, my lord, do not exile Conrad and his wife into France, as you have wanted to do, but let them remain here close to you. How can his studious, philosophizing life cause so much stir? The poor boy is bursting with tenderness. He loves both you and my mother so dearly. He is so attached to this native soil that he has never once even been able to leave it! Such a banishment would be for him almost a death verdict, Father."

"You have done your duty, Maximilian, by pleading your brother's cause; I shall now do mine by refusing you. Conrad remains obstinately opposed to dissolving his marriage, does he not?"

"I must admit, my lord, that upon that point he remains inflexible; it is, I believe, useless to speak to him further about it."

"Very well, were I to yield to him when he resists us, would not the entire nobility of Germany, solidly behind the behavior of each one of our number, fail to pardon such weakness on my part?"

"Doubtless not, but will you not at least consent to see Conrad and to hear him out in person, Father?" Maximilian replied.

"Impossible," the old Count replied, for he feared his own tenderness, "impossible."

"May Your Highness pardon me, then," said Maximilian.

"But I have taken it upon myself to invite my brother to rejoin me here. Let him not depart from here without looking for a last time upon your face. He is there, doubtless; he is just now coming towards us, and here he is. As an act of grace, receive him, Father."

"My lord," said the Countess in a low voice to her husband, "if I have always been a submissive and devoted wife, grant me (for who will know of it?) the supreme happiness of seeing my child once more."

"Let it be done as you wish it done, Gertrude, but let it be without any weakness, do you understand?"

Count Rudolph made a sign, and Maximilian stepped to the door and opened it to Conrad, who came silently across the hall and knelt at some distance away from his father.

The two brothers contrasted as completely as possible, the one from the other. As much as Maximilian was robust and resolute, as much Conrad seemed to be frail and gentle. The latter's pale face, framed with curly blond hair, lively only because of large brown eyes that sparkled as if afire—all this seemed to make the older brother's sharp features stand out as even less refined and his tanned bronze skin and his sturdy build seem even less graceful. One of the older brother's hands could easily, without any special effort on his part, have reached around both girlish hands of Conrad. Thus, while the one almost appeared frightening in his person, the other was immediately charming.

They made as they paused there together what was a grand, solemn, and still tableau of a family: the older brother standing motionless, a more or less detached and indifferent spectator of this scene that his carefully calculated clemency had craftily prepared; the young brother, one knee on the floor, anguished, trembling, but even so upheld by some inner faith that gave almost as much shine to his eyes as did his tears; the father, a tall patriarch with white hair and a white beard, seated in his sculpted chair, full of majesty in his outward appearance, full of trouble in his heart, but forcing himself not to yield to his own desire to express his love; then the mother either almost collapsed upon an ottoman or having slid down from it upon her knees, furtively wiping away her tears, looking back and forth, in fear toward her husband, in love toward her son; as a background, finally, a dark antique wood paneling against which the almost living portraits of their ancestors stood out as witnesses and judges.

"You may speak, Conrad," said Count Rudolph.

"My lord," said Conrad, "three years ago, when I reached my twentieth birthday, I became possessed of a dreamy temperament, and then I felt oppressed with the desire to fall in love. While my brother Maximilian hastened through Germany and France and was swept back and forth by the fiery blaze of his own particular youthfulness, I had always been pleased to stay close to you and close to my mother's side so that in my own desire to stay at home, I had not only refused to become a cultured diplomat by frequenting the imperial court, but I even refused similarly to frequent the society of our neighboring castles. I need no wider horizons to content my heart; the only thing is that if my feet were too lazy to move, my thoughts and my heart were, I assure you, not only active but impatient for life. The only woman I had ever known was my own mother; and so, when I found upon my path a young maiden as lovely as my mother must once have been and as kindhearted as my own mother, I took no care to inform myself about the family name by which this young girl was called—for love only knows baptismal names—and so I fell in love with Naomi because she was so charming and because she was so virginal."

"Oh! If only I had been there," Maximilian murmured. "With what pleasure I would have rid your Naomi of that last condition, which seduced you so powerfully, my poor brother!"

"Nevertheless," continued Conrad, "as I do not wish to offer any argument that may not be accurate, my lord, I will confess to you that I did not yield blindly or immediately to that passion which kept sweeping over me; no, for as I calculated the distance that separated Naomi from me, as I imagined your grief, I struggled to cast off this love from my heart, but it only flowed over me all the more violently because I had restrained it. An irresistible power drew me incessantly towards Gaspard's dwelling, and one day, finally, Naomi was conquered and told me that she loved me also."

"What an ambitious girl!" murmured Maximilian.

"Then what was I to do?" Conrad continued. "Should I have fled from her, mother of mine? I was not strong enough. Betray her, do you say, Maximilian? I was not so cowardly. Should I have come to you, Father? Should I have revealed all this to you? I did not dare do such a thing. I married Naomi secretly; thus I avoided your wrath, and thus I spared you the suffering of the moment, and so doing it seemed to me that I offended neither God nor men. I was doubly mistaken. A son was born to me, and I was obliged to choose between your anger, Father, and the dishonor of my wife. I chose your anger, because it had to fall upon me only, and despite all the attempts of mankind to sever what God has joined together, I choose it still today, and I shall choose it still tomorrow. But you see, my lord, that I find your anger justified and that I had foreseen it, alas! It is therefore not in order to turn this anger away from myself that I am on my knees before you. Only, once I am banished from your presence, as I have expected to be, I should very much like to know, as I depart, that I do not carry your contempt along with me."

"Conrad," the Count replied in a slow and hollow voice, "we come, both you and I, from an historical race to whom deviation is not permitted. Fate has placed us high enough for the rest of the world to see us, and high enough for us to set our example in the eyes of the world. Probably that is a fatality, but we must bow beneath it, and you have eluded its control. You have thus rendered yourself guilty of a crime, of the violation of our own nobility, of *lèse-noblesse*, Conrad.

"The wind of Revolution, which blows upon us today from France, should have been sufficient to warn you to stand your ground before it. More than ever before, we should, when they become dangerous to us, guard our hereditary privileges. As a gentleman and as the father of a family, responsible for the deeds of my own family members, it becomes me to repair your weakness by my own severity and to see that the old man draws himself up to his full height whenever the young man has staggered on his feet.

"Therefore depart. Go into France and serve to the best of your ability King Louis XVI. My best wishes will follow you. You have asked me if I scorned you, and I answer you by justifying myself. When your nurse first brought you to me, Conrad, I took you into my arms, and raising you above my head, I offered you first to God, next to the Emperor, next to the nobles of Germany, and then finally in service to each of our illustrious ancestors. Today, since I am still on earth, it is to the ancestors, to the nobles, to the Emperor that I am obliged now to give an account of you, and I disown you. Tomorrow, from above this earth, I shall perhaps glory in you before the Lord God Almighty."

"Father," cried Conrad, "I worship and adore you. You are a great man, a terrible and good man, and as you crush me with your death sentence, you make me proud of you. My lord, I will be worthy of you. I owe this expiation to our family, and I will acquit myself as an Eppstein. Farewell forever."

Conrad bowed low before his father, but even so, without moving any closer to his person. The old man made a gesture of final farewell with his hand, but he did not speak, for overcome with emotion as he was, he feared lest he throw open his arms to his son. As for the Countess, she dared not even look at Conrad. She had her head lowered while her tears bathed her aged face and while, hands joined, she prayed. Conrad bowed to her from his distance, but despite the etiquette tacitly agreed upon for this last interview, he could not help blowing a kiss from his hand toward her who had carried him in her womb. Aside from this other deviation, the proud young son modeled his own conduct upon the Count's and remained apparently unperturbed. The father was satisfied with his child's conduct.

"Accompany your brother to the threshold," he told Maximilian, who, throughout this novel and imposing conference, had remained mute, biting his lips.

"If Your Highness will permit me," the elder brother of the Eppsteins said, "I shall return to speak with you later on."

"I shall await you," answered the old man.

And the two brothers left the hall, one of them never to return.

What took place between the father and mother when these two grief-stricken parents remained face-to-face, no one can say, for God alone saw their tears and heard the sobs of their broken hearts. When Maximilian reentered the hall a quarter of an hour later, the two old persons had regained their serene attitude and their trappings of parental authority.

"I may now agree, my lord," Maximilian remarked, "now that your decree can never be revoked, now that I have seen Conrad depart along with his wife and his son, that what you have done, you ought to have done."

"Is it not so, Maximilian," the Count replied with a bitter smile, "is it not so that this is your opinion, certainly?"

"Yes, Father, for the Emperor would not have pardoned indulgence on your part; and certainly he would for a long time have withdrawn his favor from our family."

"I acted for the sake of honor and not for such honors," the Count said.

"The way the times are now, Father, that amounts to the same thing."

"What did you wish to consult me about, son?" the father asked soberly, thus interrupting Maximilian.

"This is it, Father. In spite of the wisdom of your severity towards Conrad, your status has nonetheless suffered some debasement. I have thought of a way to raise it. I only lost my wife Thecla about a year ago, and reassured by the birth of my son Albert that our name was reestablished for another generation, I had not thought previously of a second and last marriage for myself. But now that the time has come to regain the Emperor's good graces, I find presented before me the most desirable party that one could wish for—the daughter of one of your old friends, the daughter of the Duke of Schwalbach, who is currently all-powerful at the Viennese court."

"Is this Albina von Schwalbach of whom you speak?" inquired the Countess.

"Yes, Mother. She is an only daughter and will bring great wealth to our house."

"My sister the abbess," continued his mother, "in whose convent Albina was educated, and whom I often consulted for news of my friend's daughter, spoke to me of this young girl. She is a peerless beauty."

"And," added Maximilian, "she has as her dowry the magnificent domain of Winkel, right at the gates of Vienna."

"My sister added that Albina's grace was only the dressing over the most charming goodness of her nature."

"Without counting the fact," pursued the young man, "that the Duke of Schwalbach will easily obtain—will that not be true, Father?—the right to transmit, after his death, to his son-in-law his title of Duke and his estate."

"What a blessing," the Countess said, "for me to name

this child my daughter and to take the place of the mother that she has lost."

"And what an honor to be allied to the Schwalbachs!" added Maximilian.

"Yes," said the Count. "The Schwalbach line is one of the grandest and best branches of the German tree."

"Well, Father, have the goodness to write to your old companion-in-arms and ask him for his daughter's person for your son."

To this request there followed a rather long silence.

The old Count had let his head fall upon his chest and appeared lost in deep thought.

"Well, what! Father, are you not going to answer me? Well, what! My lord, you seem to be hesitating? Such a union, which would bring so much splendor into our family, cannot, ought not to, displease you."

"Maximilian, Maximilian," Count Rudolph began again seriously, "can I not use your own rules of conduct, which I personally do not consider valid, to say that, if as a nobleman your conduct is above reproach, as a man, alas, you have frequently failed, Maximilian? Will this child be happy with you?"

"She will be the Countess von Eppstein, Father."

There was a second silence. Certainly the two men bore no resemblance the one to the other and understood each other not at all, united as they were, as if by the world's laws rather than by the ties of blood. The son looked down upon his father because of his old-fashioned prejudices; the father scorned his son for his misbehavior of various sorts.

"Take care, my lord," Maximilian warned, "lest when the opportunity arises for adding to the renown of our name, you reject this opportunity, you the guardian of our glory, you, responsible towards our own family members as well as for acquiring honor as for erasing spots upon our escutcheon."

"Your father knows what he must do, sir," replied the old

Count, sorely hurt by his son's threats. "Leave for Vienna and you will find waiting when you arrive there a letter of recommendation to the Duke of Schwalbach."

"Therefore I shall, if you please, leave the castle within the hour," said Maximilian. "A so noble heiress must be quite surrounded, and pray God that my suit does not arrive too late."

"Do as you please," the old man replied.

"Will you condescend, Sire, and you also, Mother, to give your blessing to him who now departs?"

"Bless you, my son," said the Count.

"Maximilian, may God guide you!" said the Countess.

Maximilian kissed his mother's hand, bowed respectfully to the Count, and left the hall.

"The other one," said the old man when he was alone with the Countess, "the other one, who left first, did not even dare ask you for it, did he? For your blessing. But he had it, did he not, Gertrude? He had yours and mine, and God hears a heart which remains silent better than lips which speak."

CHAPTER

II

And now, if we leave behind us the banks of the Main and the gloomy Castle of the Eppsteins in exchange for the delightful suburbs of Vienna and for the charming country mansion of Winkel, we shall find there, running among the flowers, her hair flying free about her face and her cheeks all rosy, the delightful sixteen-year-old child named Albina von Schwalbach. At the end of the garden path along which she is flying sits her father upon a stone seat, a less grave, more outgoing Duke than the solemn Count Eppstein. The Duke watches his daughter, who as she runs this way and that in front of him, blows him thousands upon thousands of kisses. The Duke of Schwalbach is a dignified German councilor.

"What have you done all morning, Father?" the girl asks him as for a second she suddenly stops running back and forth, this way and that, in front of him for the twentieth time because she had surprised a certain smile on his lips that rather much intrigued her. "You keep looking at me, I seem to see, in a very mysterious, strange way. What are you dreaming about?"

"About that large letter sealed in black which you said smelled of the Middle Ages and which came from so far away and sent me into so long a meditation."

"Good! So I shall no longer ask you to tell me your secret, Father, for I most assuredly have no connection whatsoever with this very respectful missive," the girl told him as she prepared to run another race around her course.

"On the contrary," the councilor told her, "a most directly related connection."

Albina stopped short and opened her astonished eyes very wide.

"A connection with me?" she exclaimed as she drew closer to the senior nobleman. "With me? Oh, show me how that can be. Show me quickly, Father. What is it all about? Tell me! So tell me!"

"It is about an offer for your hand in marriage."

"Oh, that!" she cried, pursing her lips with a charming little grimace of disdain. "Oh, is that all it is!"

"What do you mean, 'Is that all it is!'?" her aged father asked her with a smile. "Ah, me! What question will you treat with importance, then, if you speak of marriage with such unconcern?"

"But, Father, you already know ahead of time that I shall refuse. All these old starlings around Vienna, councilors at court, councilors at the Foreign Office, councillors in private practice, all curled up and empty-headed, do not suit me the least little bit in the world, and never will suit me ever at all, you know that, do you not? I have already told you all that, and I thought we had settled all that between us and that you had agreed never more to speak to me about it."

"But you forget, dear child, that the letter comes to us from very far away."

"Ah, that's true. So in that case, I should have to go far away from you, and that is even worse. I do not want to leave you. I do not want to do it! I do not want to do it!" the girl kept repeating as she set off in pursuit of a butterfly that soon flew high up in the air, like a flower wafted away in the wind, and disappeared from sight.

The Duke waited for a moment and then, when his daughter had run back close enough to hear what he said, told her:

"Little hypocrite," he called. "You fail to state the real reason for your refusal."

"The real reason for my refusal!" Albina cried in her astonishment. "And what is this real reason?"

"Your deep and irresistible passion."

"Oh! You are going to tease me again, Father," Albina told him, and she came up close to him so that he would be gentler to her.

"This passion you feel, and it is a hopeless love altogether, for Sir Götz von Berlichingen. You are madly in love with the medieval Knight with the Iron Hand. But alas! He perished in the days of the Emperor Maximilian."

"But he came back to life under the pen of the poet, Father; and even now he is alive and very well in the historical drama of our poet Goethe.* Well, yes, and a hundred times, yes. In spite of all your teasing I do love Sir Götz, and I admire him because of his noble heart and loyal service. He is a true hero, so pure and so sublime, who loves so faithfully and who strikes his enemy so hard! What do you expect of me? I know it is a pity, but all I can say is, that old as Sir Götz is, for you are always reminding me that he is an old man, as if age had anything to do with such poetic heroism, well, then, old as he is, he makes all these little men at the court look so prosaic. Yes, Götz von Berlichingen, Götz with the Iron Hand, that's the man for me, and up until now, you will agree, Father, will you not, you have only presented me with doll faces, not with stern men of poetry."

---

*Goethe's historical drama *Götz von Berlichingen* of 1773 is also generally recognized as having launched the historical novel first created from this drama by Sir Walter Scott. Goethe's hero, based on a real knight of the late Middle Ages, typifies the charisma of the "daemonic" individual.

"Girl! Girl! You have not even reached your sixteenth birthday," the Duke said, "and you want a husband sixty years old."

"Of sixty or of seventy or of eighty, just as long as he resembles my savage, loyal, and valorous Knights of the Rhineland, such as Götz of the Iron Hand or Franz von Sickingen or even Hans von Selbitz."

"Well, then, my dear Albina," the Duke began with the gravest look on his face, "then this falls wonderfully for you, for this is a marvelous man of that ilk, a man cut from the very stuff of your desires, and he is asking for your hand in marriage."

"Oh, what a teasing you are giving me, Father, and what fun you are making of me!"

"No, truly. Just look at the signature at the bottom of this letter and you will see."

And the councilor drew the letter from his pocket, unfolded it before her, and showed the signature to Albina.

"Rudolph von Eppstein," the young girl read.

"Well, then, my pretty Amazon, that is the man to suit you. I hope so, at any rate," replied the Duke. "This man fought in the Seven Years' War, and fully as well, from what people have told me, as if he had been born in your fabled fifteenth century of barbaric memory. He is not quite as old as you wish, I admit, but what difference can that make to you, with your sixty years or seventy years or eighty years, just so long as he resembles one of your heroes, as you said. . . . Rudolph von Eppstein is seventy-two years old, so that gives you a good full measure, and as for his courage, his loyalty, and his nobility, I hope that you will not deny them."

"Do you suppose, Father, that I know my Germany so little as to ignore the fact that Count Rudolph von Eppstein wedded, almost thirty years ago, the sister of my good aunt, abbess of Holy Linden?"

"Then, since one can't deceive such a learned person as you are, it is for one of his sons that my old comrade-in-arms requests your hand. The son who aspires to you is hardly thirty years of age and has as yet few white hairs, and if he is not such a medieval hero himself, at least he belongs to their race. Be easy on one score; his thirty years will increase in number, and his black hair will turn white. Add to that, silly girl, romantic dreamer that you are, an ancient castle in the Taunus Mountains, only a few miles distant from the old Rhine that you are so much in love with, which comes with a legendary history as fantastic as any. They have a chatelaine who wakes from the dead because she died on a Christmas Eve, which in my opinion is rather inconsequent. But, as you would be the first to know, both poetry and reason are two heavenly twins who are themselves more like dreams that awaken us, as they come to us the one out of the Gate of Horn and her sister from the Ivory Gate. Thus, both exit from the same otherworld place, but with their backs turned completely the one to the other."

"And what is their old legend, Father? Do you know it?" the girl asked, and her eyes as she said the words gleamed with new curiosity.

"No, not well enough to instruct you in it. I have heard tell of it, but some long time ago, from my old friend von Eppstein, during the long evenings we spent in bivouac. But as to the rest of it, your fiancé will teach that to you; I will advise him that this is how to pay his court to you."

"My fiancé, do you say, Father? Does this mean that you approve of this union?"

"Alas, yes, poor child. I should be cruel to you were I to rob your love of this attraction. That would have been very intelligent of me, would it not? To have thwarted your inclination, to have brought you to a secret marriage, and my posthumous pardon! But what can I do? As misfortune will have it, age, birth, fortune, all combine to make me desire this marriage, with my old fondness which for almost fifty years I have particularly felt for Count Rudolph von Eppstein. The only detail which I might want to quibble about is the fact that the young Count is a widower who already has a son; but my dear Albina, who has such a brilliant future, most assuredly fears no comparison whatsoever with any past; and, after all, as added surety, my dear child, you shall yourself judge your prospective fiancé in detail, since the letter from his father only precedes him by a few days."

"And how is he called, this proud pretender to my hand, who must erase Götz from my heart by becoming in his person another Götz von Berlichingen?" Albina asked.

"Maximilian," the Duke replied.

"Maximilian? It is a promising enough name . . . to frighten his enemies but not so promising as far as I am concerned; for if he does fulfill my dreams, this man, who is iron when he enters combat, must prove a tender and submissive lover to his lady. That is the magical spell promised to noble ladies and reserved for them alone in exchange for all the pains that await them in love. They alone shall tame wild lions and make that man tremble who makes men tremble with his sword. And look here, Father," Albina continued with a comical sort of seriousness, "I do really prefer him to be young, the more I think about it. I shall participate that way in his martial glory; it is while pronouncing my name aloud with his lips that he will win his first victories, and I shall be, like the medieval Elisabeth,* the witness of his prowess and its reward."

"Dear child," said the Duke with a shake of his head, "do you really and truly believe that the days of medieval epic

*Perhaps Queen Elizabeth of Hungary, who died very young in 1231 after having given all her goods to the poor.

poetry, with its great sword wielding on the battlefields, can really come again?"

"Why ever not?"

"Oh! It is the invention of gunpowder that caused the collapse of chivalry. There are no more heroic Rolands, no more Renauds, and no more Oliviers; these epic warriors, whatever their especial strength could be, are only equal before a cannonball; see in their places later French soldiers like the great Marshal Berwick of France and Marshal Turenne of the Thirty Years' War."

"But when such grandiose saber rattlers fail us, we can always fall back on our own great captains, Father. Nowadays military skill has replaced brute force, and not having had another sword like Roland's magical Durendal or Renaud's Balizarde or Astolphe's enchanted lance, we can fall back upon our own commanders, great soldiers like King Gustavus Adolphus of Sweden, General Wallenstein of Bohemia, and King Frederick the Great of Prussia. I can hardly say from where this idea comes to me, but I have high hopes for our own new century so soon about to commence."

"That's a good girl," the Duke told her with a laugh. "We'll have your prediction printed in the next *Almanac* published at Gotha."

Then, consulting his watch, he continued. "Meanwhile, let us go in to dinner, my pretty sibyl, for at my age—and I am very annoyed to have to disenchant you about the future—a man does not feed any longer on prophecy, perfume, poetry, and sunshine."

Albina took her father's arm with a little determined nod of her head, which meant that age meant nothing to her, and they both returned to their castle.

The day after this conversation, where we have tried to give an idea of the original and ready imagination, as of the innocent and poetic reveries of Albina, on the very next day, Maximilian von Eppstein arrived at Vienna, already preceded and prepared for, one might say, by the dreams of this girlish and graceful intelligence. We have sketched his portrait already. It is easy to see, therefore, that he pleased the father much less than he pleased the daughter. The father, who was an accomplished diplomat well used to stripping off a man's mask so he could penetrate down to his real face, found in Count Maximilian more ambition than real merit, more arrogance than intelligence, and more calculation than love. But where Albina was concerned, thanks to the powerful physique, thanks to the pale, clouded brow, he cut a glorious figure compared to the pallid lovers she had glimpsed in Vienna. She saw Maximilian through a cloud of poetry that was inside her. She took his abruptness for candor, his boorishness for simplicity, his coldness for nobility.

"This is a high-mettled, archaic sort of man," she used to tell herself, "whose only fault is to have a soul that antedates by three hundred years the gallant courtiers of Vienna."

Then she confided to Maximilian the romance that she had promised for her own life, and Maximilian took care to conform to her notion of his conduct, to affect the most profound contempt for protocol and treaties, and to move so that he made his sword rattle heroically and his spurs jingle.

Finally, one day Albina begged him to recount to her the legend of Castle Eppstein, so eager was she to know if her notions of chivalric romance corresponded to the young Count's temper. Maximilian had only a slight acquaintance with that aspect of rhetoric that is called "discourse", but he spoke rapidly, with thrust and a colorful vocabulary. More than that, Maximilian wanted to please. He therefore narrated the legend of Castle Eppstein with conviction, with feeling, and with such enthusiasm that these stylistic characteristics completed his subjugation of the starry-eyed little girl. This is what he construed as the legend of Castle Eppstein.

———————————

This castle had been built in the heroic times of German history, which is to say, during the era of Charlemagne, and it was constructed by a direct ancestor of those who today inhabit it. Then the builder was a Count von Eppstein.

They knew nothing more about such primeval times except that a prophecy of the Magician Merlin said that *"every Countess von Eppstein who would die during the Eve of Christmas would only half die."* Like every horoscope, this prediction was more or less obscure; thus, nobody understood it for a long time, until there died the wife of a German Emperor. Nobody remembered the Emperor's name anymore, but the Empress was named Ermangarde.

Ermangarde had been raised with the daughter of the Lord of Windeck, and the latter had become Countess von Eppstein. Now, as they became the one a Countess and the other an Empress, the two young ladies, and this despite the difference in their ranks, had lost none of their friendship. And as the Empress dwelled in Frankfort and the Countess resided in her castle, which is situated only ten or so miles from that city, the two former companions saw each other frequently. Count Sigismond von Eppstein stood, moreover, very high at court so that the Emperor had attached him particularly to the Empress's suite.

Suddenly, during the night of December 24, 1342, the Empress died. Such an unexpected death threw the court into deep mourning. The Emperor in particular adored the Empress and showed on her account every sign of the most profound regret. According to the custom of those days, the Empress was laid out on a bed of state, and all the lords and noble ladies of the court were admitted there to kiss her hand.

Court etiquette prescribed that this viewing ceremony should be conducted in this way: The Empress lay in state alone in the Burning Chapel, stretched out upon her bed of state, clad in her imperial vestments, her crown upon her head and her scepter in her hand. One of her noble attendants kept vigil outside the door, relieved every two hours by another servitor. This chamberlain introduced into the mortuary chamber each person who came to render homage to the deceased lady. This visiting person knelt down, kissed the hand of her who had been his Empress, walked back across the chamber and rapped at the door, which was then opened; and thus, as he left, each person made room for the next. These courtisans of death only entered the chamber one by one.

It came the turn of Count Sigismond von Eppstein to stand guard near the door of Ermangarde. Twenty-four hours had now passed since the death of the Empress. It was the last day before Christmas.

Count Sigismond had begun his vigil at noon. It was now 1:15. He had already introduced into the chamber near to the dead Empress eight or ten persons when, to his great astonishment, he saw appear at the door the Countess Leonora von Eppstein, his own wife.

We say this caused him a great astonishment because he had not had his Countess notified, having reserved it for himself, once his guard duty was done, to mount his horse and go break the news to her himself. For knowing the close friendship that his wife felt for the Empress, he wished, as much as his skill would allow, to soften the blow that was about to strike her.

Sigismond had not erred in his precaution. The blow must have been terrible, for the Countess Leonora was as pale as death. Her pallor stood out even more strikingly, as she had robed herself in the long trailing weeds of mourning.

Her husband threw himself toward her, and as he knew what pious duty brought her there, without inquiring how she had learned the fateful news, he conducted her, mute and bathed in tears as she was, to the door, which he opened and then closed again after her.

Generally speaking, such visits were brief. The nobleman visitor or lady visitor bent the knee, kissed the hand of the Empress, and left immediately thereafter. But Count Sigismond knew that it would not happen in such a fashion with his wife. It was not a performance of duty according to etiquette alone that the Countess was performing; it was the need of the heart that brought her there. He was not surprised, therefore, when after several minutes inside the chamber she had not come out. However, when a good quarter of an hour had slipped by without his having heard the Countess rap at the door in sign that she was ready to leave, he began to become worried. He feared lest the impression had been too great for Leonora to bear, and not daring to open the door without her call—which would have constituted an infraction of the rules of etiquette—he stooped down to look through the keyhole. He trembled to see that the Countess had fainted away near the dead Empress.

But to his great astonishment, that was not the case.

After having looked through the keyhole for several seconds, he stood up, his forehead bathed in sweat, his own face as pale as that of a cadaver. This alteration in his expression was so obvious that several courtiers who were there, awaiting their turns, asked him what the matter was.

"Nothing," replied Count Sigismond as he passed his hand across his forehead. "Nothing. Absolutely nothing."

The courtiers went back to discussing their own affairs, and Count Sigismond, who thought he had seen wrong, a second time pressed his eye up to the keyhole. This time Count Sigismond was convinced that he had not been mistaken, for this is what he saw:

He saw the dead Empress, still crowned with her crown, still holding her scepter in her hand, but she was seated upon her mortuary bed and was chatting with his wife, Countess Leonora.

The event was so strange that the Count could hardly believe his own eyes. He thought he was dreaming, that he was bound under the spell of some delusion, and so he stood up again, even paler than he had been the first time.

At about the same instant, his Countess Leonora rapped on the door, in sign that her visit to the Empress had been fulfilled. Count Eppstein opened the door for her and cast a rapid glance into the interior of the chapel. The Empress was once more stretched out, motionless, upon her mortuary bed.

The Count gave his wife his arm and, conducting her back along her way, asked her two or three questions that she answered not at all. His duty recalled him for another ten minutes at the door of the Empress. He therefore left the Countess in the antechamber, thinking that her silence when he had asked her the questions had resulted from her affliction, or rather not realizing any of this at all, so overturned were all his ideas at that time.

The courtiers continued to enter, the ones after the others. During each visit Count von Eppstein looked again through the keyhole, but the Empress stayed motionless where she was. Two o'clock rang. The master of arms, who was to replace him in his functions of escort into the chamber, entered. The Count took the time to greet him properly, handed over his tour of duty, and then, rushing headlong from the chamber, ran to the Emperor's apartments, where he found the Emperor himself in the depths of sorrow.

"Most Holy Majesty," he cried, "no longer weep in this

way! Instead, send your doctor as fast as you can to the Empress. The Empress is not dead.''

"What are you saying, Sigismond?" cried the Emperor.

"I am saying that just a few minutes ago I saw with my own eyes, that I saw, for sure, the Exalted Empress Ermangarde seated upon her funeral bed and chatting with the Countess Eppstein."

"Which Countess Eppstein?" asked the Emperor.

"Countess Leonora von Eppstein . . . my wife."

"My poor friend," the Emperor told him as he sadly shook his head. "Grief has caused you to lose your mind."

"How is that, Sire?"

"Countess Eppstein, you say! May God grant you the strength to endure this tragedy!"

"Why, what about Countess Eppstein . . . ?" Sigismond inquired with anxiety.

"Countess Eppstein was pronounced dead this morning."

Count Sigismond screamed aloud. He ran to his town house, jumped on a horse, crossed the intersections of Frankfort like a wild man, and a half hour later entered Castle Eppstein.

"Countess Leonora?" he cried. "Countess Leonora?"

As he ran through the castle, he met several of his own servants, none of whom replied to his calls. He burst into his wife's bedchamber. There she was, lying on her bed, clad all in black, just as pale as when he had seen her three-quarters of an hour earlier. At the foot of her bed the chaplain was intoning prayers from the Bible. The Countess had been dead since morning.

Having been unable to locate Count Sigismond, the messenger from Castle Eppstein had delivered his sad news to the Emperor in person. The Count inquired if, since the hour of midnight, when the Countess had actually passed away, anyone had observed the slightest movement on her part.

"None," he was told.

He then asked the priest who was praying beside her bed if he had once absented himself from beside that bed.

"Not for a second," said the priest.

Then the Count remembered that they were exactly on Christmas Day and that an old prophecy of Merlin had foretold that those Countesses of Eppstein who died during Christmas Eve would only half die. Leonora was the first Countess Eppstein who died during the night before Christmas. Sigismond had made an error: It was not Ermangarde who was alive; it was Leonora who had passed away; the dead Countess had come to kiss the hand of her dead Empress, and the two phantoms had spoken together for ten minutes.

Count Sigismond thought he would go insane. People assured him that his Countess, whose soul had been granted the privilege of forming a relationship with the living, had, during the course of the illness that struck the Count as a result of this occurrence, visited her husband's bedside several times.

One year later, Count Sigismond retired from the world into a monastery, leaving his title to his eldest son, and his fortune to him also, both of which he abdicated in order to devote himself to God.

These visitations took place, people said, inside what is called the Red Chamber of the castle, and which, by means of a door that opens in the wall and which leads into a secret staircase, offers another access to the tombs of the Counts von Eppstein. They added that over three generations the Countess appeared to the oldest members of the family in times of crisis but that finally, after the fourth generation following that of her death, the apparitions ceased.

Since that time nobody had ever seen Countess Leonora again; but her tradition was perpetuated in Castle Eppstein, so that the eldest son had preserved the custom of sleeping in the Red Chamber. As for the rest, no other Countess von Eppstein, from that period onward, had ever died during an Eve of Christmas.

─────────────

One can easily understand what an effect such a narrative had upon Albina; her soul, which flamed up at any poetry at all, simply blazed at this fantastic legend as it was unfolded word by word. Sitting there musing upon the fact that she was going soon to be addressed as Countess von Eppstein and dreaming of how she was going to dwell in this ancient castle that was contemporary with Charlemagne, she believed herself almost returned backward in time, in actual fact, to this Middle Ages, which was the historical period of her predilection.

Meanwhile, as Maximilian would not have been able very long to sustain the role that he was playing in the forewarned and clairvoyant eyes of Albina, he was, happily for him, called home after a fortnight by a grave matter requiring his attendance upon his father. He departed, bearing with him the young girl's confession of love and the consent of her father the Duke, who in any case was holding to a year hence for the celebration of the marriage.

In this interval, Maximilian went several times to Vienna, but always in the nick of time disappeared from there. First of all, there was the death of his mother, followed by that of the Count as he joined her. Before their deaths, however, the two noble old persons had written to their son's fiancée letters as kind as their hearts, which not only maintained but even increased the illusions of the poor, enthusiastic girl. Across the gulf of their separation, Albina, who was faithful to the beloved figment of her imagination such as her own sublime soul alone had created, still considered her Maximilian to be superb. She could hardly wait to console him for all the sorrows which cast him down, and to go in person to people his sad solitude and make it lively with her presence, queen and fairy as she thought herself, in his ancient Castle Eppstein.

Then very often she thought of Countess Leonora's legend and frequently caught herself praying to God to let her die during some evening before a Christmas Day, so that possessing the ancient privilege granted to the Countesses von Eppstein who would die on that night, she might, after her own death, rise out of the tomb to go and call upon her spouse.

Finally, toward the close of the year 1791, the long-desired wedding ceremony was performed at Vienna. The Emperor witnessed the marriage contract, and the two newlyweds departed for Castle Eppstein.

The first request Albina made as she arrived there was that she be shown the Red Chamber.

It was, in any case, the one Maximilian had been using since the death of his father.

We are acquainted with this bedchamber, and we have already heard it described. It was then exactly as it is still today.

Fifteen days after Albina's departure, the Duke of Schwalbach suffered an attack of apoplexy from which he never recovered, as if the father's protection was henceforth no longer needed by his daughter. That was the first severe grief in Albina's life, which was to be a lifetime of severe griefs.

Nobody ever heard a word more about Conrad and Naomi. The new Count von Eppstein never again spoke of them.

CHAPTER

III

One year later everything was vastly altered at Castle Eppstein as in the rest of the world. Albina trembled before Maximilian, and Europe trembled before France.

The French Revolution had not yet broken out in all its fury. The King was not dead yet, but he was already a prisoner. The grumbling of the thunder announced what a storm was about to strike, and just as an oncoming tide batters the seashores, so France was already overflowing her frontiers onto the Rhine provinces while she waited to drown the whole continent. General A.-P. Custine had already, in 1792, seized Mayence and was threatening to attack Frankfort.

Inside Castle Eppstein the turbulent, fierce temper of Maximilian, even though it had not yet dragged him into his former debauchery, had already come to light, so that Albina by now had seen expire one by one all her chimerical imaginings. The noble, poetic knight of whom she had dreamed in girlhood now appeared before her rather what in actuality he was, which is to say, a vulgar schemer and a lewd rake to whom marriage was nothing more than a stepping stone and a wife nothing more than an object upon which to vent his pleasure. At first, Albina had suffered deeply, but then she had become resigned, so that now, without a murmur, she permitted the soft flowers of her being to be trampled by his brutish feet. She hardly found time now for pain or regrets, since the events on the political scene stepped faster than her anticipation.

Once Mayence, or the German Mainz on the left bank of the Rhine, had fallen to the French, the banks of the Main were occupied by the French Army of the North, and the old imperial troops beat a retreat before the new soldiers of revolutionary liberty. Frankfort could only hold out for a few more days. Count von Eppstein, whose castle was directly adjacent to the theater of the war, would have been a prisoner of some note, and he thought of himself as an even more important personage than he really was. In any case, they were recalling him to Vienna. He therefore considered himself obligated to leave his territories until the whirlwind had passed them by. To attempt holding out against the French Army inside his own castle was manifestly impossible, and steadfastness in such desperate circumstances would have been nothing more than incautious folly.

But Maximilian had already delayed considerably; French scouting parties were even then cutting the route to Vienna; his escape had already become chancy, his road already sown with perils of all kinds. The presence of Albina would have doubled his own danger during his flight. Maximilian therefore resolved to leave his wife in the castle.

Albina did her best to persuade her husband to take her with him. Finally, on the eve of his departure, she begged him insistently by all he held sacred not to abandon her alone there. Unfortunately, decisions taken by Maximilian were irrevocable. He remained unmoved by her tears, deaf to her pleas. His wife begged him in vain.

"What are you afraid of," he asked her, "and what is the meaning of these childish terrors? If we flee together, we shall cause the loss of the one and of the other. You know the plan, that I shall make my escape tonight with Daniel, that I will dress as a peasant. After daybreak, even so, we shall not easily manage to throw off suspicion. What would be the case were we to have you along with us? Once I am out of their reach, what can they do to you? Does one take women prisoners? No. The French are not devoid of generosity. Make them honor you and they will honor you. In any case, all discussion is useless, for we have no choice. If my life were mine alone, I would drive an easier bargain with you; but I consider my person not without usefulness for my country. Come along, Albina. Have some courage and realize that I am confiding to your care what are my dearest possessions in the world, my son and my honor. Tomorrow, Albina, you will be widowed and alone," he added in a voice that was almost gentle as he kissed the poor waif. "Let me forget tomorrow since today still remains to us."

As always, Albina bent low in obedience before her master. The next day, Maximilian departed. Three days later, Albina received a letter announcing that he had arrived safely. But during those three days there had occurred at Castle Eppstein an event that was to bring with it a radical upheaval in the life of the miserable Albina.

Before he gave the order to march toward Frankfort, General Custine thought it prudent to reconnoiter the perimeter of that city. He deployed two companies to search the passes of the Taunus Mountains. His precautions were reasonable. The French discovered an ambush that had been set up to catch them on the wooded slopes not far distant from Castle Eppstein.

During the ensuing combat, our boys were forced by a heavy enemy contingent to fall back upon the general's main body. But the enemy's strategy had been laid bare, so that as a result, they could, without the risk of being caught in a crossfire, launch their main offensive against Frankfort. The next day they took it. The only thing is that during their hard-fought skirmish the two French units suffered the loss of a good number of men plus a few of their gallant officers.

Among the latter category was a young captain known

only under the name of Captain Jacques, who had up until that time stood out only because, as the Army of the North crossed the Rhine, that is to say, at the very moment when the French first set foot on German soil, he had cast his sword into the river. He wore henceforth only an empty scabbard by his side. Although now deprived of his defensive weapon, which, as far as that goes, was rather a sign of their rank rather than a real defense to them, the young captain had, because of his bravery, his sangfroid, and his personal knowledge of the countryside, also rendered noteworthy services. He was the one who had walked straight toward the ambush, but he had also received the reward for his daring at the first salvo that the imperial forces launched upon our republican troops. The captain fell, struck on the forehead by a bullet. Both our side and the enemy had left him for dead on the battlefield.

It was only toward evening that one of the new servants, coming home to Castle Eppstein from Falkenstein (at the death of his father Count Rudolph, Maximilian had hired all new servants, keeping only the old steward Daniel and the forester Jonathas) heard moans and found Captain Jacques still alive and breathing. Assisted by two peasants, whom he enlisted, the servant transported the wounded French officer into Castle Eppstein. There Albina ordered that the most sophisticated care at their disposal be afforded him.

The chaplain was an expert surgeon. He examined the young officer's wound, put on an emergency dressing, and from the next morning declared that he would answer for his life.

Albina showed a personal concern for the wounded young man, bustling about him with speed, first of all because she was a woman and therefore touched by suffering and next because the presence of a captain instituted a safeguard for herself against marauding bands of French soldiers. One has to admit that the conquering French soldiery did not use their victory with all the moderation that Maximilian had assured his wife that they would use. Whenever pillagers came pounding upon the castle portal, Jacques was alerted. He rose out of bed, and despite all the protests of the chaplain and of Albina, he dragged himself up to them, and pale though he was from the loss of blood, he managed to raise his voice enough for them to hear him and, thus, to safeguard from every peril both castle and chatelaine.

From that time onward, both gratitude and pity as well induced the youthful Countess to redouble her attentions to him who had saved her life, and, possibly, more than her life.

Captain Jacques had, on top of that, a most loving nature, and even a most passionate nature, which responded, you might say, most empathetically to the gentle, fervent personality of Albina. The only reproach one might have made him was that he tended almost continually to lapse into melancholy and that he presented, because of this tendency, a somewhat too effeminate appearance for a military man. But sadness became his pale face, and everybody knew he was as brave as a lion. People thereabouts had seen him standing calm and unconcerned amid bullets and cannonballs, so that his men regarded him, a man who appeared to be so delicate but who was in reality so strong, with an admiration that verged upon veneration. On the other hand, Captain Jacques was very well liked by his fellow officers because of his wide, helpful knowledge of military matters, which caused him to be forgiven for certain of his rather eccentric notions or opinions. His education made his fellows more or less unable to follow him upon the terrain of imagination or into imaginary landscapes where wild poetry ran rampant. While his men called him Captain Jacques the Hero, his fellow officers called him Jacques the Dreamer. It was obvious, in actual fact, that Jacques had gone to war for an idea, and for nothing else, and that the specific quarrel between the crowned heads of Europe disappeared, as far as he was concerned, under the general question of people and populations.

One ought to be able to understand now how such a person moved in harmony with the kind of person Albina was. Jacques was truly the man of her dreams: brave, faithful, and as daring as Götz von Berlichingen, as handsome and as literary a man as Max Piccolomini in Schiller's *Wallenstein* trilogy.

Thus, to the chaplain's great amazement, because he knew how distant the Countess kept herself, an obvious familiarity soon grew up between the young officer and the Countess. After a few days more, the Captain called the young lady Albina, and the young lady called the French officer Jacques.

In addition, as Jacques seemed to wish not to be seen by the people living in the area around the castle, he practically never left his apartments, where Albina kept him company. The castle servants could freely enter, at all hours, the drawing room where the youngsters stayed; they would always find them laughing and talking. Their safeguard was the perfect innocence of their thoughts.

You could have said that these two soulful persons, both so white faced, so similar the one to the other, so familiar in their contacts, had known each other before, inside some better world, and were rediscovering each other in this world. Long, long hours passed by, then, in conversations full of charm for them, without Albina and Jacques realizing the flight of time.

And so Jacques appeared to awaken from a dream when they notified him that he was ordered, two days hence, to leave the castle and return into France with his troop. His convalescence of two months had passed as swiftly as an hour.

Albina escorted the young officer to the exterior stairway. There he took leave of her, kissing her fingers and naming her his sister. Albina wished him all sorts of good fortune, calling him her brother. Then, as long as she could follow him with her eyes, she kept bidding him farewell and then waving to him with her handkerchief.

Two weeks after Jacques's departure, Albina received a letter from her husband. The French retreat now allowed Maximilian safely to regain his castle. So he wrote her to expect him from one instant to the other.

Since one could not reach Castle Eppstein by carriage, Albina dispatched Tobias (who momentarily had taken over the functions of Daniel after his departure from the castle) to await Maximilian at Frankfort with two saddle horses. Maximilian recognized in this action one of Albina's customary kind offices, but he was one of those egotistical men who always think people only do for them what they ought to do anyway. He mounted one of the horses while Tobias mounted the second. The rest of the Count's suite were to make their way to the castle as best they could.

The conversation on the way home came naturally to turn upon the sojourn of the French in that area. So hardly were the Count and Tobias en route but the Count gestured to Tobias, who was keeping a respectful distance behind him, to take a place at his side and to maintain his pace.

Tobias obeyed.

"Well, then," inquired Maximilian, "the French, according to what the Countess wrote me, therefore respected the castle?"

"Yes, my lord," answered Tobias, "but thanks to the protection of Captain Jacques; for I believe that without him things would have turned out badly for us."

"What's that about this Captain Jacques?" Maximilian replied. "The Countess mentioned him in one of her letters. So, then, he had been wounded?"

"Yes, my lord. Hans found him dying at about five hundred paces from the castle and had him transported to Eppstein. For the first night, he hovered between life and death, but our reverend abbot treated him so skillfully day and night that at the end of a month he was perfectly healed."

"And then he removed from the castle?" asked Maximilian, who had imperceptibly wrinkled his brows at the mention of the care that the Countess had arranged for the wounded officer.

"No, he stayed on another month."

"Another month yet! And what was he doing there?"

"Nothing, my lord. He stayed almost the whole time in Madame's apartment, and when he left it occasionally, it was during the evening, and so he only went out after dark to stroll in the grounds. You could have said that he feared being seen."

Maximilian's lips grew white, but without the slightest alteration showing in his voice.

"How long has he been gone?" he asked.

"Only eight or ten days."

"And what manner of man was he?" asked the Count. "Young or old, handsome or ugly, sad or happy?"

"Why, my lord, he was a young man of twenty-six or twenty-eight years of age, more or less, blond, pale, and slender, and who always seemed very sad."

"Is that so," said the Count, biting his lips but continuing the interview in spite of himself, and with that persistence that sets the heart upon knowing those details that will cause it to burst. "Is that so? Then he must have been very bored at the castle."

"No, my lord. He seemed to be sad, but not to be bored."

"Yes," Maximilian continued, "his comrades came to see him. That was a distraction for him."

"Oh, as far as distraction is concerned, he never sought any, for on two occasions only, during all the time that he stayed at the castle, his sergeant came to Eppstein, but it was neither about a billet nor because he had been summoned, but just to bring him his orders from his colonel."

"So, I understand. He went hunting, then."

"He never held a gun, nor once went riding, and Jonathas told me yesterday that for the two months he was there, he personally never saw him."

"But what was he doing, then?" inquired the Count, still trying to control himself; for, despite himself, he felt his voice losing its calm.

"What was he doing? Oh, that's not a long story to tell. In the morning he was playing like a child with my little Lord Albert, who had become very attached to him and who ran to his bedroom every morning as soon as he was up. Or he was conversing with the reverend abbot, who was amazed at his learning. After lunch he made music on the harpsichord, either singing himself or accompanying Madame. And then those were hours of entertainment for all the rest of us, for we listened to their voices outside the doors to the drawing room and thought we were hearing angels. Then, when the concert was terminated, they almost always read aloud to each other, and every evening, as I told my lord, but rarely, they went for a walk in the garden."

"That's some strange officer," said the Count bitterly, "who plays with children, who talks philosophy with old men, who sings with women, who reads books out loud, and who goes for walks all alone."

"All alone?" Tobias exclaimed. "But Madame always accompanied him."

"Always?" replied the Count.

"Or at least almost always," continued Tobias.

"And that's all you know about this officer? Nothing of his birth, nothing of his family? Is he noble or plebeian, rich or poor? Answer me."

"As for all that, my Lord, I know nothing. But Madame Countess, without any doubt, will be able to inform Your Excellency about those matters you wish to learn."

"And where did you get such an idea as that, if you please, Master Tobias?" Maximilian said, casting a sidelong look at his indiscreet speaker in an attempt to discover what lay behind his last remark.

"Why, that idea came to me, my lord," Tobias replied with that affected affability expected of servants who because of it almost always hate their master, "from the belief I have that Madame Countess and the young officer knew each other from way back."

"And from what indications were you able to judge that, sir physiognomist," replied Maximilian in a mocking tone of voice the depths of which Tobias could hardly grasp, "that this young officer and Madame Countess had already met prior to the event which brought them together again?"

"Because the Countess called this officer Jacques and because he addressed Madame Countess as Albina."

With a mechanical motion, Maximilian raised the crop that he held in his hand, intending to cut this clever observer of his, who rode there beside him, across the face. But he contained his wrath just in time and spoke immediately again instead.

"That's fine," he said, whipping his horse instead of whipping Tobias. "that's fine. That's all I wanted to know for the moment, and you are correct, Tobias. Madame Countess will tell me the rest."

The horse leaped forward, and Tobias again found himself behind the Count. Then, since his master made no other sign to him and ceased from that moment to speak to him, he followed, keeping his distance respectfully.

Maximilian's face remained noncommittal, but hideous suspicions gnawed at his heart, at this heart so impervious to love, so prompt to feel anger and to hurl accusations.

Meanwhile, he lacked certainty, and so, while urging his horse to move faster, he kept saying to himself:

"One proof, one proof of her dishonor, one proof which which will permit me to crush the guilty woman!"

And as for that proof, he almost longed for it.

As soon as he arrived at the beginning of the promenade that led to the castle, he saw Albina on the stone stairway, waiting impatiently and happily for him, and with a convulsive thrust of his heels, he drove his spurs into his horse's belly.

The poor woman believed that the Count had put his mount into a gallop out of impatience to see her again.

As soon as the Count set foot on the ground, Albina threw her arms about his neck.

"Pardon me, beloved husband," she told him. "Pardon me for not having gone to meet you. I am not well. But what is the trouble, Maximilian? How careworn you seem and how preoccupied! It is politics, no doubt. Oh! I shall bring back serenity and happiness to your forehead. Come, Maximilian, come and let me tell you privately my great secret, a sweet secret that I keep saying over and over to myself. For I am drunk with joy. It is a secret which has helped me to endure your absence, a secret so charming that I have not wanted to trust it to a letter, for I promised myself the delight of telling it to you in my own voice. It is a secret which I was not able to reveal to you when you left, because I did not yet know it myself. Listen to me, Maximilian, and drive away your dark ill humor. Do you remember that night we said our farewells, that night which was so sweet and yet so painful . . . ? Kiss your wife quickly, for in six months, Maximilian, you will kiss your child.

CHAPTER

IV

You will kindly allow us now to leave for a moment the old turrets of Count Maximilian in exchange for the modest lodging of the forester Jonathas. Castle and cottage have had and will again have, as you will see in the rest of this story, more than one connection with another, so much so that the history of the cottage will be obliged to rub elbows, at more than one point in time, with that of the castle, the one throwing light upon the other.

The little chalet of the keeper of Eppstein, situated at a hundred paces from the wrought-iron gates of the castle grounds and at the entrance to its demesnial forest, backed up to a wooded hill that preserved it from the north winds. This little dwelling was old and decrepit, and yet it seemed young and smiling, such harmonious hues had the bricks with their various shades of red, the shutters painted dark green and the woodbine, which twined capriciously along its walls, acquired under the workings of that great painter that is the weather.

The four huge linden trees that had been planted as a sort of cool antechamber before the front door, the welcoming bench placed near the doorsill, the brook, the neatly disposed courtyard, the little garden, which was small but bright, tufted with plants, full of fruit, flowers, and birds—all that attracted the visitor, all that delighted the eye. In the interior, the same order without affectation, the same cleanliness without gloom, downstairs the family room and the father's bedroom, upstairs the children's room, white, darling, well kept, made bright by a songster in a cage, made perfumed by a pot of flowering plants; there where you see on any windowsill a rose and a chaffinch, you may tell me that the inhabitants of this cottage are wiser and better than their neighbors.

From the year 1750, Gaspard Muden was forester for Count Rudolph von Eppstein. In 1768, at the age of forty, he took a wife. After five years of the calmest and happiest union, the housewife died, leaving Gaspard with two little girls, Wilhelmina and Naomi.

Gaspard was as solid a man as he was faithful, a man according to Our Lord. He read again the Book of Ruth in the Bible and vowed to live henceforth for the sake of his two orphaned daughters. He therefore lived, and lived simply and with dignity, a noble example for his children, who, under his honest and fatherly instruction, grew in virtue and at the same time in gracefulness.

Wilhelmina and Naomi were both pretty, both hardworking. Wilhelmina was the more playful; Naomi, the more thoughtful. When Wilhelmina, who was the older sister, reached the age of sixteen, the question was which of the country lads would win her in marriage. Among all the suitors, Gaspard chose Jonathas, whom he loved because of his hardihood and his good luck as a hunter. Hunting was old Gaspard's passion, and he obtained for his son-in-law the inheritance of his own appointment. Meanwhile, Jonathas was raised to the rank of adjunct forester.

Without complaint, Wilhelmina took the spouse whom her father presented to her and found the arrangement satisfactory. Jonathas was the best fellow in the world, perhaps a little simple, a little too carefree, except for anything concerning his deer and wild boars, but as husbands go, he was devoted, with eyes for his wife only. He came to live there at his father-in-law's.

As for Naomi, the spoiled child of Jonathas and of her older sister, she was much less docile than Wilhelmina and refused all suitors. The gentle glance of Conrad von Eppstein had already pierced her through to the depths of her soul. The pale, melancholy youth, whom she had often met in the woods and who, at each encounter, had turned away from her with so much confusion, filled all her thoughts without her knowing it.

One day a violent storm drew the lonely youth, who had been walking alone in the woods, into the shelter of the forester's cottage, and from that day forward, encouraged by the father's cordial hospitality, fascinated by the girl's beauty, Conrad returned every week, and then every day.

With his good sense as a countryman, Gaspard had not failed to notice Naomi's emotion when the youth arrived, her reverie when he was no longer there. He would certainly have shown the door to a known philanderer like Maximilian; but the serious demeanor, the austere and dignified character, of the young scholar, as he was called, inspired the forester's trust and virtually his respect. When Conrad was not there, Gaspard spoke angrily of him, to Naomi's great fright, and swore that he would never again receive in his cottage the young and noble Lord Eppstein, whose proper place was in the castle. Conrad came, and Gaspard awkwardly tipped his hat to him and disappeared somewhere grumbling.

We know the rest. When Gaspard learned of his daughter's secret marriage, man of honor that he was, he had nothing to say; as a faithful servant, he trembled at the thought of his master's wrath. He justified himself easily, however, before the noble good sense of Count Rudolph, but the father in him had to suffer, for he had to bid a sad adieu to his darling Naomi, banished because she had fallen in love. Naomi so resembled his dead wife that he felt, when he saw her go, as if he had lost his mate a second time.

Nevertheless, in that second trial, the Christian in him

bowed his head before the decrees of Providence. Without shedding a tear, he kissed the daughter whom he was never to see again and read the Biblical story of Hagar cast out into the wilderness.

Naomi departed, and days, months, long years, flowed past without their receiving a single letter from Naomi. All they knew was that Naomi was in France.

When she thought about her sister, Wilhelmina wept; but also, it should be noted, she only wept when she thought of her sister. She was, aside from that sorrow, happy; and she loved her husband, who adored her.

We have spoken of the death of Count Rudolph and of his wife. As he took over the management of his household, Maximilian excepted both Jonathas and Gaspard from his general dismissal. Were he in service under a new master, Gaspard could have talked about his stepson and Jonathas about his brother-in-law. Keeping them in his service, the Count obliged both to be closemouthed.

When Albina came to dwell in Castle Eppstein, she found the sweet, good Wilhelmina much to her taste. The nascent jealousy of Maximilian caused him to forbid his wife to frequent any of the castles thereabouts, but he did not forbid her the cottages; and Albina was less lonely in the attractive, little house of the forest warden than in her own black, dismal fortress. She had at Wilhelmina's house her own flower plot, which she watered herself, her own birds that recognized her. The little bit of fresh air, sunshine, and freedom that were left to her now were all to be found only at Wilhelmina's house. It was only there that she once saw by chance one sunny day such as she had known at her home, at Winkel.

However, at the arrival of the French, which pressed the Count to leave for Vienna, he rigorously commanded his wife not to set foot outside the castle. Her housekeeping chores kept Wilhelmina in her own place, and so poor Albina was more lonely and more disconsolate than ever, up until the moment when there arrived at the castle the French captain Jacques.

Persons whose hearts ache tend to feel pity for all suffering. Albina took a keen interest in the poor, wounded youth. For his part, the wounded officer openly expressed an oddly personal attraction toward Albina. One evening, Captain Jacques told Albina the story of his life. Doubtless there were in his recital, which has not come down to us in any part, however, certain aspects of intense interest for her, because, from that evening on, a true friendship seemed to reunite, as it were, these two young charmers.

From that time onward, Albina's thoughts seemed to have food, and her life became more interesting to her. She no longer so much regretted that she could no longer take long rambles through the forest; she stopped urging Wilhelmina so urgently to come and see her in the castle. The forester's wife never even once saw the wounded officer during all the time he was in Castle Eppstein. She only caught a glimpse of his brilliant uniform the day he left to rejoin his regiment at Mayence.

As soon as Captain Jacques left her alone, Albina drew close to Wilhelmina once again and made her swear to steal away from her little cottage as often as ever she could. While these two young women were separated by both birth and education, they got along so very well together because of their similarity of thought that from this point of comparison they were like two sisters. The chatelaine had recovered some of her old exuberance. She confided in Wilhelmina, but in Wilhelmina alone, her secret hope that caused her suddenly to be so happy. Jonathas's wife, too, was expecting a baby, about a month after the Countess. So imagine what a lot of plans and dreams and excitement there was between the two of them!

"Our two children," Albina used to say, "shall be raised together and shall have the same schoolmasters. I wish it. Do you hear me, Wilhelmina?"

"Yes, madame," Wilhelmina would reply. "But I have thought of one thing. You are too delicate to be able to nurse your baby. So, then, I will nurse yours just as long as I am nursing mine. As for me, I am a peasant woman with big breasts, and I am very healthy, too, and so you can rest easy on that point. These babies will never lack the proper care and feeding, neither the one nor the other. The only danger is that I shall not know which of the two of them is my own baby."

Right in the middle of all these plans and of all this hopefulness, Count Maximilian returned from Vienna.

The day after this return, when Wilhelmina presented herself at the castle, as she usually did, she was notified that Madame would no longer receive anyone, and this by direct order of the Lord von Eppstein. She insisted and was virtually turned out of doors. She went home to her own cottage extremely worried and completely bathed in tears.

From that day on, Count Maximilian, who had only rarely hunted up until that time, went out hunting every single day, always accompanied by Jonathas. As far as Gaspard was concerned, he hardly left his house anymore. He found himself very happy to be replaced by his son-in-law.

In these daily hunting expeditions, Count Eppstein now displayed a fierce savagery that nobody had ever seen him reveal before that time. This cruelty on his part grew more bloody day by day. He seemed to have in his heart of hearts a need to cause suffering. When either the stag or the buck was brought to bay, instead of sparing them their long and excruciating death throes by means of a bullet or a stab from the hunting knife, he let them be torn apart alive and devoured by his dogs, not without the leaders of his pack being gutted in the process. As for him, always hideous, he laughed at the sight of it. Otherwise, he stayed speechless for the length of entire days, without ever uttering a word. One time, Jonathas, who had been won over by his wife, asked him for news of the Countess. At that Maximilian grew visibly paler and in clipped tones accompanied by a threatening stare: "Shut your trap," he had said. "What the hell is it to you what the Countess does or does not do? That's none of your business." And so from that day on, the poor forester had never again ventured to ask questions that were so badly received.

Several more weeks slipped by. They were at the end of December. The time for Wilhelmina's lying in had arrived. On the morning of Christmas day, the Count had notified Jonathas to present himself for a consultation. The latter waited in vain for his master for two hours without Maximilian having appeared at all.

Soon after, in the place of Maximilian, Jonathas saw a messenger arrive who announced to him that Wilhelmina was calling for him with loud screams. Wilhelmina's labor pains had commenced. With as long strides as he could manage, Jonathas sprinted home along the path to his cottage. Just as he was passing the threshold, Wilhelmina was giving birth to a daughter.

Wilhelmina's first thought thereafter was for her husband. The second was for Albina.

"Let the Countess be notified," cried Wilhelmina, radiant in the midst of her suffering.

But no one answered Wilhelmina's words except by tears and silence.

Really, there had taken place that very morning in Castle Eppstein a terrible confrontation.

CHAPTER

V

Albina had thought that when she revealed to her husband the happy news that filled her motherly heart with joy, Maximilian would share this intoxication with her, that he would press his wife in his arms, that he would shout with such happiness as only two lovers understand and treasure, and that a new era was about to open in her love.

"I must have misunderstood the Count," Albina told herself in the quiet dialogues she held with her generous nature. "He is noble and good and a devoted husband. The only thing is, I was all the time comparing him to the ideal man of my girlish dreams, comparing him to the chimerical fancies of childhood. I was expecting life to make the capricious fantasies of my imagination come true, as if a great statesman like my husband were the hero of some medieval romance, as if men of the eighteenth century could resemble those of the sixteenth century. I was crazy, but now I have reached the age of reason. Now I am strong and a woman. Now I am soon to become a mother. No more silly demands. Now I have only duties to perform. I can no longer allow myself to judge him severely, since now I, too, am responsible for ourselves. In addition, I feel that I should want to pardon everything to him who has fathered a child for me, to him who has given me the happiness of becoming a mother, which is the purest happiness there ever can be in this world."

It was thus with a watchfulness full of impatience that Albina longed for the Count's return. It was with a haste that was totally joyous and totally confident that with a smile she whispered her darling secret in his ear. It was with a child's innocent and teasing gracefulness that she stole a look at his face to spy out the effect upon him of her wonderful news. She hoped that he was going to kiss her with abandon, that he was going to call her all sorts of pet names, that he was going to ask her one thousand questions arising from his tenderness and his concern for her well-being.

Instead of that, Maximilian grew deathly pale. Raging, he squeezed the hand that Albina had extended for him to kiss. Then, because he perceived Tobias at some distance behind him, and his retinue beside him, feeling the necessity of controlling himself before them, he passed by his wife, where she stood stunned. Wordless and icy, he threw himself forward in one burst of speed.

Albina remained standing where he had left her, motionless and then icy cold herself, still in the same spot, like a statue of grief. She drew her hand across her forehead. Yes, she was awake well enough. It was not some awful nightmare. Her heart leaden with horror and sick with anguish, she managed to retire to her own apartment.

What had she done? What fault on her part had drawn down upon her head her master's wrath? Or rather, what crime on her part? For, that such anger could have been proof against even her news of happiness, which she had only just then first announced to him, it must have been some very capital offense on her part that had caused it.

Albina interrogated her conscience as rigorously as she could, but to no avail. She truly could not find anything in her life that could have occasioned such intractability on his part. Perhaps her sin was having for such a long time kept silent about her condition; but really, if she had done it, it was for the purpose of announcing the good news to the Count personally, and surely such a slight fault hardly deserved such a harsh greeting. Lost in a thousand fearsome misgivings, the poor Countess, solitary in her bedchamber, had no idea what was going to happen to her and crouched there trembling at the slightest sound.

After an hour had gone by so, the door opened. It was a servant, who entered and handed her a letter. This letter came from Maximilian, and contained the following:

Madame, I confine myself to acquainting you with my wishes, my express wishes, do you understand? Here they are.

You shall never again leave the walls of this Castle. You shall never appear before me again. You are free to walk in the galleried courtyard whenever I am outside the Castle, and I shall go out every day. However, on pain of your life, I order you not to take a step beyond that courtyard. I also require that you do not write to anyone and that your Wilhelmina shall not present herself ever again for admission within this Castle. You know who I am and what I am. Obey me and do not compromise yourself with my anger at its peak, or else I will not answer for what follows a new outburst which you will have brought upon yourself.

After reading this letter, not a word of which she could understand, except that she herself was utterly ruined, the Countess remained in collapse.

We have already explained the kind of violent power that the implacable will of Maximilian exercised upon everyone and how people everywhere bowed low, almost despite themselves, to this undeniably gross authority, which one no more thought of being able to outwit than one could hope to escape the blind, inevitable decrees of destiny.

This was true to the degree that Albina, even though she was certain of being guilty of no crime, still bowed her head low, as one does before death, and waited.

We must observe, however, that in the calm of her attitude, for she had chosen to remain outwardly composed, there was as much dignity of bearing as there was resignation. After all, she was upheld by her belief in her own innocence, so that, not loving her husband any longer, she cared less for the Count's esteem than for her own self-respect.

"If Maximilian no longer respects his wife," she told herself, "it is his wife's duty to maintain her respect for herself and, by her undeviating and confident composure, to protest against an unjust condemnation. I do not even know what crime Maximilian accuses me of, but the future always advances torch in hand to illumine the past. A day will dawn, therefore, when Maximilian will recognize his error. Until that time it becomes me to remain undisturbed and assured."

Was she not counting too heavily upon her own strength, inexperienced girl that she was, who until the day of her wedding had seen all persons and events yield before her girlish frailty? The wrath of such a man as Maximilian ought assuredly not to be treated lightly, for once this degree of wrath is aroused, it will not halt halfway along its course or allow itself to be rerouted by any roadblock. No, it would crush through the roadblock in order to arrive at its destination.

The Count realized all this so thoroughly that he frightened himself and trembled before the knowledge of his own virulence. Overcome with rage at the moment his wife naively announced to him what was for her a happy condition but what he judged a dishonor for himself, he had in a very real way fled before his own vengeance. If he had only listened to his own instincts for violence, he would under the press of the moment have killed outright this woman who had cuckolded him and who, after having deceived him, insulted him. Had he slain her then and there, he would only have proclaimed his own disgrace. What he did was to dominate his own wrath. Provisionally, he only sentenced his wife to prison, as one does any other felon.

Once his threatening letter was sent to Albina, he, too, on his side, waited.

Both continued to live under the same roof, morning and night also, both of them. Albina could hear Maximilian as he passed along the corridor. He proceeded always with the same slow, somber steps. Not one single time did he halt before her door or ever evince the least desire to halt there. For the next several months they did not see each other a single time; if they did not see each other, they thought about each other, and certainly as much or more than lovers would do, or the most devoted couple.

The Count tried in vain to dispel by means of physical exhaustion all the dark ideas that obsessed him. He found them impossible to dispel. The outrage that he considered he had received was of that sort that men of his stamp resent too terribly for them ever to forget it or to pardon it. On her side, the Countess in vain tried to take refuge in her clear conscience and, thus, to shield herself from any thought not directly connected either to her baby or to God. Even so, the mystery of why Maximilian had reacted as he did horrified her despite her efforts and continually came to upset her, shattering in the daylight hours her hopefulness and at night breaking into her sleep with nightmares.

The outward calm that both demanded of themselves amounted to nothing more than the deceptive calm that precedes hurricanes; both of them knew this prefectly well. Both of them quaked under the pain and fever of the long wait. Maximilian and Albina were no longer alive. Both of them, with a semblance of tranquillity upon their faces but death in their souls, shuddered frequently before the dumb terrors that weighed upon their chests. As for him, he shook, without even realizing why, before the halo of purity that he knew bound the white forehead of his wife. She, for her part, well acquainted with her husband's violent bouts of fury, expected that the worst would happen the very first day they would meet each other.

And yet it was to Albina that this state first became unbearable. Strong in her own innocence, she resolved to go before the unknown danger that she felt closing in upon her from all sides. She came to have such a strong conviction of this peril that once she had finally decided that she would demand an explanation of his conduct from Maximilian, she took action. She wrote a letter first before demanding this explanation from him. Her letter was, as we shall see it, rather more in the style of a last will and testament than in the style of a letter:

It has been forbidden me not only to see you, my dear, good Wilhelmina, but more than that, even to write to you. Thus, this letter will only be handed to you if I die. Death, it seems to me, ought to release me from any obedience.

Do not be astonished by my sad apprehensions, dear Wilhelmina. One must foresee all eventualities in the condition in which I find myself, and I should not like to leave this earth without bequeathing to you, to you, dear, who have always been so devoted to me, the legacy which all dying persons who have loved someone must absolutely will.

Dear God. I do not know why these words come so sadly to my pen. I am perfectly easy and tranquil. Please believe it, my pretty farm wife. So, well, I am even able to smile at this very moment at the thought of the happy plans we used to make two months ago.

"Do you remember, dear friend? In any case, I am

going to remind you of them, for, on both our parts, these projects amounted to firm commitments.

You swore to me, Wilhelmina, that you would nurse my baby if I were unable to do so. Do not forget this promise, for I am depending upon it. Do you hear me plainly? I shall live, I hope that I shall survive, to make you remember it in person. Just the same, I shall be calmer up here when I shall have recalled this promise to you, and which in a minute this resolution that I have just taken will solemnize.

That is not all, Wilhelmina. Listen. If God calls me to Him, I am sure that Count Maximilian would raise my child with care and care for him as a noble child should be cared for; but all the same, the education of a child's soul, do you understand me, the education the child receives at his mother's knee, only a woman knows how to give.

Men know how to teach about life, but only women know how to teach about heaven. . . .

For instance, because you know me, you would speak to my child of me better than his father would do, for he has never known me. Speak to my child of me, Wilhelmina. Do it often. Do it always. Try to make him know me as if he had actually seen me. Then, the hugs and kisses which are no less necessary to little ones than are a mother's milk, do not withhold them, either, my good-hearted Wilhelmina. The poor orphaned baby! May he grow up in your tender care and in your love. Last of all, be to him not only a nurse. Be a mother to him.

Is this really all I had to say to you? Yes, because if I have forgotten something, your heart will guess all the rest of my thoughts.

But you are probably finding me selfish, for I have not spoken to you at all of yourself. Please forgive me! I have been speaking of him, of the baby who is in me.

All the same, while recommending my child to you, you will see that I have not forgotten yours. You will find enclosed under this envelope two other letters, the one addressed to the mother superior of Holy Linden, the other to Major von Kniebis in Vienna.

If a daughter is born to you, you will send her, as soon as she is five or six years old, with the first of these two letters, to the care of my dear Aunt Dorothy, who has been a second mother to me. Answering my request, Wilhelmina, my aunt will welcome your daughter immediately into the same convent where I was raised beside the first heiresses of Germany. Oh! What a happy time that was for me, when I used so joyfully to sing the hymns of Our Lord and where the loss of my pet dove was the greatest sorrow I ever had. There, dear Wilhelmina, rest easy. Your girl will receive the best and most holy upbringing.

If you have a son, send him to the major, who will either enroll him in a preparatory school or who will place him in a military academy! This beloved major was the close, personal friend of my father. Not a day went by but he called upon us at Winkel. I remember what pleasure I had teasing him and with what gracefulness and what kindliness he took part in my childish games, or even started them. Who in the world would say, were they to see me today, that I was once the silliest and most giddy of little girls?

The major will certainly not have forgotten his little Albina, and he will greet your son as if he were my own.

I wish we could have had each one of us either a son, or both a daughter, so that our children could be brothers or sisters.

Do for mine if I die what I will do for yours if I survive.

Farewell forever, my dear Wilhelmina! Before all

eventualities I have one firm conviction: I believe that the soul does not die and that my soul will never in this world leave that soul which will never in this world leave my child.

I am folding inside this letter, for my beloved little angel baby, a lock of my hair. It will only come down to you if I depart from this earth.

Farewell once more. Farewell forever! Do not forget anything! Do not forget anything!"

Albina von Eppstein, *née* von Schwalbach.
December 24, 1793.

P.S. I was forgetting something. It is a childishness on my part, but if a son is born to me, I desire that he be named Everard after my father. If I have a daughter, I desire her to be named Ida after my mother.

Once this letter was written, Albina felt a little calmer.

Nothing so much refreshes the soul as a resolution made; and Albina had decided to force Maximilian to break this somber, obstinate, and terrible silence, even though the first word that she should utter struck her dead, like a strike of death-dealing lightning.

That long day sped by more quickly for Albina than the other long days of her captivity, for she kept thinking ceaselessly that each passing minute was bringing nearer the decisive hour and her supreme moment. The last hours of that day flew past on wings.

Night fell. The Countess had several tapers lighted; it seemed to her that the more brightly lit her bedchamber, the more clearly the serenity of her forehead would be seen, that the more deeply the innocence of her soul would be plumbed, the stronger she herself would be. At last. At the accustomed hour, she listened. She heard the sound of Maximilian's footsteps. She threw open her door and stepped out into the corridor.

Maximilian appeared there at the top of the staircase. He was being guided by a servant, who proceeded him, lighting his way. When he glimpsed Albina, he halted for an instant, astonished. The valet continued on his way, bowed as he passed in front of the Countess. Then came Maximilian's turn to pass her by.

He intended to pass her without uttering a word; but with a firmness of which Albina herself would not have believed herself capable, she laid her hand upon his arm. At the touch of this hand, the man of iron shuddered.

"What do you wish, Madame?" said Maximilian.

"A moment's conversation, Count," answered Albina.

"And when that?"

"Instantly, if you are so kind."

"What! This evening?"

"This evening."

"Madame!" said Maximilian in a menacing voice.

"I beseech you."

"You recall the advice I had given you to let my anger lie sleeping. You have just awakened it. You are the one who wishes that, Madame. Well. So be it. I am at your command."

They stared at each other, both of them, there in the flickering light of the torch. They were as white faced, the one as the other. This decisive moment, so long dreaded and which they knew was inevitable just the same, had come. Possibly, in the depths of their hearts, after having more than once longed for it, they would now, both of them, have desired to postpone it. But it was too late. An impulsion, which was stronger than their wills, drove them forward.

"Madame," the Count said after some hesitation, and his voice thirsted for blood, "there is still time. Tell me to withdraw and to pass on into my own apartments. I sense that you are ill, and, to speak plainly, I am now warning you. Madame, I will not be answerable for my actions. Pay strict attention to this caution. Look here. So you really desire that instantly we should once more confront each other, face-to-face, or rather would you prefer that we should adjourn and once again delay this business?"

"No," replied the Countess. "No adjournment. I have waited long enough as it is. I have nothing to fear, for my part. . . . Therefore follow me, if you please."

The Count signaled his valet to bear the torch into his bedchamber and then followed her inside hers. The Countess, who had entered first, closed the door after the Count.

So much authority on her part almost made Maximilian tongue-tied. He stared at her in amazement. Then, seeing that the Countess had positioned herself opposite him, face-to-face with him, and that she had leveled her quiet eyes full upon him:

"Madame! Madame!" he said, "be on your guard! I am about now to demand from you a rigorous account of your actions. I mean, of all your actions."

"And I also, sir," the Countess said. "I am obliged now to accuse you of yours. You may slander me afterwards if you so wish."

"Speak first, then," said the Count, "but you are pale and ill. Sit down therefore . . . for heaven's sake," he added with a terrifying gallantry as he drew forward an armchair for the Countess.

The Countess was seated. Maximilian remained standing, his arms crossed over his chest, his lips pressed tightly together, his eyes dark.

They were in the grandiose Red Chamber, the family lying-in chamber where the Countess had continued to dwell during Maximilian's absence and which Maximilian, upon his return, had left to her.

This chamber was lighted by four candles, but it was so vast that the light hardly even reached the far walls on its other sides. The state bed stood out in relief, despite the darkness, because of its massive hangings; and before the windows the swaying curtains shivered whenever a gust of winter wind rippled across them.

There was a moment's pause. Then, in a measured, confident voice the Countess began her charges:

"Sir, I lived close to my father, a calm, happy, and beloved girl's life. I used to laugh. I used to run. I used to play. My soul spilled over with happiness, and my heart spilled over with the love of life. Such enthusiasm is by no means a vulgar virtue in a girl. Believe it, sir. And yet this is the very enthusiasm, or love of life, which then caused my downfall. You came, and poor idealist that I was, I discovered that you resembled all my dreams. I saw in you a true nobleman, chivalrous, courageous, fervent; however, you, sir, you married me for my riches and for a title. . . ."

"Madame!" the Count interrupted in a voice that was hollow and more than a little mocking.

"As soon as I became your wife," Albina continued, "you did not even take the trouble to hide your true nature from me and to keep alive my illusions which at once became henceforth useless to you . . . Dear God! it seems to me that something could have been made out of my life."

"You don't say!" Maximilian cried with a burst of sarcastic laughter.

"I saw with my own eyes, sir, I saw," the Countess continued, "my ideals fall like petals from a flower, one by one, and I would once have thought that it would have been impossible for me to live without them. Then I remembered words of advice which my beloved mother superior, abbess of Holy Linden, gave me: 'My child,' she told me on the day I left her side, never again to see her once more, 'if ever you lose happiness from your life, take refuge in duty.' "

"Oh! Yah!" interrupted the Count.

And his sardonic tone of voice carried also something even more frightening to hear.

The Countess continued with an angel's serenity. "Devoted to this memory, I have placed my entire life into obedience and all my strength into resignation. Thus, I steeled myself against being forgotten, but not against hatred, not against indifference, and not against contempt. I do not reproach you for my disenchanted youth, nor for my ruined dreams, nor for my existence, which has been lost. I do not clamor for love from you, knowing that such love is impossible for me to receive. But I do have the right, at least, to lay claim to your respect. I do not wish to have to blush before my own people. Is that too much to require from you, Sir Count? Answer me. Say!"

"I shall commence by telling you that I have in no way to concern myself with your boarding-school childishness about which you entertained me in your first sentences. A man's time is otherwise sufficiently precious, I presume, not to be squandered on such chimerical nonsense; and if I have not realized the dreamings of your tender affections, have you, may I now inquire, realized the projects of my ambition?"

"Oh, Father! Father! You had foreseen all this for me," Albina cried. "A man ambitious for decorations, a man ambitious for titles, whose every effort is bent towards his becoming grand marshal instead of commander, of becoming Duke instead of Count! And he calls that ambition! And he comes talking ambition to me!"

"Wait, Madame," the Count said, and he flushed with anger and stamped his feet. "That's not all of it, what you have just said, that in the grand total it is all about, and you know that perfectly well."

"No, I do not know it. I have desired to have this interview with you so that I could learn what it is all about."

"All right. Then I am going to tell it to you. I have entrusted my name and my honor to you. What have you done with them, Madame? Do not lie to me. Do not hesitate. Do not put on your saintly airs and your pretended martyrdom. That's all useless. The question is clear. So, answer it clearly."

"Even in the most trifling matters I have never lied."

"All right. Then tell me, you faithful wife, you. Tell me what that man was, what he was, that Frenchman, that Captain Jacques?"

As soon as he had said that, Albina understood everything. She smiled, and for one long moment looked pityingly at the Count.

Then she spoke: "That Captain Jacques, sir, was a wounded man whose life I probably saved and who most assuredly saved my honor for me."

"And that is why he called you by your name Albina? That is why you used to call him Jacques. That is why you used also to call him 'mon ami,' my lover. That is why, not venturing so far as to call you 'his lover,' he used to term you 'ma soeur,' my sister. That is why he was all the time inside this chamber with you. That is why you two never left each other's side even for a minute. That is why you wept when he departed."

"Oh! sir," said the Countess, rising from her seat.

"Oh! Don't play your proud tricks on me. Don't attempt to simulate indignation, Madame," replied Maximilian, growing more and more heated as he spoke. "Don't smile at me your little disdainful smile. Don't look at me with contempt. Now I am advising you. If one of us is to scorn the other, it is the outraged husband and not the guilty wife."

"Poor Maximilian!" Albina murmured.

"Oh! Oh! Pity is it now! Take care, Madame! Do not push me to the limit with your insulting coldness. Take care, Madame! Take care! I do not have patient blood. This man has been your lover. I tell you that he has been. But I will have my revenge. Rest assured on that score. I have sworn it to myself privately, and I now repeat my oath to you out loud. Therefore, instead of smiling, madame, I believe that you would do better to tremble."

"However, sir, I am not trembling," Albina said in an unshaken voice. "Look at me. You see what I am doing instead."

"So what are you doing, then?"

"I am pitying you."

"Oh! Then that's enough from you. Hold on," cried the Count in an explosion of wrath. "Stop right there, rather, and bend your neck before my anger. You stand there, up on your feet, haughty and insolent, hoping to hoodwink me doubtless through the strength of your impudence. But I tell you once more that I know everything, that nobody deceives me as easily as you have thought to do, that you prostituted yourself to that man, and that this child that you carry is not mine but the child of adultery. Do you hear me, Madame? Do you hear me? Do you dare look me in the face now, Madame? Ah, you still dare do it. . . . She dares do it, the wretch? Will you lower your eyes before me? You will not do it, you vile woman? Still smiling, are you? Ah . . . !"

With a wash of blood in his eyes Maximilian strode toward the Countess, furiously, blinded with rage. Calm and still with her confident look on her face, Albina watched the storm draw nearer and nearer. She still kept her same little smile on her lips. She smiled and stood her ground without flinching. She spoke not one word. She raised no hand to protect herself. The Count halted one step away from her, shaking, aflame. For a second they stayed there, that way, standing there face-to-face with each other, both carried away, he calling upon hell and she praying to heaven. But Maximilian could not long endure her wordless insults, which came plain enough to him from such supreme self-confidence so that, placing his two hands down upon the shoulders of his wife, he shouted to her.

"One last time," he shouted in a voice of thunder. "Bend your knees. Beg pardon of me on your knees."

"Insane wretch!" Albina said.

She had not even finished saying these words when a terrible swearing echoed thoughout the chamber and the two rough, profane hands of the count had already bent her down to the floor like a reed in a wind, and there lay the frail girl who had defied him. As she fell, Albina's head was knocked back against an angle of the heavy armchair where she had been seated only a moment before. The blood spurted from her head. As she lost consciousness, she kept saying in a low voice:

"My baby. Oh, God! My baby."

Maximilian stood for a while still over the lifeless body, his eyes bulging, motionless, and as if stupefied by his own crime. Then, rousing himself from this lethargy, he rushed out of the bedchamber, crying:

"Help! Help!"

Servants came running at his shouts. They lifted the Countess up and placed her, still unconscious, upon her bed. And then somebody ran for the chaplain, who, as we have already said in connection with Captain Jacques, had previously also studied medicine.

"I don't know how it came about," stammered the Count. "She fell and her forehead struck against a piece of furniture. I guess her foot must have slipped."

And, as the words slipped out, Maximilian couldn't help remembering poor Gretchen, the bailiff's daughter, whose foot had also "slipped" and who died a victim also, not of his anger but of his love. Thus, this man crushed all the human lives that he touched.

Maximilian became awfully pale at this thought and had to lean against the mantel as he struggled to regain control of himself. He saw that the valets were looking at him. The chaplain had just entered the room.

Albina did not regain consciousness, so hard had the blow been. And yet all the same, it was rather her soul that had broken and not so much her body. The chaplain knew no way to bring her back to life. Cold water did not revive her, and smelling salts were equally useless. But soon, this miracle that science could not work, nature finally set into motion. The pains of childbirth brought her around. Albina opened her eyes again, but her eyes would not focus. She recovered the use of her speech but not that of her mind. Delirium swept over her. The incoherent words that in her fever she let babble over her lips were incomprehensible for all the persons in attendance upon her, but for her husband, and for her husband alone, they had a terrible meaning, indeed.

The chaplain declared that if some skillful doctor did not arrive from Frankfort to lend him aid, not only could the chaplain not answer for the mother's life, but he would not even answer for that of the child. No sooner said than one of the Count's servants left for town, leading a spare horse by the bridle so as not to delay the doctor from arriving as fast as possible.

Meanwhile, the delirium grew worse and worse.

"I am dying," Albina said, and even these sad words were cut by her sad moaning, for when the logic of her mind was destroyed, it was transferred to her suffering. "I can feel my soul detaching itself from me. . . . Oh! Let not my whole soul rise up in one surge to you, dear God! Let me leave the half of it to my child! My baby! It is yours, Maximilian! Can you hear me? Yours . . . Oh! Here on the doorsill of eternity, I swear it . . . ! Maximilian, where are you? Maximilian, you have been cruelly mistaken. Dear God! What terrible pains these are! If you only knew, if you only knew, Maximilian. But the secret is not mine to tell. He made me swear not to tell you his secret. One day you will know it. . . . One day, through him personally . . . One day he will return here. Death! Death! But death is not the end of my nine months, is it, Father Chaplain? Will not my coffin be a cradle in the sky? And you, Father, my own father, good, kind Father, please give me your hand. . . . Father, I have a request to make of you, and only of you alone. Please try to see that Maximilian does not overhear what I am going to say. Please listen, Father. You will find a letter for Wilhelmina under the head of my bed. In the name of Jesus, hand it safely to her. Tell her, Father, tell her that I am dying but that I shall return to see if she does carefully everything that I have asked her to do. You know, Father, that the Countesses von Eppstein who die during the day before or the night of Christmas Eve only die halfway. . . . Oh, my child! My poor child! May Good look favorably upon my prayer! May God look favorably upon my prayer! I can feel thee, my baby, more than I can feel myself. I give thee my heart. I give thee my own life. Take it. Take it all, and let me die. Oh, dear Father Chaplain. Save him, and take no more thought for me. . . . As for me . . . I am lost."

At that second, midnight sounded, and the Count shuddered. In truth, just as Albina said in the midst of her delirium, the day of Christmas had just commenced.

The Countess now was sinking fast.

"Farewell! Farewell!" she said. "I forgive you, Maximilian. But love your son. Love him. Dear Father, here I am . . . ! Ah! Ah! It's Christmas today. Ah! I am dying."

Albina, who in the last movement of her death throes had almost raised herself upright upon her mattress, fell back upon her pillow and died.

Maximilian threw himself toward the bed and enfolded Albina in his arms, but although she was truly dead, he felt the baby squirming around in her womb, and he started backward as if horror stricken. At that very instant, the doctor from Frankfort entered the room. He made everybody leave the chamber, including even Maximilian. He was going to save the baby by performing a terrible operation:

One hour later, from the womb of the dead mother, whose body was already cold, a living child was drawn. What a strange mystery that can turn life from out of death.

Is it not true that the most intimate affinity exists between a mother and her child? And tell us whether the soul of a child, sir philosophers, or tell us, sir doctors, whether the soul of a child does not seem to you also to be the last sigh of its mother?

The chaplain entered the Count's room, where he found him with perspiration running down his forehead, and handing him the letter found under the Countess's pillow, and addressed to Wilhelmina:

"My Lord," he said, "you have a son."

The Count opened the letter, which had not been sealed, skimmed through it quickly, and replied:

"That is good. You will name him Everard."

The same day that a son was born to Maximilian in the castle of the Counts von Eppstein, Wilhelmina's daughter came into the world in the cottage of old Gaspard.

CHAPTER

VI

The following morning, the Countess was dressed in her rich finery, laid to rest upon her bed, and exposed to view. She remained thus for three whole days. Then she was placed in the coffin, already prepared as it had been, and carried down to the crypt of the family von Eppstein.

The morning after the burial ceremony, the Count left for Vienna, where he stayed for a month. During this period of time, every trace of her death was obliterated, so thoroughly, indeed, that when he returned to Castle Eppstein from Vienna, with the exception of the poor orphaned baby of whom Wilhelmina had declared herself the mother, anyone would have thought that Albina herself had never existed. The castle servants through some instinct had understood that for them to remove far from their master's sight anything that might awaken his memory of the Countess amounted to courting his favor.

All the same, in spite of all this putting away, Maximilian's emotion was powerful when he found himself alone again inside his ancient castle. His son Albert, whom he loved dearly, had been placed in boarding school in Vienna.

It was particularly when he reentered the ancestral chamber that was called the Red Chamber, it was when he stood there at the foot of this armchair against which the countess had cracked her skull, opposite this bed upon which she had died, it was then that all the memories that were associated with Albina surged back toward his heart and that he felt himself shaking despite himself.

The fact is that from times long ago, and even upon those persons whose conscience was clear, some kind of awful terror, impossible to describe in words here, fell from those gloomy draperies. On that particular evening, the unmentionable terror was only increased even more by a raging wind that whistled out-of-doors. A huge fire burned in the enormous fireplace, where gigantic quarter trunks of oak spat as they devoured each other. And yet it was as cold as always in that vast, empty chamber. A candelabrum having four branches had been set lighted upon a table, and yet no light seemed able to illumine those dark chamber walls or that high ceiling. The night recalled exactly the scene of Christmas Eve. The only difference was that the armchair where Albina had been seated was vacant.

Every now and then the hurricane increased in violence as it broke itself at the angles of the outer walls. Then it howled pitiably. It sounded like those long shrieks that only die away to commence wailing again and which were only going to hush their tongues long enough to catch their breath again.

Make no mistake about it. The count was a brave man. If anybody had told him that some man had shuddered at the murmuring voice of a breeze, he would have laughed at such a man and would have called him a coward. And yet the Count stood there shaking despite himself.

In a dreaming frame of mind, he paced up and down, his head lowered onto his chest and his hand on his chin. He strolled back and forth, the length and then the breadth of the room, without ever stepping outside the circle of light, just the same, that the candelabrum cast about him.

And even from time to time, let us admit it, he turned his gaze toward the black corners or toward the stiff, quivering window curtains.

"What a terrifying imagination we have," the Count whispered to himself, "in that we turn these long-drawn furies of the wind into the crying of all the world's dead. Their scream, always growing in volume as it comes, must be the one which glides at certain times over all sleeping nature. It is probably the same impotent anguish which has uprooted forests and moved mountains off their foundations, the same funereal call from those who lie buried in earth to those who still remain above it. What a dreadful thing to hear!"

The Count stopped short, shivering, and to steady himself, rested an elbow on the mantel. Then there happened to him what always happens in similar circumstances. The trouble was that once he stumbled upon that idea his fancy whirled him to the very bottom of the pool.

"Among all the dead who cry," he told himself, "those who bemoan their state so pitifully up and down these hallways of the castle are perhaps my own dead. Alas! They are very numerous. The merciless scythe of the Grim Reaper has made an ample harvest inside this castle. Alas! Alas! Let me see . . .

"Without counting all my ancestors, without going all the way back to the ones I never knew, there is first of all my mother. A sainted woman! When she was alive, I often made her sorrow over me! The sweeter and gentler she was to me, the more headstrong and willful I myself became. How many nights my mother spent on her knees between my father and myself, pleading with the former and soothing the latter. And my father. He, too, is there, and if he went down in an early death into his tomb, it is perhaps I, Oh, my God, who cut short his final days.

"He was a noble old man, Count Rudolph, although very austere and very rigid. He should not have taken so seriously the stormy escapades of my youth. My brother is probably there also, for since the day of his departure I have never had any news of him. My poor Conrad! Oh! As for him, no matter what my mother and father said, I loved him all right, that weak, poetic youth whom his father cursed because he married beneath him. And he has probably died the sooner because of his father's malediction. Are those all the ones I weep for? No. No. The funeral register is not yet closed. There is still my first wife, Bertha, to be mentioned.* She is a name only rather than any memory, a shadow of a woman even when she lived in this world. She was an insignificant figurant who passed by here only to leave me, and thank God for that, an eldest son to the House of Eppstein. And then, last of all, there is—"

Count Maximilian stopped. Suddenly he was panting and sensing, although he was leaning against the mantelpiece, that his legs were about to give way under him. He let himself collapse into an armchair. Then, inside his speechless thoughts, came words that the movements of his lips shaped into syllables:

"There is that one other," he said between gasps for breath. "She is Albina, Albina who betrayed me. . . . Oh! she must now be wailing louder than all the rest, that one! For her death, and her passing, was not a natural death like Bertha's. Because the disease she died of is my jealousy. For I killed her, not with my sword but with my anger. Well! So what? I killed her, or rather I punished her, and I do not repent because of it. No. If it were to be done over again, I would still do it again."

At that moment the wind groaned more sadly than ever.

The Count rose from his chair, pale and frozen.

"How cold it is in here!" he said aloud.

And with the toe of his boot he pushed a great oak stump onto the embers.

"How dark it is in here!" he then exclaimed.

---

*Maximilian mentioned his first wife in chapter 1, where he said her name was Thecla. Dumas seems not to have caught his mistake.

And he lighted a second candelabrum that had been set upon the mantel.

But what's the use of pretending we don't know? The facts are clear that it was in his heart where the cold lay and that it was in his conscience where lay the dark of night.

Meanwhile, he tried to drive his black thoughts away, but they bumped into each other within his soul, like owls against the walls of their cave. He summoned up that distraction that was always the most diverting, usually able to come most powerfully to his assistance: his dreams of personal ambition.

"Come on," he said as he caressed his forehead. "Come on, Maximilian. Aren't you a man anymore? Let all these fancies go to hell! Let's see. Let's write this letter to Kaunitz."

He sat down at a desk, took a pen, and wrote the date: January 24, 1793."

The pen dropped from his fingers.

"It was a month ago today that she died," he murmured.

And he rose to his feet, violently pushing his armchair away from him.

A singular wave of anguish gripped his heart.

Then he set himself to walking about, completely overcome and struggling in vain to recapture his benumbed thoughts. Whatever funereal murmurs there were that ran through his mind, they alerted him in some still way that there was right then commencing to occur something terrible, something supernatural, something unexpected. It was something that he could not vanquish in open combat, something that he could not escape, either, by running away. So he stood comparing the tumult that was boiling up within himself, inside his own chest, with the ghastly silence that surrounded him. The stillness in the room was only disturbed by the dying sobbing of the wind, and that frightened him out of his wits.

There are moments when, even for the most intrepid

hearts, everything collapses into sheer fright. Inside this silence the warming vibration of the clock's drum before the hammer strikes on it the twelve strokes for midnight, the twelve strokes themselves, the last one of which had just announced that he was entering upon the twenty-fifth day of January, an explosion in a stick of firewood that tossed it out of the hearth and onto the parquet floor—all those sounds triggered an electrical shock in this man who was so courageous. The distant yelping of one of his dogs in their kennel cast his heart, which was so resolute, into an ungovernable turmoil. Soon he was afraid of the hollow sound of his own footsteps falling upon the parquet. So he stood there, quite still, leaning back against the wall. But then he became afraid, even of his own lack of mobility. He rubbed his hands together. He shook his head back and forth in a kind of nervous spasm.

He wailed. He could feel something appalling draw near.

The thing is that the invisible world that surrounds us, that eludes our powers of sight, that flies from our touch, that plays tricks with our senses, was there and then shaking all around him, in that dark and silent chamber, its mute but jittering hallows. All the terrors that Dante dealt out in his poem, Michelangelo in his paintings, and Carl Maria von Weber in his music quivered around Maximilian's temples. He could almost breathe them out of the air, as it were. Of what avail was his paltry reason against all the sinister visions of his awestruck imagination?

One terrible memory set him to quaking, moreover, as it floated vaguely into his mind from some lower depths. Maximilian had brought to his mind the dismal legend of Countess Leonora, who had died on a Christmas Day. He figured it out, that Countess Albina had died on the same day of the year as Countess Leonora, and he remembered that the legend said that the Countesses von Eppstein dead upon that day only died by half.

Next, out of the shadowy depths of his own soul, Maximilian heard the voice of Albina saying: "What if I had not been guilty but was only a victim! And you, Maximilian, who considered yourself a judge. What if you had only been a murderer?"

These slow, solemn words the voice intoned twenty times over. Twenty times they fell down upon the Count's conscience. The words were heavy and corrosive, like the drops of lead Dante speaks about in the *Inferno*.

The Count rallied all his energy so as to tear himself away from this torture of the damned.

"What a strange and stupid illusion on my part!" he said out loud, doubtless to override with his speaking voice that inner voice that kept up its silent murmuring in the depths of his heart.

But, suddenly, at the moment when he spoke to himself, the wail of a little baby rose in the quiet night as if to join and swell the dying cries of the dead Countess. The difference was that this time there was no possibility of misapprehension, for the noise was real enough. It was the continuous crying of babyhood, and it issued from the apartments situated above that of Maximilian.

"Wouldn't you know it," thought the Count. "If it's not the mother, it's her son after her. Her son Everard, her son, this stranger to me, this enemy whom I am forced to raise under my own eyes, an enemy inside my own house, and as my own child, or else the shame of the mother rebounds onto me. . . . But," he continued, exasperated, "will he ever shut up, finally! Could Wilhelmina have gone outside? Could she have left him above in his cradle? Is that the way," he added with a bitter laugh, "that she follows the last instructions of her girlfriend?"

Having to deal with a sound of natural origin, Maximilian waited with less apprehension, although perhaps with more impatience. Meanwhile, the baby's crying did not cease. Maximilian took his sword, climbed up the stepladder beside the library shelves, and rapped with its hilt against the ceiling. He intended to wake up the nurse, who had apparently fallen asleep.

The baby kept crying.

Soon Maximilian's first reaction of anger began to yield to a new anguish. His heart, which for an instant had resumed its normal pulse, began to be oppressed, as it had been before the crying commenced. This uninterrupted wailing, which seemed to be a complaint addressed to God for the death of the mother and the abandoning of the son, harassed the Count to the point of driving him mad.

He wanted to get out of there. But where would he go?

He tried to call someone. His voice stuck in his gullet.

He took the bell that rested on the table. But truly, whom should he summon? Everyone in the castle was asleep except the orphan and the murderer.

The fire, which Maximilian had forgotten to keep burning, had little by little died away on the hearth, so that now the darkness was invading that chamber where only the flickering light from the wax candles struggled against the shadows. Outside, the wind bellowed still. Above him, the baby bewailed his pain, continuously making his voice resound. The Count was cold. He was afraid. And when in his near hysteria he raised his hands to his forehead, he withdrew them again with a sudden start, for he thought that his forehead was on fire and had burned his hands even though they were ice.

Then, and as if brought to his senses again by the very strength of his terror, he began to laugh, but it was a mournful, terrible laughter. He spoke out loud.

"Oh, what's that! Why, I believe, God damn me, that I am going out of my mind. Let's go see why that child is still crying. It's as simple as that." So he walked over to the wall with a totally deliberate step, put his finger on the hidden spring in the tapestry, and pushed out the little secret door before him.

This door gave access to a narrow stone staircase, which had been known from father to son by the Counts von Eppstein alone. It had no other exit but in the floor above where the baby was still howling, or in the floor below, or last of all, down inside the crypts where reposed the ancestors of Maximilian. This staircase, which sprawled inside an exterior wall of the castle like a lounging giant, missed nothing of importance that took place within.

At the moment when the door sprang open, an icy wind, a wind straight from the cold tombs, slapped Maximilian on the face and snuffed out the candle he was holding before him. Pale as a corpse, his hair standing straight up on his head, the Count remained petrified on the threshold.

Along this staircase, of which no person but himself knew the secret, which no one but he could penetrate, he could distinctly hear the rustling of a woman's dress. And then he saw a white shape gliding within the shadows before him.

The baby was still wailing. Those were too many terrors all at the same time. Feeling his legs buckle under him, the Count had to lean against the wall to keep from falling on the stone steps.

How long Count Maximilian remained there, numb with terror, unable to react, he himself would not afterward ever have been able to estimate. There are instants that last as long as entire years. At the end of a minute, at the end of an hour perhaps, he regained possession of his faculties. He was bathed in a cold sweat. He listened to the silence.

The baby was crying no longer. The wind had stopped blowing.

In one supreme effort of will, Maximilian mustered all his courage. He recovered the candelabrum that he had let fall, lighted it again, drew his sword from its scabbard, threw himself at the staircase, and climbed up to the baby's bedroom.

As he opened the secret door that afforded access to the upper floor, the candelabrum, which the Count held in his left hand, blew out again. And this time it did not blow out because of an updraft of air or because of a gust of wind. It blew out because of a supernatural ascendance.

Meanwhile, the moon, which up till then had been hidden by a dark cloud, at that hour freed herself and cast one of her pale rays across the high casemented window. And in the wan light of the pale moon, this is what the Count saw before his eyes:

The nurse Wilhelmina was absent from the chamber.

But the dead Albina, upright beside the baby's cradle, was rocking her son in it, and gently rocking it back and forth, and the baby, whose cries had softened into a kind of cooing still, was already slipping off into slumber again.

It was Albina, all right, and Maximilian recognized her immediately, even as the strange rocker of the cradle.

She was still wearing the white gown in which she had been buried. He could still see about her throat that chain made of large gold links that she had inherited from her mother. She had recommended in her letter to Wilhelmina that she be interred wearing it.*

Albina was as lovely as when she had been alive. Maybe even more lovely. Yes, death had made her more beautiful. Her long black hair flowed across her shoulders, with their skin so white it seemed transparent. All around her forehead there seemed to float a luminous vapor. But it was her eyes especially that burned with a gentle glow, and it was her smile that gleamed like a golden sunburst.

*Another error on the part of Dumas. Albina made no such recommendation in the letter as we had it here.

When she saw Maximilian appear suddenly upon the threshold, she raised her calm, proud eyes up to him, and putting one finger to her lips, as if to caution him to be quiet, she continued rocking her baby in his cradle.

Mechanically, the Count raised his right hand, which still held his sword, to make the sign of the cross; but his hand stiffened there at his forehead. It was paralyzed. . . .

The dead girl's lips were moving!

"We conjure up demons, but we may not call up the blessed," she said with melancholy, and her voice trilled through the rafters like a celestial choir. "Do you believe me, Maximilian, that God would not have permitted me to come back when I heard my baby cry if I had not been received among the body of the elect?"

"Among the elect?" murmured the Count.

"Yes, Maximilian, for God is just, and he knows that I have always been a chaste and faithful wife. I told you that with my last breath, and you did not believe me. I repeat it for you today that the Lord God has chosen me by divine election, has drawn me into his bosom. The dead do not lie. Now, Maximilian, do you believe me this time?"

"But what about this child?" objected the Count as he pointed with the tip of his sword toward the baby Everard.

"This child is your child, Maximilian," replied the Countess. When I was alive, appearances bore witness against me. My presence here tonight exonerates me, does it not? It seems so to me. I tell you, Count, that this child belongs to both of us and that he is legitimately connected to you by birth, just as he is connected by birth to me."

"Is it the truth? Is it the truth?" Maximilian said

over and over, like a madman. He was in some sense out of his mind, so that he spoke as if driven to do so by some irresistible power.

After a moment's silence he began again to speak, or rather to babble:

"But the, that man, that Captain Jacques. What was he?"

"You shall one day know it, but it will probably come too late. All I can tell you is that an oath obligates me as much now that I am dead as it bound me when I was alive. The gist of the matter is that this man was not and could never have been to me anyone but a brother."

"But in that case," cried Maximilian, "in that case, I must have suspected you unjustly, then? How does it happen that you did not avenge yourself, then?"

Albina smiled at this mention of vengeance.

"Oh! I forgive you for having caused my death, Maximilian," the dead girl began again. "The storms of human passions do not disturb the celestial spheres where we repose after life. Only try to soften your violent, fierce moods where your son is concerned. Maximilian, never raise your hand to him as you raised your hand to me. There is a reason why you must not, for Jesus has accorded me the privilege of continuing, even from beyond the grave, my maternal services and my watch over father and son, to protect the one in case of need and to punish the other when necessary. For I died on Christmas Eve."

"Almighty God!" murmured the Count.

"Thus," continued the dead Countess in her solemn, dignified voice. "thus, as Everard's beloved nurse, Wilhelmina was retained near her wounded husband this evening, and this in spite of her desire to remain here, I came to rock and calm my baby. . . .

"But here comes Wilhelmina back again. I am going

to return to my tomb, where I shall listen, always ready to rise out from it, think of it, Maximilian, at the first cry from my son. Farewell!"

"Albina! Albina!" cried the Count.

"Farewell, Maximilian," Albina said again in hollow tones. "Farewell, and take care lest it be only a provisional good-bye. Farewell and silence. Remember me! Remember me!"

The ghost then left the side of the baby's cradle, in which he had fallen asleep again with a smile on his face, and advanced toward Maximilian. He moved aside to give it space to pass. Again she put her finger to her lips as she approached the Count. By then he was aghast. And she faded from view down the staircase.

Worn out by so many emotions, Maximilian was no longer from that time forward aware of his actions. Probably, when he, too, heard the sound of the nurse's approaching footsteps, he mechanically shut the mysterious door to the staircase. Probably guided by blind instinct, which sometimes survives the loss of one's reasoning power, he was able to make his way back to his own bedroom. It is true all the same, however it may have been, that upon awakening the next morning, and he had spent a feverish night, he found that he lay completely dressed upon his bed. He told himself:

"I had a terrible nightmare."

However, when he interrogated Wilhelmina, he found that effectively she had been retained for a part of the night in her own cottage and that this had been due to a wound that her husband Jonathas had suffered during the previous day. A wild boar, brought to bay, had turned on the dogs and then on the forester, whose thigh he had ripped open with his tusks. When she returned to the castle, Wilhelmina had found the baby as peaceful as when she had left him.

It had not been a dream. It had been an apparition. But that conclusion was too awful for the Count. He kept repeating:

"I dreamed it! I dreamed it!"

CHAPTER

VII

Events that for the past five years, sinister or pleasant, and more often sinister than pleasant, sped by with such rapidity at Eppstein now slowed down a little after this solemn apparition of Albina. Since that lugubrious Christmas Eve, any sojourn in his Castle Eppstein had become unendurable to Maximilian. Each night he was there, he would awaken with a start, thinking he heard steps on the staircase inside the castle wall. Each day he would tremble whenever Wilhelmina and her nursling met him along a passageway. Last of all, he simply could not hold out there, and so he escaped from his remorse. One morning he called for his carriage to be made ready, and an hour afterward, he was on the high road to Vienna. He took his son Albert along with him that time.

All the Count's hope for the future as well as all his tender affection was henceforth concentrated upon this elder son. This child, at least, was really his own son, and Maximilian loved to repeat that by right of birth as by the laws of primogeniture, this son would one day become head of the House of Eppstein, that he would continue his father's ambitious plans and that he would succeed to all his father's titles. The Count had resolved to give Albert the most thorough education and the most brilliant, the education of a gentleman, of an officer, and especially that of a diplomat. As far as the rest went, this beloved son, who was an only son, for his younger brother did not count, had not lost too much, any more than had his father, from that alliance with the Schwalbachs. It may have been an unfortunate marriage from the point of view of a family life together, but it had been advantageous in its political repercussions. The Schwalbachs were all-powerful and very well connected. All anybody at Vienna knew about the sad fate of Albina was that she had died in childbirth. Everybody pitied this poor Count, widowed a second time, after two years of marriage.

"What is the worth, after all, of dishonor which nobody knows about?" Maximilian used to ask himself.

And, as his conscience was rather deaf where that was concerned, he was not slow to grow giddy in all the noisy diversions of the imperial court and in all the grandiose projects that he concocted for himself as for Albert.

As for the stranger child, as for Everard (it was that name with which the chaplain had baptized Albina's son), Count von Eppstein hardly afforded him a thought, never gave him any care whatsoever, no more concerned with him than with his brother Conrad or with his dead first wife or with the dead Gretchen. The rumor that circulated at Vienna suited the Count. The younger child's delicate health, it was said, required his being left at home in the pure mountain air. This was a new reason, as a result, why people should look with sympathy at this unfortunate father who was now forced to be parted from one of his sons.

Fortunately, while Maximilian received these complimentary opinions, condolences, and kept leaning for all he was worth upon the relatives of Albina, Everard had found a mother. Wilhelmina reread every day the Countess's letter and piously executed the sacred last will and testament of her benefactress. Accepted as Everard's nurse through the disdainful indifference of the Count, she had lavished more care and more love upon Albina's son than upon her own daughter. In this she showed her exaggerated or excessive love, for she was a fine woman, generous, and kind-hearted. At the end of seven months she had already weaned her little girl, Rosamund, but for a year and more she continued to nurse at her breast her adoptive son, the baby of her heart.

"Now listen to me, Jonathas," she used to caution her husband, who was slightly jealous of her preference, "our daughter is our own daughter, and we have to answer to no one as far as she is concerned. But this poor orphaned baby, who has only us and God in all the world, if we were to neglect him now that his mother is dead and his father has forgotten him, what would Madame think? And then, too, he is so frail, the little darling! While our Rosamund is so sturdy and the picture of health.

Thus, for Everard, Wilhelmina became the most loving and devoted mother, and aside from such a time as the fateful hour when she had been obliged to leave him so she could care for her wounded husband, she hardly ever left him even for a quarter of an hour. Thanks to this care minute by minute, the baby came along so well that it was a marvel to see him grow. It was so sweet to see them together, Rosamund and he, white and charming little creatures, frolicking on the lawn.

Long years went by, and Everard's tastes grew to be more or less those of a wild creature, not very scholarly. He learned well enough and at the same pace as his foster sister. He read and he wrote, but since Rosamund was taught neither Latin nor history, he refused to have himself taught those subjects that only boys of his class studied. The chaplain, Dominus Aloysius, felt it was essential to teach him these other subjects. Everard preferred running through the woods with Rosamund or following Jonathas on his little boy's legs when the forester went after game. This love of the outdoors did not stop him from considering it a great treat when in the evening he could listen to stories. Seated close to Rosamund and at the feet of Wilhelmina, who used to spin after dark, he would hear some tale of ghosts or of fairies as told by Jonathas or by old Gaspard.

As for the rest, if the education of the mind was lacking in his training, that of the gentle heart, the very education his mother had requested for him from Wilhelmina, had been abundantly provided. First of all, he had only to look at the God-fearing wife of the forester, and to watch her live her life, in order to absorb instruction in gentleness and religion. Then, every evening and every morning, as soon as Everard was old enough to comprehend, Wilhelmina took him to say his prayers in the funeral crypt of Castle Eppstein. She spoke daily to him of the angel he had lost on earth but who watched over him from heaven.

"Think of it, Everard," she used to say to him. "think how your mother sees you, follows you ceaselessly, that she is present in all your actions, that she smiles at all your good thoughts and sheds tears at all your faults. Think how her body lies in the tomb but that her soul is all about you, wherever you are."

The child strained to behave like a good boy so as to make his dead mother smile down on him. When he had committed one of the naughty tricks usual to children of his age, he blushed and turned to look behind him as if he would encounter the sad eyes of his invisible witness. This thought haunted him until it became his second religion.

His boyish imagination was so impressed that he even thought he glimpsed more than once, or (who knows?) that he perhaps saw, in the still of night, a white shadow, which did not frighten him at all, standing right beside his bed, gazing raptly at him with eyes of love. Then she used to say:

"Sleep, my Everard, sleep. Slumber is good for little children."

And he would go sweetly back to sleep, and, those nights, he would dream the most fascinating dreams.

The next day, he would not fail to tell Wilhelmina all about it, and Wilhelmina never disillusioned him. The worthy woman saw no danger in that, and was there any harm in it, really? Where did he run any risk, this young soul, if he believed in the presence of a celestial angel guardian of his childhood? Wilhelmina was, in any case, first to believe in it.

"Madame used to say," she thought, "that she would abandon neither nurse nor nursling."

Very frequently she, too, happened to speak out loud to the dear departed and to ask for her assistance and counsel. Everard also became accustomed, following her example, to call upon his mother, and he prayed "Dear Mother" as one says "Dear God." The dead mother continued alive in both their hearts.

We shall speak no further of little Rosamund. She was even so becoming, as she grew in years, as pretty as a love and as good as a little angel. A graceful and loving little girl, she was all gentleness and all sweetness. Everard adored her and yielded to her in every instance. Wilhelmina wept with joy to see, one Sunday in chapel, these two children kneeling a few steps in front of her and praying both of them for her as she was praying for them.

Count Maximilian remained absent from Castle Eppstein for seven years. Politics had swept him up in its whirlwind. At the end of this period, he came to spend two weeks at Eppstein not in order to see his son but to collect his tenants' rents and renew his farm leases. He hardly even asked to look at Everard. He had eyes only for his son Albert, anyway, and the latter, who resembled him in every aspect, played a thousand mean tricks on his little brother and on all the people who worked at the castle.

The chaplain took it as his duty to inform the Count of Everard's resistance to any sort of further learning.

"Oh, my God, let him alone," said Maximilian to the great astonishment of the Dominus Aloysius. "Leave him be. Let him do what he wants to. Let him become whatever he can. It makes no difference to me. . . . What need has he to know anything, since he is destined to be nobody, anyway?"

At the end of a week's residence at the castle, Count Maximilian, accompanied by Albert, set off again for Vienna.

Two more years sped by just as tranquil and happy for the forester's household, which the two youngsters made ring with their bubbling laughter and which they perfumed with their pure breath. Everard and Rosamund were both ten years old by now. Grief first announced its return among them by the sudden death of their tutor, Dominus Aloysius. The venerable old man, loaded down with years as with virtues, passed gently away while turning the pages of a great book upon the pages of which he was thought to be asleep, when in reality he was dead. That was Everard's first heartbreak. He could not help crying over his dear master, who had only been too weak and too indulgent toward him.

This first sorrow was nothing compared to what was awaiting him, the poor boy! Master Aloysius had served during a long career, after all. His death occurred in the natural course of things, and he remained the last survivor of all his fellows. He had been a contemporary of old Count Rudolph and of the old Countess Gertrude, both of whom were already asleep, and for the last ten years, in their tombs. He closed the era of their generation. But was not Wilhelmina still essential? Was not this good housewife, this skillful manageress, was not her young life not still necessary yet for the two youngsters? Did she not belong by her breast and her womb to the whole family?

And yet God called her to him, although she was a

woman only twenty-nine years old, and she died at almost the same time as the oldster aged eighty. The members of Wilhelmina's family all died young. Her own mother had been even more prematurely deceased, just like, there is little doubt of it, her sister Naomi. Wilhelmina went to rejoin them all, and even so, to rejoin her mistress whom she had so faithfully served all the way to the very tomb itself.

For a long time, her health had given grave signs that had concerned them all. All blond and rose as she was, she had been seen by Dominus Aloysius to show the symptoms of those diseases that attack frail bodies and sad hearts. For a long time Wilhelmina had been growing paler day by day, and yet, from day to day, whenever she felt the least emotion, bright red spots would come and go on her cheeks. Every autumn she grew visibly weaker. One would have said that living the same cycle of life as flowers, she would vanish along with the lilies, with whom she shared her white skin and her modesty, and with the roses, whose pearly sheen and whose fragrance she shared. Every spring, as if this regenerating life that spreads throughout all nature whispered confidently to her also, she took on a better semblance of health, but it was nothing more than an even more burning fever. Because the two children ignored the causes of her feverish beauty then, they looked at her anew and used to exclaim, as they threw their arms about her neck:

"Oh! how beautiful you are, Mummy!"

Their Wilhelmina, who had no illusions about her real state, would smile at them sadly. She would draw her darling little ones to her heart, and when they asked her, looking up at her in amazement:

"Why are you crying?"

She would reply:

"Because I am just too happy."

Toward the first part of the year 1802, Wilhelmina began

to sense, because of her weakness, which was increasing, that her disease was about to make rapid progress for the worse. From then on, so as not to squander the little bit of strength she had left, Wilhelmina gave up taking long rambles in the forest. It was these excursions that sent her two children into ecstasies. She shut herself up in her bedroom without voicing any complaint, for a complaint from her would have awakened suspicions, and as a consequence, sadness throughout her family. She shut herself up, well and truly, inside her bedroom, which under her hands, with its white curtains, its palm fronds blessed at Easter time, soon took on the appearance of one of those street altars that they build up in country villages on the feast day of the holy sacrament, after Pentecost. At such shrines God stops a moment, between the perfume of incense and the perfumed flowers.

Alone of the whole family, only the old man, because he was himself closest to death, realized that her death was drawing near. During the fine, long evenings of summer, while they used to sit awaiting Jonathas's return home, and while the old man stayed on his bench in front of the cottage door, where the last rays of the setting sun could warm him, he watched the two children running, picking Michaelmas daisies in the grass on the forest floor or chasing fireflies carried aloft by the evening breeze. Then Wilhelmina would appear suddenly on the doorsill like a paler vision of her old self. She would come quietly and sit down at her father's feet and rest her head, bent down, upon his shaking, old knees. Then, without taking his eyes off the sky, the old man would let his hand fall upon his daughters's head. Wilhelmina could feel his hand trembling and, without changing her position, either, would reply to his unexpressed thoughts in words that were barely understandable:

"Why go against it, my father?" she would mumble. "It must be for the good, since God wills it thus."

And the old man did not reply, for a father never understands that God should wish his child to die.

As for the two children, they noticed none of this. They kept playing their games. They kept singing their songs. They were happy.

Finally, Jonathas noticed, in his turn, how weak his wife was, and fear overcame him. He said a word or two about it to his father, who then informed him that he had guessed it long ago. The next morning, Jonathas left the cottage as usual, as if he were going to make his rounds of the forest, and toward noon he returned with a doctor whom he had gone to Frankfort to fetch. At the sight of him, Wilhelmina began to shiver, for she understood then that her husband now knew everything, and the poor wife suffered for his pain.

If they had been wealthy people, the doctor would have hidden the truth from them. He would have given them reasons to hope so as to afford himself an opportunity to come back once more; but poor people are favored by truth.

The doctor told them all about it.

At first, Jonathas refused to believe it. He had feared some indisposition on her part, nothing more. The very idea that his beloved Wilhelmina could be taken from them in the first third of her life had never presented itself to his mind. He then examined the poor, sick woman with closer attention, and he saw plainly what awful inroads her disease had already taken. Then, like all men who are robust and accustomed to physical fatigue but whose spirit has never had occasion to combat emotional suffering, Jonathas collapsed all at once. He never spoke again all that livelong day and all that next night, but sat looking at Wilhelmina. All night long he stayed awake, watching beside her bedroom door. Then, when day came again, he unhooked his gun as usual and took four steps outside the front door. But he lacked the strength to go any farther. He came back inside the house and put his gun back up in its place; and as soon as Wilhelmina arose from her bed (each day she got up later and later), she found her husband seated on a stool in front of the fireplace, his head in his hands.

The unfortunate wife walked straight up to him.

"You can't do anything about it, Jonathas!" she told him. "You must have courage."

Jonathas wanted to answer her, but feeling that he was about to break out sobbing, he rushed out of the house.

From that day onward, the poor forester's life was completely disorganized. He went out every morning with his gun, but he never went far away from the little cottage. He could not make up his mind to go out of sight of it. In spite of the precautions he took to hide from her, Wilhelmina often saw him slipping across some clearing, or else the two children came home all upset, holding each other by the hand and asking Wilhelmina:

"Mummy, what's the matter with Jonathas? We saw him lying up against a tree trunk, and he was crying."

At last, the day came when Wilhelmina ceased getting out of bed at all. Only in the evening, as the sun was about to set, they opened her window so that the dying woman could smile regretfully upon its last rays. Then everybody gathered in her bedroom. The children brought her great bouquets of flowers that they laid upon her bed. Jonathas brought in the Bible, which he handed solemnly to his father. The old man would read some holy and sublime story from the book while Wilhelmina said her prayers, while Jonathas wept, and while the two children kept very still. They would sit side by side in an armchair that had been pushed up against the bed.

One morning, Wilhelmina felt worse than usual, and so it was herself, on that day, who asked Jonathas not to go out at all. The two men therefore remained almost all that day long right beside her. As for the little ones, they spent their time in the usual way, coming in and going out again, carrying out their faded flowers and bringing in fresh ones. The nearer she drew to death, the more Wilhelmina loved flowers. For the last few days she had only known she was still alive because she could smell their fragrance.

That evening, the reading took place as usual, but at the end of the reading Wilhelmina lost consciousness. They noticed it from her light sigh. Jonathas threw himself over her. At first thought, he believed that she had died, and he cried aloud.

From the depths of her fainting spell, Wilhelmina heard his cry and opened her eyes again.

"Poor beloved!" she said, holding out her cold, damp hand to Jonathas. "Poor beloved! Me, too. Believe me. It breaks my heart, too, to leave you so early and while you still need me, you who have loved me so dearly. But the Lord wishes it. Be strong. Be a man. Happily for me, the hardest part of my task on earth has been accomplished. The children are already half-raised and are both healthy. I have never had the courage to separate myself from Rosamund. That was a fault in me, and when I shall no longer be here among you, dear husband, I beg you to conduct her to Vienna, to the convent called Holy Linden, where you will entrust her to the mother superior and hand her the letter from my good mistress. They will undertake to raise our child according to the laws of God. Do not fail. Do you understand? Watch over Everard all the time. You must take my place close to him, and his own mother will keep you company the while, as she has accompanied me wherever I went with him.

"Now, Everard, you also must listen to me. . . . Now you are a tall and a reasonable boy, and you will be all right going by yourself morning and evening to pray at your mother's tomb. Do not miss a single day as long as you remain here at Eppstein, my child. Respect your father but love your mother. I recommend to your good offices your sister Rosamund.

"And you, Rosamund, my daughter, do not cease to love God and to be charitable to others. Show that you are worthy to be received in the holy abode which you are going to enter. Keep always before your eyes the example of the noble protectress whose virtues I have often told you about."

The children began to cry without really grasping what all that meant to them but because everybody else was crying.

Following her last words, Wilhelmina turned toward her father, Gaspard, who stood behind her husband. He towered over him by a full head, standing there motionless and collected, an old oak that saw all its younger shoots now perishing.

"What shall I say to you, to you, father of mine? What to you, who like a living figure of grief, must bury all your children!"

"Say good-bye to me, my daughter," the old man replied gravely, "for it is I who shall rejoin you first. If these old fingers are to have to sew your shroud around your young self, at least our separation will be the least long. That you die a holy death is a consolation to me. We shall find each other once more, at the feet of God, Wilhelmina. I should go forth completely calm in my mind, alas!, if I knew that your sister Naomi has died an equally Christian death, as pure and innocent a death as yours."

"Do not doubt it, Father. Do not doubt it. As for me, I am only dying. Naomi had also to suffer. But do not speak to me yet of rejoining me, dear father. Live to teach Jonathas resignation. Live to watch over my two children. They have only their lifetimes to be with you, poor ones. Both Naomi and I will have all eternity before us, while we wait for you."

Then, sensing that she was growing weaker and weaker and wanting to spare her husband from bidding her a supreme farewell, she spoke once more.

"I think I am feeling better. Why don't you go away now. I would like to sleep a little."

Jonathas reached over to lead the two little ones away.

"No, leave them here with me," Wilhelmina said. "They will fall asleep in the armchair."

The poor woman did not want to die alone.

Jonathas withdrew, truly believing that she wanted to sleep, but Gaspard understood the real reason. He bent down over his daughter's bed, kissed her on the forehead, and pressing her hand in his, bade her farewell.

"See you again in heaven!" he told her.

Wilhelmina quivered. Then, in an even lower voice, so low that her husband could not hear her, she bade him farewell also.

"Good-bye forever!" she told him.

The two men stepped away from her room. Crushed with fatigue, Jonathas went to bed and fell asleep. Gaspard went upstairs, too, and knelt in prayer.

After about an hour, hearing no more sounds, Gaspard stole back downstairs and gently pushed open the door to her chamber. Wilhelmina seemed asleep. One would have said there lay a beautiful madonna on her bed that was covered with roses. In her hands she held the two hands of Rosamund and Everard, that she had joined together.

The two children were not asleep. They were wide-eyed.

"Oh, Grandpa," they said as soon as they saw Gaspard. "Look. We are afraid. Our Mummie does not answer us, and her hand is so cold that it is freezing our hands."

Gaspard drew close to the bed. Wilhelmina was dead.

The next day, as he returned home from burying his wife, good Jonathas, a much weaker man than old Gaspard, let himself fall to his knees in the place where his wife always sat. . . . Suddenly he felt little arms thrown around him and two pairs of rosy lips kissing his tanned cheeks down which his tears were falling fast. He looked down at these two little ones and found that he was a good bit comforted.

That same year, Count Maximilian von Eppstein also received his consolation. He was named personal and high privy councilor.

CHAPTER

VIII

I t was a new and awful suffering for Everard when he had
to be separated from Rosamund. He had only just made
acquaintance with death. Now he would be obliged to experience the pains of absence.

Even so, and despite the tears and pleas of Everard but
in order to fulfill the last wishes of Wilhelmina, Jonathas
escorted his daughter to Vienna. Just as poor Albina had
foreseen, her letter opened the gates of the Convent of
Holy Linden to her goddaughter, and Rosamund was received by the lady abbess as if she had been the real daughter of the late Countess von Eppstein.

For some time Everard had thought that he would make
up one of the party for this expedition to Vienna, but the
forester had finally made him understand that he had not
the right, without the Count's permission, to take Everard
to Vienna.

Everard stayed home, then, alone and disconsolate, beside old Gaspard.

Jonathas's return had not even brought back Everard's
natural joyousness. All the youngster had done was to make
Jonathas tell it twenty times over where this convent was
located and how Rosamund's chamber was furnished and
decorated. Now the cottage, once so gay, had become
gloomy and silent. The inhabitants remained for the most

part, all three of them, taciturn and somber as they faced each other: an old man, a mature man, and a boy.

Gaspard no longer ventured beyond the house and its garden. Almost all the time now he stayed seated on the bench beside the door, at least when it was pleasant, and on a chair near the hearth when it rained. There, lost in thought, his eyes closed, he looked inside himself to see his memories come alive again and to catch the smiles of his two darling daughters, Naomi and Wilhelmina.

No matter what the weather was like, Jonathas threw his gun across his shoulder every morning, whistled up his dogs, plunged into the forest, and more often than not, returned home at night without any game. He had spent the whole day tramping through the darkest forest glades, or he had just let the time slip by him as he lay full-length at the base of a tree. . . . The soul of these three males was like a clock that keeps poor time, you could say, or that has stopped because of some shock. Since the pain of that blow had sunk deep inside them, they seemed no longer to exist. All they did was breathe.

In the case of Everard, he was too young for his spirit and his healthy body to remain so chilled by sorrow forever. Even so, in his deep retreat, away from all other human contact, without relatives, without a close friend, having seen nothing of the whole world but this castle and the forest of Eppstein, having known no men but Gaspard and Jonathas, having no other love in his life except a son's love that he felt for the dead Wilhelmina and a brother's love that he felt for the absent Rosamund, he, too, was cloistered inside his own mind, you might say. He had no outlet at all for his affections. So he let his personality take the shape of his instincts. He grew up to have a character that was basically generous and forthright but which was at the same time contradictory, uncivilized, strange. Since he was now always alone by himself, he had only his earlier impressions from childhood to color his convictions as a youth, and he grew up with sets of passions and beliefs that became fixed. The affective side of his being functioned upon a basic set of emotions that were not only naive but false and which he himself would have seen collapse all by themselves had he found them set forth in books where he could have compared them with others, or he would have seen them collapse in real life with the help of some other person, like a counselor, or a guide.

As a result, his imagination replaced what would have been a young man's judgment. Clinging to the terrors and loves of early childhood, which Wilhelmina had seen fill his earliest being, he still saw before him, always, everywhere, an image of his real mother. Thus, he now had no other one to love, no other thought, no other happiness except in this imaginary mother. He lived day by day ceaselessly, with this dead mother. Thus, finally, his entire life was merely a vision.

Witness to his doings, bosom friend to him, aider and abettor of this constant, adored ghost was the old leafy forest of Eppstein.

We have already attempted to paint this enormous woodland for you, dark, black, deep, lonely, sublime as it was, and almost holy. It was holy and thus similar to the ancient Roman *lucus,* or grove, sacred to the deity whose temple it surrounded and where the wind in earlier days blew with the same sighings of souls in grief. You could find everything in this woodland, just as you can in the rounded personality of a human person: There were ravines so deep the daylight never reached their bottom; there were bubbling springs that sang to the birds; there were vast granite domes that shone white in the moonlight, gray in sunlight, like nature's architectural ruins; there were also sections of masonry that had crumbled, the eviscerated keeps of castles, which were vestiges from lost ages. Other uneasy watchtowers that still leaned over valleys whose access roads they once barred looked as if they were looking out to see if the barbarian hordes were not returning. Ghosts must have loved to reappear in the midst of these relics from history, ghostly survivals themselves from elapsed times.

Very soon Everard came to know his vegetable universe in all its leafy confusion: clearings, thickets, stands of young trees. None of all this held secrets from him. He had scaled all the trees. He had lowered himself into all the deepest chasms. He had scanned all the horizons that bounded his domain. He was seen running along the cliff edge of the ravines, going downstream along the stony beds of cascades, leaping in one spring from oak to poplar. He played games of skill against the forest, as a child plays with its nursemaid; and the forest respected him, cherished him, and smiled at him.

Everything there he found familiar and beneficent. And as for him, from his side of it, he remained always kindly and protective of all that surrounded him. He pulled no branches off trees. He took care not to crush flowers with his feet. He hunted no wild creatures, as Jonathas hunted both stags and does alike. He even sympathized with the owl and pitied the spotted adder. He would gladly have joined that charming Saint Francis of Assisi, whom, by the way, he had never heard of: "My brothers, little goats! My sister swallows!" Thus, the roebucks that came down to the stream to quench their thirst passed near where he was sitting without becoming alarmed, and the tiny songbirds did not take flight from the tree at whose feet he was resting but continued, on the contrary, to rustle their wings and sing their songs. All the hosts native to these heavily shaded groves did where he was concerned the honors of their refuge, divining in him doubtless a creature as good and as innocent as they themselves were.

This ancient wood was not merely a retreat for this youth, moreover, or not only one, nor a house, nor a nest.

It constituted yet something other than them, something more even than them. It was, along with the funeral crypt of the castle, the spot where he came daily to see his mother once more. Inside her tomb, his mother lay dead. Under the forest canopy, she became alive, like him, and beside him.

Once Everard had pushed on down some very peaceful track, if he wanted to see Albina, he had only to close his eyes. Sometimes even, with his eyes open, from his mortal eyes, he could also see her, heavenly soul though she was. It was she who steadied him when he dangled from some tree root that thrust out over the precipice, when he crossed chasms, when he ventured out upon a crumbling rock face, and she did not stop there by simply appearing to him or by assisting him, either. She often spoke to him, and she was always counseling him. Those times the voice she borrowed was one of the forest's own voices, a tone both sweet to hear and affectionate also, sometimes low and serious, sometimes rumbling and awesome.

At dawn, for example, at the dawning of a day in May, as soon as the sun, blasting the horizon, had turned each drop of dew into a diamond, had made each tree into a feathered orchestra, had blended each flower into a perfumed sachet, when everything sang, scented the air, glittered, and when the forest breeze, as soft to the touch as the girlish lips of your beloved, caressed Everard's forehead, our lonely hero, as he lay full-length upon the grass, thought himself clasped in his mother's arms, throwing a thousand kisses to her and stretching up to hear her tell him: "Everard, my darling child, how beautiful you are, and good. I love you! Smile at me. I love you! Look at me. I love you!" And she kept on with all sorts of such flattering, fond words mothers use to rock their babies asleep as they hold them on their lap. The higher the sun rose in the sky, the more warm and melting grew the mother's expression and the more lively and heated grew the son's appreciation of her whose passion for him had awakened his love in the first place. That was happiness. That was a delirium of joy for him. Everard would therefore have been astonished to be told by someone that he was an orphan.

Almost as much as the finest days of the summer season, he loved certain winter days, particularly when it snowed. So sad a sight when it falls on a city, the snow over country woods is always so pleasing! This white mantle that clothes the earth is almost as cheerful as the green dress of summer. Those days, too, Everard believed that his mother was satisfied with him, and he was happy to believe it.

Albina did not always speak to him as a mother to her child. She was not always like a mother to him, but sometimes like a teacher, and so there were times when, in their serious conversations, she tried to make him better and stronger. That occurred, for example, during the solemn hours of evening, when the twilight descends upon the earth like meditation into the heart. All around him is falling asleep while man himself remains in thought. Then, with the last rustling of the leaves, with the last peeping of the birds, with the last rays of the sun, the mother shares her wise precepts with her son. He would find her eloquence inside some old ruin he had stumbled upon, in some strong, straight tree of the evening that the wind next morning had broken in two. Often also the horizon widened before Everard. He had climbed to the summit of a mountain, and just as his eyes encompassed the whole forest, he heard, down there in the far distance, a deep, continuous murmur that he took for the song of eternity. But it was the Main River rolling along calm and powerful, silvered by the first rays of the moon. Thus, between the dead lady and the dreamer, everything acted as an internal diary, everything, even the rain and its gray misery, the fog and its chilly moroseness that drove him back inside himself, everything, all the way to the cyclone where he heard just reproach and when he took its salutary chastisement to heart until it was eventually dispelled by the touch of a sunbeam streaking through clouds.

In such ways Everard's education progressed, and his soul had for masters only the will of the wind and the shade of a departed lady.

In addition to these, he saw no one and heard no one. His father! Did he even know that he had a father? From time to time, he heard it said about him: "His Highness the Count will not come down to Eppstein this year." What did that matter to him? Such words awakened no corresponding echo in himself and no memory at all. He felt neither sad nor glad for the abandonment in which they left him. This abandonment was what he was used to, and he was neither surprised nor resentful. He never referred to "My father!" Like everybody else, he said: "His Highness the Count."

In the castle were two or three valets whose function was to air the bedrooms and maintain the garden, but Everard paid them no attention, and they left him alone also. He certainly had his own bedchamber at Eppstein, but he slept there rarely. Most often, he returned to spend the night under Jonathas's roof. There he was nearer his beloved forest; moreover, all summer long, when the weather was at least passable, his bedchamber was the forest itself.

In the thick of the woods, on the bank of a stream that at that particular spot, where it was wider and faster, boiled up into almost a rapids, he had discovered a sort of natural grotto formed by the water's excavation under a lofty, sheer cliff escarpment. Even at first these strange, savage surfaces of bare granite had delighted him, and when he exposed a comfortable refuge hidden from most eyes by a hawthorn bush and a wild fig, he thought that when in this cave he was safe in a real paradise. On the opposite bank rose the sheer side of a mountain, clad in gigantic spruces. Their dark green needles and branches harmonized with the lugubrious howl of the rapids, adding to the scene what amounted to a stark sublimity. It was all too severe and too grand to be commonplace.

The severity of this scene was not unenlightened occasionally, in actuality, by some lovely golden reflection that slid down the gray mountain wall like lost sunshine, or that faint perfume exhaled by a thunderstorm, and like a good deed that has not been trumpeted. Nowhere better than there was Everard able to capture that sweet, haunting music that, he said, played an accompaniment to his steps wherever he went and set the mood for all his acts and all his ideas.

"Do you not hear it?" he would ask.

"No."

"Well, I hear it. I do. It leads me on. It surrounds me. It is inside this land of melody which steps alongside me, everywhere beside me, and from its land I can open my heart to my mother, tell her all my longing, my grief, my joys, and ask her advice."

In this corner of a lost valley Everard passed most of his nights and the greater part of his days. That is where he grew to manhood, that's where he lived his happy youth, remembering his mother and Wilhelmina, and, we must admit, waiting and hoping for Rosamund. One regret, one dream? Is that not what all life is about? And when our dreamer had searched the world in travel, in motion, in the disturbances of the heart and of pleasure, could he have found something more than in his sweet-scented solitude?

Yes, he ardently desired Rosamund's return. The small companion of his childhood had not gone from his memory. With her black beret on her head, he could see her there, before his eyes, her blond curls dangling from inside her cap, with her pink little heart-shaped face, her pouting lips, her cunning smile. He remembered all their games, their quarrels, and the sober, protective stance he took when she was around. It was of her alone that he spoke to Jonathas and old Gaspard; when they replied, it was only a question of her. Thus, Rosamund was the only link that attached Everard back to real life of this world. As for the rest, he was in every aspect exactly like Jonathas, his fourteen years exactly like the latter's forty, and also like Gaspard, who was by now a man eighty years of age. Just as sober and taciturn as the man and the senior, he would come in and take a seat by their hearth without uttering a word, and they would no more question him than he, them. Nobody ever asked him where he came from, what he did, what he planned to do.

When by chance they received a letter from the boarder at the Holy Linden convent, then there was rejoicing in the forester's house. The boy jumped for joy, the father wiped away a loving tear, and even the ancestor himself awoke from his ecstasy of contemplation. Then Gaspard and Jonathas listened devoutly to the reading of the blessed letter already captured by their young friend. Rosamund spoke of her companions, of the progress she was making, of the care lavished upon her, as if she had been a Duke's daughter. She was studying history, French, drawing, music—all of which were disciplines whose very names were barely known to Everard. Also, what made her happiest was when she returned in her thoughts to Eppstein, near her old grandpa, near her father Jonathas, and near her dear brother Everard. The letter was read, then read a second time, then commented upon, and then reread once more. Those evenings the lamp and the fire burned late in Jonathas's wood-paneled family room.

It is in this absolute retirement, in this unquestioned freedom, in the midst of manifestations, in the middle of centenary pines, and at the divide between the wonderland and heaven that Everard's dreaming childhood extended. For years on end he never opened any other book than nature displayed open before him at every hour of the day. He never addressed a word to any other persons than his two almost dumb and very sober friends, Gaspard and

Jonathas. Whenever a lumberjack or a countryman from the area crossed his path, Everard fled like a startled fawn. When old Gaspard's Bible happened to fall into his hands, he never turned the page that had been marked, satisfied to follow the black printed characters mechanically with a passing sweep of his eyes, thinking how he had seen Wilhelmina's fingers touching the tiny hands of Rosamund on that page as the young mother taught her little tots to spell.

And yet we cannot believe, can we, that his soul was speechless, even though it was the soul of this ignorant sublime youth who had once learned to spell from the Bible and to read in a castle moat? Was his soul sterile, made up of faith and love, as it had been? It was a soul fertile in amazement, used to astonishment, to supernatural fairy beings, such as one would meet only in *A Thousand and One Nights*. This soul of the boy was as naive, as pure, and as chivalrous as someone's in a legend on the banks of the Rhine; finally, it was like a Spanish cathedral where an Arabian Nights fantasy of delicate flower tracery has been overlaid upon a grayer Christianity.

However that may be, the days at Eppstein passed sweetly by. So it happened one morning that five years had already gone by without having brought any change whatsoever there, as we have said at our beginning. Only now Everard and Rosamund were fourteen years old, and Jonathas, to Everard's great delight, spoke of setting out to fetch Rosamund from her convent.

During these five years, which is to say from 1803 to 1808, Napoleon had accomplished the best half of his *Iliad*. That great and terrible drama played between France and Europe does not directly concern us here. We are historians only of a castle and a cottage between Frankfort and Mayence. There five years, which were so revolutionary for the world, were for this castle and this cottage so slightly affecting that it is hardly worthwhile even mentioning them.

Toward this period, old Gaspard, who grew weaker day by day, could not find the strength, on a certain morning, to leave his bed and go sit down upon his bench beside the kitchen door, or even to go as far as his easy chair near the hearth. He called Jonathas.

"My boy," he told him. "I feel that I am going out and that the cold of death creeps upon me."

"Only a momentary weakness, Father," the forester told him. He was upset beyond belief, although he would not have wanted it to show. "We shall keep you with us for a long time yet."

"No, Jonathas," the old man told him in a firm, calm voice. "I only have, I am pretty sure of it, a few more days to live. I do not complain. Rather I should rejoice. Nevertheless, before leaving this world, I would like two things still. Why not! Man asks eternally. Even one's death agony has its desires. I should like to know, first of all, what ever happened to my daughter Naomi, who disappeared into that turmoil which is France in our times. I want to know whether I am to look for her up in heaven and if she died a Christian death, like her sister. This wish on my part will not be answered, alas! And yet God only knows how the fulfillment of this request would make my death twice as peaceful. But as for my second wish, you yourself can make it come true. You, Jonathas."

"Tell me, Father."

"Jonathas, am I never to see one last time my own Wilhelmina's daughter?"

"Father, I will start for Vienna tomorrow."

"Thanks, Jonathas. God will bless you for having with one word understood the dying, and he will grant me, I hope, the grace to await your return."

The very next morning, in truth, the forester set out. Everard followed him until about midday. He would have liked to accompany him to the very end of his journey, and doubtless he would have been able to do so, for who at the castle would have noticed his absence? Jonathas refused him permission, however. Someone had to stay and watch over the grandfather. At about 3:00 P.M., then, after having shared his spartan meal with him, Everard embraced the traveler, loaded him with a thousand good wishes and loving messages for little Rosamund, and then, with lagging steps, followed the track back to Eppstein.

When he arrived at the forest, it was already 9:00 P.M. Darkness had fallen completely, but the darkness of a June night, liquid, calm, and blue. From a lookout point where he stopped a while, Everard could encompass in one glance all the harmonious undulations of the treetops as they turned white under the moon. This grouping of valleys and hillsides really looked like a seascape. All you could hear was the chirp of the cricket as a shiver of wind barely skimmed the treetops. In the sky the stars shone brightly. Down below him, in a hollow, a still pond gleamed like a silver mirror. Inside that diaphanous shadow, the houses, which showed up paler than the woods, seemed asleep, and the silent, cultivated fields seemed dreaming. It was enough to send the viewer to sleep or into a reverie before this fantastic landscape, which sent a religious peacefulness deep into the heart.

Everard sat down upon a grassy plot and reflected. A neighbor woman had promised to stay the night near the sick man, and the air was so perfumed, so moist, that the youth decided not to return home until morning.

He needed to stay alone in order to think, to speak to his mother, who must be sending kisses to him along the evening breeze. He needed to recapitulate his own lifetime, to look back the length of his past, and to imagine what his future would be. It seemed to him that a new era was about to open before him and that he as the climber who has come out on the mountain's summit casts a last glance down to the valley he has crossed, he, too, was bidding a last farewell to days gone by. Very few happenings but a great many thoughts and sensations had filled his existence up until then. For this reason, he was both naive and philosophical. His was the child's inexperience attached to the passionate heart of a young man. That particular night, being both heart and brain, he felt himself troubled to his very core, as one is before some crisis brought by destiny. The beloved or unloved who had crisscrossed his days once more filed past his eyelids and greeted him. All the while Albina kept close to his side, as a faithful witness should, he saw through a kind of luminous dream first his second mother Wilhelmina and then his good, old schoolmaster Aloysius. Next, in the far distance, his father, his eyebrows squinted, and his brother, mean and mocking. But from them he averted his gaze fearfully, to bring his eyes back with love in them for the noble and fine figure of a man who was old Gaspard, and then turned toward the kindly, sad face of Jonathas.

Then, descending deeper and deeper into himself, this lad, who had been loved only by two icy dead women and by two taciturn men, discovered how alone he was in the world. He felt then how much he lacked, that there was an emptiness in his chest, a vacuum that remained unfilled and which his soul told him could, if filled, constitute a new life. He reproached himself for such an idea. He fought it. But it swept over him again, all the same. He wondered if his mother was not displeased because of his ingratitude, and he dared neither close his eyes upon her or turn away his head. He feared to see her severe toward him, and angry with him. He was wrong. He saw her calm and smiling. All the dead are not burdened with the petty jealousy of the living.

Happy at not being guilty of coveting what he did not have, Everard set to dreaming then of his little child friend of other days, whom he was soon to see again, and a wonderfully unknown joy flooded his heart. He never imagined her grown taller or changed. No. He still imagined her as the pretty, saucy child she had been five years previously when he carried her in his arms whenever the fraidycat refused to cross the streams. He was going at last, then, to dare being young again, playing and laughing fit to burst. They were the same age, born on the same day; they would understand each other, and they would talk to each other. God knows! It is not with Rosamund that Everard would take it into his head to remain taciturn or to philosophize, as he did with the men who had grown sorrowful or whose nature it was to be tongue-tied. Near his vivacious and joyous childhood friend, how he would run, how he would live again, how he would love, how joyously he would do her the honors of the familiar forest!

He envisioned nothing else, nothing more or beyond that. For the moment, this notion sufficed, and at this very thought a thousand hopes and a thousand pleasures sang in him like birds at the first rays of the sun. Though it extended no further than a few days, his future was nonetheless immense. He was drunk from this divine waiting, and in his fanciful delirium, it seemed to him that in future he would have two hearts.

All the same, the hours of his poetic wakefulness passed quickly, and the dawn crowned the mountaintop with a bright flash across the very spot where Everard had sat down. The boy passed his hand before his eyes and offered, according to his daily habit each morning, his soul to God and to his mother before beginning the descent into the valley in the direction of Eppstein Village.

The beloved grotto lay on his road downhill. Everard did not wish to pass it by without a hello to his favorite haunt, especially since he might not visit it again perhaps even for several days. He might be needed to watch beside Gaspard. Before long, he could distinguish the murmur of the spring that watered his kingdom from about two hundred paces distant. Soon he had it all in sight. But he drew back suddenly with a cry of surprise and of indignation; his flowery

refuge, of which no living person knew, had been dese-
crated. A man, a strange man, was seated there, his forehead in his hands, there on the bank of the stream.

Everard's first reaction was that of jealous anger. He
advanced rapidly toward the unknown man. His footsteps
were absorbed by the thick velvet of the spring grass, so
that he made his way thus right up to the intruder without
his being aware of it. But then all the young boy's wrath fell
from him. The man was weeping.

He was probably about thirty-five or forty years old. He
was small and delicate looking, but he seemed nervous
also. The lines of his face were attractive but also powerful.
His clothing was as sober as his face: a green redingote
buttoned up to the throat, but with a bit of red ribbon
showing there. Altogether, there was something military in
both his posture and his outfit.

CHAPTER

IX

One glance sufficed for Everard to draw these conclusions, and immediately he felt himself overcome by an inexplicable feeling of identification with this stranger, a sense of attraction due perhaps to the tears that he saw running down his cheeks.

After having studied him for a few minutes in silence, feeling sympathy mixed with respect, Everard told him in his quietest voice:

"Blessed are they who weep!"

"Who's that speaking to me thus?" the traveler said as he turned around. "A boy . . . ! do you come from around here, young fellow?"

"Yes, sir."

"Then you will be able to give me the information I am searching for here. Tell me . . . but wait a second . . . until I catch my breath. Give me a second to control myself a little."

"Yes, take your time, sir," Everard said, for he was moved by the stranger's real grief. "Wait until you feel better and have wept all your tears. Tears are almost always good, I think. Do you know the legend concerning the waters of these mountains?" he added, as if he were talking to himself.

"An evil and sacrilegious knight told a holy hermit the

story of his filthy life, not because he repented but because he scorned the saint.

" 'What should I do, Father?' he said with a laugh, 'to rub out so many nasty crimes?'

" 'Nothing but fill this gourd,' replied the holy hermit.

" 'What? So little! And for that penance you will absolve me?'

" 'As soon as the gourd will be filled, you will be absolved. But give me your word as a nobleman that you will fill it,' said the hermit.

" 'I give it to you. This spring that I can hear bubbling is not very far away.'

"But the spring dried up at the knight's approach.

"He went to the brook. The brook dried up.

"He went to the torrent. The torrent ceased running.

"He went to the stream. The water would not run into his gourd.

"He went to the river. The gourd remained empty still.

"He went to the sea. The gourd did not even grow damp there.

"So, after the passing of a year spent in fruitless pursuit, the evil knight came back near the hermit's cell.

" 'Old man,' he told him, 'you made fun of me. But you shall not have done it unpunished.'

"And he slapped the holy man across the face.

" 'Have pity on him, dear God!' said the hermit.

" 'Pray for your own grace rather,' replied the knight.

"And he pushed the hermit so savagely that he fell down upon the sand.

" 'Oh, God!' said the solitary man. 'Take my whole lifetime of prayers in expiation for his lifetime of sins!'

" 'Will you shut up, finally!' shouted the knight in a fit of rage.

"And he slashed at him with his sword.

" 'Oh, God!' said the hermit as he fell. 'Pardon him, and I, too, pardon him.'

"So finally, as soon as he heard this evangelical cry, as soon as he saw this old man weeping for him who had wounded him, he felt a great ripping sound come from his knight's soul. He began to shake all over like a child, and he fell down on his knees near the saintly man. As he fell, he shed one tear, which dropped silently into the arid gourd. At once it was filled. Meanwhile, the knight kept crying all the time, and not only was he saved and absolved by his tears, but his tears of remorse, which flowed forward until they mingled with the spring which previously had dried up, gave to all the waters in these mountains the property of being able to cure wounds of the body as they have also been able to heal wounds of the soul.

"Therefore cry all your tears," Everard added. "Tears bring peace to the heart. They console us."

The stranger, who had at first listened absentmindedly, had ended by raising his head in surprise. He looked with a smile at the young shepherd who was holding forth with such a mystical sermon. In fact, Everard was dressed like a countryman native to these mountains: leather leggings and belt, wide trousers coming down to mid-calf, jacket of brown velvet, shirt with dropped shoulders attached at the collar with a gold ring, and a hat of gray felt, decorated with a long black feather. But under these rough country clothes the inborn elegance of the youth himself was very obvious. That steady, thoughtful look of the eyes certainly did not belong to some village lout. The pale, fine skin of his forehead indicated a strange gift of poetry. Under the frail envelope of flesh that clad this delicate youth, the stranger could feel the power of his mind. Last of all, in the shy bashfulness of the boy's approach, he could see a perfect honesty and sincerity.

It was therefore with a marked deference that the traveler said to the boy:

"And who are you, young friend?"

"The son of Countess Albina von Eppstein," Everard replied.

"Albina's son . . . And where is she? Where is your mother?"

"Dead for all, except, of course, for her son," the boy answered in all seriousness.

"What do you mean?"

"Do not the dead live forever for those who love them?"

"Albina still lives for me!" cried the stranger in a deeply sincere voice, "for God knows if I have loved her, the noble and sainted creature . . . ! And when did you lose her, alas?"

"The day I was born."

"At least something of her still remains on earth, then. Allow me, my dear child, to heap upon you all the love and affection which I had once pledged to her."

"I acknowledge you," said Everard, "you who have known and who have loved my mother. I love you, then, also."

And the inexperienced youth and the sober gentleman shook hands on it, like two old friends.

"You resemble Albina. Truly," said the stranger.

"Really? Oh, how happy you make me by telling me that!"

"Yes. There are her large, clear eyes, a mirror of her celestial being. There is her voice, which I hear again every time you speak. It goes now, just as it used to so long ago, right to my heart. My son, what is your name?"

"Everard."

"Everard, I'm telling you. Your mother has come back to life again in you."

"And she has come back to life for me, too, sir, for, I assure you again, she has died only as far as others are concerned. But where I am concerned, I can hear her. I can see her. She is my confidant and my protector. She is the one who at this early hour of the day put into my thoughts all the confidence I have felt for you, and all my sympathy towards you, for I usually fly from strangers. I am usually like a wild creature. You would not have deceived me, or been able to do so. Go on with you. I can see through you because of my mother."

Then Everard told his newfound friend all about his own life from the beginning, if one can call such an existence between the tomb and the earth a life, if one can call life this unceasing vision of death, where the dead mother shared an existence with a living child, where the living child was halfway down into the death of his deceased mother, where the child, too, seemed almost a phantom, where the mother seemed almost reality.

Charming are such spirits from Germany! Angels and nymphs of nature and of life, sylphs, ondines, sylvan beings, salamanders! I can believe that all of you may have loved and spoiled this boy child, who was never less gracious than you yourselves. And you yourself, *Germania,* old pantheist who took the universe for your religion and for your ideal. Germany, European sister of India! How you must have recognized yourself in this child who fell in love with riplets and with clouds, who was smitten with palpable infinity, and so tenderly respectful of a mother at once invisible and everywhere present!

The stranger listened to Everard's bizarre account, gravely and without a smile, like a man who has sounded the depths of incertitude and weakness in the human spirit without ever having been able to measure the omnipotence of God Almighty. According to his habit, Everard hardly mentioned Count von Eppstein. The secret of Maximilian's jealousy and of Albina's last hour had remained between her and God, so that the stranger wept for her strange, sudden death without ever suspecting a crime at that time.

He appeared no less keenly interested in everything to do with the forester's family.

"You must have known my other mother, too, Wilhelmina, since her premature end touches you so deeply?"

Everard told him. "She and my mother, you weep for them both truly as for two sisters of yours."

"Just like two sisters, truly. . . . But you say now that old Gaspard Muden is still living and that Wilhelmina left Jonathas a daughter?"

"Yes. My sister, Rosamund. Jonathas left yesterday to go to Vienna and fetch her. And I was telling my mother, just this last night, it seems to me that her return is going to bring about for me a new era in my life."

"And will Jonathas return soon?"

"Ah! I hope so. He must hurry if he wants to fulfill one of the last requests of Gaspard, who lies presently upon his deathbed and who would very much like to see his granddaughter before he dies. Whatever men can do to make the dying happy, they must not fail to do. The other desire of the ancestor depends only upon God, however. That would be for him to know if his second daughter, Naomi, died a good and Christian death or lived a prosperous life. But Naomi is in France, and so this last wish of the poor old man cannot be brought to pass."

"On the contrary. It can," said the stranger.

"And who is there to bring it about?"

"Me."

VOLUME
II

CHAPTER

X

Everard offered the stranger the hospitality of the forester's house, and his new friend accepted the offer eagerly.

"Only," he said, "I should like not to appear before old Gaspard until Jonathas returns home. Then, at the same time as the presence of his granddaughter fulfills one of the old man's wishes, I give you my word that I shall grant his second wish."

The unknown traveler spoke with such confidence and authority that Everard opposed no objection to his stipulation and walked pensively along with him to the side of the cottage. As they drew nearer and nearer, the man slowed his steps and seemed to be breathing with more difficulty. A strange emotion constricted his chest. When he arrived before the chalet, covered with its green vines, he stopped suddenly and could not go forward anymore. Although Everard watched him with astonishment, he hesitated to question him. The stranger composed himself at length, entered the cottage, and allowed his young guide to show him into a bedroom very distant from that of the sick man. There he spent the rest of that day either resting or writing letters. Then, when night fell, a night as transparent and clear as the preceding night had been, he requested Everard, who had come in to pay him a visit, to introduce him into the castle itself. The boy had a key to a small door in the woodland wall, and as we already know, the two or three servants left at Eppstein by Count Maximilian were never surprised or worried by the presence or absence of their master's son. Everard was thus able to grant the stranger's request and to allow him entrance into the ancient dwelling of his family.

The man and the boy first entered by way of the garden.

At that spot, there commenced for Everard a series of amazing discoveries. This garden itself seemed to recall to his companion a thousand memories. He halted at each shrub, at each clump of trees, and passing through an arched trellis, he dropped down on a bench and broke off a twig of honeysuckle, which he brought to his lips. From the garden they passed into the castle. Nothing had been altered there since the death of Albina. The stranger walked straight to the oratory. The tiny chapel was only lighted by a ray of moonlight that passed through the stained-glass panes and fell to rest upon the velvet kneeling chair where her Bible still remained open at the last text read by the dead Countess. The stranger knelt upon her kneeling chair, let his head fall upon the holy book, and prayed earnestly.

Everard remained standing at the door, staring at this man whom he had never before seen and to whom each object, even so, seemed to be remembered or to constitute a memory. After his prayer of a quarter of an hour, the stranger rose to his feet. It was then no longer Everard anymore who guided him but he who led Everard. He took the direct route right to the great master bedroom, toward the family bedroom, toward the Red Chamber.

At that door, and as he reached out to turn the key, Everard laid his hand on the man's hand.

"This chamber was my mother's room."

"I know that."

And he entered. The boy followed him.

The chamber also was only lighted by the rays of the moon, but they cast a sufficiently bright glow about so that each object in the room could be distinguished from another.

The strange gentleman went over to lean against a massive oak armchair.

"That armchair belonged to my grandfather, Count Rudolph," the boy said.

"I know it," answered the unknown stranger.

Then he pulled that chair over close to another similar armchair.

"This second armchair belonged to my grandmother, Countess Gertrude," said Everard.

"I know that also," answered the stranger.

Then the stranger turned toward the door, and from there, looking across at the two armchairs set near each other as they were and which doubtless, by this particular positioning, brought to his mind some deep memory, he put his hand to his eyes and began to weep again.

Then, after some moments of silence, he spoke again.

"And now," the stranger said, "let us go down to the tombs."

Everard started to leave the room, for he knew of no other entrance into the family's mortuary crypts except the access from the chapel itself. The stranger stopped him, however, and took him by the hand.

"Come this way," he said.

Astonished as he was, the boy let himself be led by this man who seemed to be better acquainted with the castle of his ancestors than he himself was. The stranger proceeded toward a section of the tapestry located between the window and the head of the bed. He leaned his hand against the wall there. To the great amazement of Everard, the wall yielded to the touch. A gust of damp air rushed with a slap across his face, and his eyes, which were accustomed to darkness like the eyes of the animals with which he spent his nights roaming the forest, plainly made out the first steps of a descending staircase.

"Follow me," said the stranger.

And the boy, more and more amazed, walked along behind the unknown man.

As the two nocturnal visitors slowly descended the stair steps that had been built along a corridor worked into the interior of the castle wall, a pale glow seemed to come from in front of them. It was the light from the lamp burning inside the crypt, which, by express order of one of the ancestors, was to burn there eternally.

Everard and the stranger came to the small wrought-iron grille. This grille was closed. The unknown man reached up his hand and from behind an angle of a column took a key from the nail where it hung and opened the grating. Everard recalled having often noticed this iron barrier but without ever having worried about where it led.

The boy knelt by his mother's tomb, and the stranger knelt by that of Count Rudolph. From this tomb he moved next to that of Countess Gertrude, and then, last of all, to Albina's tomb. The boy was so absorbed in his prayer that he did not even hear the stranger's steps drawing close to him also.

Having arrived thus close to Everard, the unknown man listened to the prayer that the child uttered. To his great astonishment, it was not a prayer at all. It was a private conversation. The boy was not praying as one prays beside the grave of a dead mother. The boy was talking to her as a person talks to a living mother. From time to time he paused to listen to her replies, and he smiled. The stranger knelt on the far side of the tomb.

They remained in prayer thus for a fairly long time, each of them seeming entirely forgotten by the other.

Finally, the stranger stood up and tapped Everard on the shoulder.

"Come," he told him. "It is late, and you need your rest."

The boy had fallen asleep, his head leaning against his mother's tomb.

The following day and the ones after that, the stranger became more and more like a family member and more like a father to Everard, who, for his part, had, since the scene at the tombs, shown him much affection. The stranger took advantage of this good feeling on the boy's part to question him about his father, Count Maximilian. But in this regard, alas, Everard was very ignorant.

"Truly," the boy said. "I do not know if I would recognize him myself. So many years have gone by since I have seen him, and he left here so fast. All his affection, as is right and proper, had already been lavished upon my elder brother, Albert. I have no complaint about that. In that way he left me entirely to my mother, and my mother loves me enough for two."

The stranger had already noticed how the boy spoke of his mother, not as if he were speaking of the deceased but as if she were still living. This sort of struggle, in which a child seemed to want to dispute his mother's love with death, made the youth even more interesting to the stranger, who, as far as that goes, was himself capable of deep love also.

However, as he penetrated deeper into a friendship with Everard, the stranger began to remark, and this to his great astonishment, the ignorance of this boy, who was often so astute, so reflective, and so subtle in his arguments. One day, the unknown pronounced the name of Napoleon in front of the boy. The boy asked him who that man was. Everard could have been the only person in all Europe who ignored that man and that name Napoleon. It was a name that every echo in the world was repeating endlessly during that period in history.

The stranger taught Everard all about that magnificent epic career, during which Egypt constituted one campaign and one stanza in the hero's poem. The victory at Austerlitz made only one episode. He told Everard that Napoleon was one of those rare men of genius who appear throughout history at certain times that summon them. Napoleon was also a meteor sent by Providence to enlighten whole peoples. Earlier such meteors were named Caesar or Charlemagne. But the boy no more knew the names of Charlemagne and Caesar than he had known the name of Napoleon.

It was the same when the stranger spoke to Everard of Napoleon in the Alps, in Italy, and in Egypt. The boy now heard the first repercussions of history in his solitude, and he was thunderstruck at his own simplicity. He heard all that just as he would have heard the tales from *A Thousand and One Nights.* His thoughts had been large and deep, however. His life had prepared him for the marvelous and the infinite. He soon stopped being astonished and listened only with admiration.

CHAPTER

XI

He died a beautiful death, did Gaspard Muden, such a death as even kings, surrounded by princes and servants, rarely have. From each side of his bed, Conrad von Eppstein and Rosamund held his hand, representing for him on earth angels of heaven who were yet invisible: Wilhelmina and Naomi. At the foot of his bed, Everard and Jonathas wept.

The two wishes of Gaspard's last days were thus fulfilled. The happiest death crowned his life, where he had been sorely tested, so that his last sigh was lightened by a divine smile, like a dawning in the sky that colored his face rosy even while still here below.

Thus, the children's grief at losing their father was tempered by heaven knows what serene assurance. This ending, calm and beautiful like an autumn sunset, seemed to them a reward. And when next morning at dawn, according to the custom of hardworking countrymen, they accompanied to its grave the body of their ancestor, their tears did not lack a certain sweetness that was filled with a vague hopefulness.

It is across these tears moderated by faith that Everard first perceived the white glowing face of Rosamund. As we have said, in his innocent exhilaration, a joyful, laughing girl was the one he had known. He imagined he would take her by the hand and talk baby talk to her as formerly and that he would greet her first, when he first went up to her, by a big, friendly, brotherly hug. But the girl-child had become a young lady, and as he separated this girl from his past memory of her, Everard remained shy and speechless, without daring to take a single step toward his sister now so transformed. His silent ecstasy must have been very complete, for now she made him forget, for one entire minute truly, but for a whole minute, both the old friend whom he had just lost, and his father's brother whom he had just found.

In truth, Rosamund was a ravishingly lovely creature. Already tall and well developed for her age of fifteen, what struck you at first glance in her general appearance was her glamour. She also charmed because of her modesty and her wholesomeness. There was something about her that was both imposing and yet lovable. In her whole bearing reigned an admirable aura of chastity, just as in her face and profile an infinite calm predominated. Her smooth fore-head and her blue eyes seemed the seat of all peacefulness and all gentleness. She was beautiful with that eternal beauty that statues have, but she was brought to life by her proud grace and her modest playfulness. Only Raphael has caught these same traits in his divine Madonnas.

Let us just imagine the daze that this dazzling apparition descending into his solitude must have brought over our wild Everard! Completely unassuming as Rosamund was in her carriage and in her dress, she must have seemed a queen to him, or a fairy, or an angel to this young person living in the forest of Eppstein. And so this first revelation of an ideal beauty filled him with an unknown uneasiness. It appeared to him, the son of a Count, that this daughter of a peasant had been elevated to a height that he would not attain. He measured, like an abyss between her and him, the innocent admiration she inspired in him, and he told himself that he would never be able to fill this immense space.

Thus it was Rosamund who, seeing that her childhood friend failed to recognize her, advanced to him and held out her small white hand, saying softly:

"Hello, Everard."

The spell was broken. The first words that Everard exchanged with Rosamund were still marked, however, by the strange respect that he had felt come over him at the first sight of her whom up until then he had called his sister. The first rapid exchange, spoken in a low voice, with a red blush on his forehead, was soon interrupted. Moreover, the day that Gaspard passed away had to be filled with prayers, with sobering thoughts, and with tears. The evening meal was shared by the family but eaten in silence.

The next day, upon their return from the cemetery, while Rosamund remained kneeling in the bedroom occupied formerly by Wilhelmina, on the kneeling chair used by her mother, Conrad von Eppstein took Everard aside, and Jonathas, to share his secret with them along with his farewells. He was obliged to leave immediately for France, where duty called him. He had already delayed too long in order to attend the burial service for Naomi's father, but he wished not to leave Albina's son and Wilhelmina's husband without saying something about his past life and his future.

"I was struck out," he told them, "from my family and from life. Outside yourselves, not a person cares about me in all the world. You alone therefore even know that I exist. I have resolved to die while still alive, to extinguish both my name and my self, to wipe myself off the earth. My story is a sad and fatal one, of which you know only a part. I am going to complete it for you and bring it to its end. My father exiled me because I fell in love, with a love that was pure and holy. Therefore, I sought refuge in France, where I closed myself off in my love. Although a gentleman, I hid my rank and assumed a vague name, a bastard's name. Thus, the world forgot me, and for a certain time I even forgot myself. But revolution began to growl all over

France, and it is difficult to preserve the pure flame of love from the breath of the hurricane. Almost unconsciously, I, too, breathed in the electrically charged ideas that reached us from the stormy tempest. I read Jean-Jacques Rousseau. And I read the economist Mirabeau. I familiarized myself with the daring thinkers of the eighteenth century. The studies and dreamings of my youth had prepared me, moreover, for this apprenticeship. A German, and yet banished from Germany, a nobleman repudiated by fellow nobles, I chose philosophy for my ancestral family and liberty for my fatherland. Free from the instincts that had now been denied me, from the prejudice that had been forbidden me, I was better able to judge from the outside those who had driven me from their ranks. And I saw distinctly, at the same time that I saw their glory, the faults of their past and their inclinations as contrary to the future. I took in my hand again not a Count's sword but a soldier's saber, and I enlisted in the service of the young French Republic, offering to it whatever existence there remained to use.

"Naomi, whose tender heart convinced me better than my proud reasoning could do, let me do as I wished, without jealousy on her part. She allowed herself only a sad smile at my decision. That noble woman was almost happy to see me live again with this new enthusiasm. I had only done my duty towards her, certainly, but she had sworn to reward me by constantly sacrificing her happiness to me, her soul, her life. She kept her word exactly! She therefore encouraged me to do what brought hope back to me, and she seemed to share my illusions without ever complaining about the desertion in which I left her. How blind I was! I never understood her abnegation, and I went. I went without worrying about her quietness. It was not long before I awoke to my double error. Even the most generous wines have their special drunkenness.

"The first fumes of liberty drove reason out of France,

and I recognized soon enough on the straw of a prison floor the nothingness of my dreams also.

"You know the rest of my misfortunes. My Naomi did not allow herself, in her devotion to me, to be distracted by death. In exchange for my name, which I gave her, she gave me her life. For the next three or four years, I do not know what became of me, what my acts were, what my thoughts were during this terible widowerhood. I no longer remember. What dreams then possessed my sleep, I forget.

"It was at the news of Bonaparte's first victories that I shook myself out of my torpor. My admiration awoke me then, living corpse that I was. The revolutionary principles I had once believed in were not chimeras, after all, since they produced this man and since they disposed him to-wards the conquest of the world. I felt that my own life, abandoned and lost as it was, could still be good for some-thing and that in the grand epochs of history one can always fill one's role and be of use, were it only by devoting oneself in the manner of the German philosopher and historian Ernst Curtius.

"I had no hold on anything, and nothing held on to me. I gave myself, like a cipher, to what they called the Emperor Napoleon's ambition. I abdicated my past, my old convic-tions, and my person more or less to plunge into the person of that conqueror who was to personify the thought of his century, myself to become an instrument of his projects, a means of his genius. It seemed to me that in obeying him, I obeyed an unconquerable destiny. He led me, to be sure, but it was God. It was God who led him.

"There are many of us who follow him in this same way, as we follow him at a word, at a gesture. All those who pass under his eye are fascinated. All those who breathe air from his sky go to him as iron goes to the magnet. But I have the pride to believe that I gave myself to him because of reason, and not because of instinct, like the others.

"Where will he lead us? I know not; I shall go with him to the ends of the earth. I even hold the notion that I shall not die until or when my task is accomplished and that then he shall have no more need to use me.

"He was not long to perceive my passive obedience, which came from a watchful understanding on my part, for this is a man whom nothing escapes. He knows that he is my goal, my master, my family, and my fatherland. He tells me: 'Go there!' and I go; 'Do that!' and I do it. When he shall command me: 'Die!' I will die, and all without a word in reply on my part. He is my will.

"That perhaps astonishes you, that a descendant of the Counts von Eppstein acts and thinks in such a servile fashion. But I am no longer Conrad von Eppstein; Conrad is dead. With what name did you call me, Jonathas, and how did you believe that you recognized me? Conrad is dead, I tell you! He died two or three times. He died the day his father drove him from his door. He died the day his wife died. He who stands before you and who speaks to you is a French colonel in the service of the Emperor Napoleon and currently returning from a secret mission in Vienna.

"Napoleon, who up until now had only asked from me for my blood on the fields of battle, wanted to utilize, this time, my intelligence in a negotiation, and I followed his orders, as always. They received me better there in Vienna under my simple baptismal name than as if I had introduced myself as one of the sons of Count Rudolph von Eppstein. It appears that Austria has resolved to turn Germany into another Spain, and that, being an old dynasty jealous of yesterday's empire, Austria wishes to back the peninsular insurrection. Austria has covered Germany with agents and with pamphlets, has prepared an army of four hundred thousand men, and has renewed her alliance with England. I went to Vienna to ask for explanations, and they replied with protestations. That is why, before a year is out, perhaps before six months, war will be declared, war against Germany, my old fatherland. But I prefer the country of my choice to the country where by chance I was born, and my real mother, to whom I owe my life, above all, is revolutionary thought and ideas.

"Jonathas, Everard, you now know all. I felt myself obligated to offer some consolation during the last moments of Naomi's father, and I have not been able to stop myself from revealing my life to you, who are so guileless and so affectionate. But keep my secret, I beg of you. There are two men in me, and I wish to forget the former. This month just passed here in this cottage, I choose to consider a passing dream. Now comes the awakening, and I no longer remember the dear ghosts that have obsessed me. I shall resume my new character and return to my work, for I am a new person.

"Dear friends, not a word about what has passed between us, I beg you to swear it. Let me rest buried in your hearts, and especially let my brother ignore my passage. If I had found him unhappy like you, Jonathas, I should not have been able to resist the desire to embrace him perhaps, but he is happy, I know. Let us not trouble his happiness. Now, friends, farewell! I must leave instantly. Shall I see you again? That is as it shall please God. However, something tells me that I am not leaving Eppstein for the last time. So good-bye, Jonathas. You will recommend my secret to your dear Rosamund, will you not? You, Everard, to whom I owe one other revelation, will you come back up the Rhine with me as far as Worms and keep me company for a few days?"

Conrad added in a whisper:

"We shall speak of your mother."

"Oh! dear Uncle, I desire it as much as I love you."

"Well, that's agreed. In an hour we shall set out. Within eight days you will be back here."

Everard was especially pleased to leave Eppstein, as one can well believe, in order to put a distance between himself and Rosamund. He was almost afraid of her and also afraid of himself. He trembled at the thought of reappearing in front of this charming, poised lady, and he accepted joyfully all that could delay the moment when he would find himself before her, and alone. His preparations were promptly and joyously made. His farewells to Rosamund took place without too much embarrassment, along with those of Conrad. He never noticed the frank disappointment on the young lady's face when she saw him going far away so fast and so merrily.

CHAPTER

XII

Eight days later, as Conrad had figured, Everard had returned from Mayence, having seen more country in a week than he had done up until then in his whole life.

Before returning to Eppstein proper, he stopped for a while, according to his custom, in the forest, and once arrived inside his beloved retreat, he sat wondering.

How many happenings in just one month! The departure of Jonathas. The arrival of Conrad. The fabulous tales of the colonel. The death of Gaspard. The return of Rosamund. The uncle's revelations about his first trip to Eppstein, a trip that had preceded his own birth by six months. The real world already glimpsed. The past brought to light. The future still in shadow. How many events! How many new ideas!

It was particularly what he had just learned from Conrad about his mother that preoccupied him. Old Gaspard and Jonathas had often spoken to him of Albina, no doubt, but that was the one speaking through the ices of old age, the other across the rather crude envelope of his own personality. While Conrad spoke, it was with the eyes of a brother, the heart of a poet, and the temperament of a dreamer who had spoken to him of his mother.

Then this strange story of the loves of Conrad and Naomi, this union of castle and cottage, this past of another person who, one would have said, was revealing his own future to him, Everard. It was a revelation that set his own heart to beating faster. What a strange business! This memory, which stood there like a lighthouse to mark the reef, instead of frightening him, drew his boy's mind forward like a magnet, like a promise, like a seizure of vertigo. And this terrible example, which seemed sent expressly by God to frighten him, appeared to him vaguely more like a ready-made justification: Conrad had loved Naomi. A young man, a Count von Eppstein, having gone forth one day from his castle, had encountered a poor girl of ordinary birth who came from the cottage of their forester Gaspard. The youth had loved her; he had made her his wife. This was the entire example of what had happened as Everard saw it.

All that disturbed him, oppressed his young spirits, tormented him until the boy became feverish. He felt himself transformed, exalted, larger than life-sized. He thought himself stronger than before and was proud of his force. All these confused calls to action, confused hopes, new sufferings, he confided to his mother, along with his novel sort of delirium, which he felt for the first time. Everard was happy without knowing why he was happy. Up until then he had only lived and thought. Now he felt a need to act. He had so clearly understood, and so quickly, too, the great deeds that they had shown him for the first time that without yet being at a height that would lead him to action, it seemed that he could reach his goal entirely through the power of thought. What now would he not undertake? What obstacle could stop him? Before whom would he tremble?

At that moment, he realized that he was no more than a mile or two from the forester's cottage and that he was going to see Rosamund again. He stopped short and grew pale.

Yes, without a doubt, he would have stood up to all the rest of the earth, but as for her, for Rosamund so beautiful, so grown-up, so well educated now, how could he dare appear before her! And, from instinct alone, without realizing why, instead of returning, as was his habit, to sleep in the forester's cottage, he set off toward the castle.

Night was falling as Everard came to the little gate into the castle precinct, and our dreamer, who was so preoccupied with the huge events he had just seen and with the grand plans he had contemplated, did not notice a considerable and unusual bustle that was occurring through all the castle courtyards and corridors.

Absorbed by his thoughts, which continuously formed a barrier between himself and all about him, when what surrounded him was not his beloved forest, he entered the great hall without seeing or hearing. His head was low on his chest, his inner being felt proud and daring, and his whole self seemed to him to have been renewed.

"Here is Master Everard," said a valet as he opened the door from the corridor into the Red Chamber.

The boy entered without knowing why he was being announced. A man of very great height, whom Everard did not know, was seated before the fireplace where a great fire was blazing; for in this chamber, with its tremendously wide outer walls, a fire was lighted at all seasons of the year. Only, since even this huge fire lighted the room but sparingly, the servant had lighted the four candles of a candelabrum; its four candle flames cast a circle of light that reached to about a third of the room's surface and which also cast only a faint glow into the rest of the towering shadows of the vast chamber.

"Ah! Yessir! Here is our Master Everard," the stranger said in a sardonic voice as he rose to his feet. To the boy's great surprise, he seemed to have moved into his mother's private chamber, where his mother had died.

"Yes," he said. "Here I am. What's going on, and what is wanted of me?"

"What's going on? What's wanted of you? We want to know where you are coming from, like this, vagabond?"

"Why, from wherever I please," replied Everard. "And, upon this point, it seems to me that I have always been free and that I have never given any account of my actions to anyone."

"What kind of insolence is this?" said the stranger as he wrinkled his brows and grasped the back of the chair with a hand that was knotted in wrath. "Sir, have you no idea to whom you speak?"

"No, in truth," replied Everard with the best faith in the world and more and more surprised.

"What do you mean, no? Oh! You take it as a joke when I question you. You are amused when I accuse you!"

"Doubtless, for I have no idea where you derive this right to question me and to accuse me."

"Where I derive this right . . . ? Are you insane, sir? To me, Count Maximilian von Eppstein . . . you speak so to me . . . your . . . father?"

"You are the Count von Eppstein? You are my father?" cried Everard, who was aghast.

"Ah! Now you have recognized me, have you not? Your excuse was a good one, I would say, and particularly filial."

"My lord, pardon me, but I swear to you, in this dark chamber and at first sight—And, moreover, it has been such a very long time since I have had the honor to see you, . . ."

"Shut up," cried the Count, who was furious at this justification where his conscience showed him blameworthy. "Shut your mouth! And try to reply like a submissive son instead of speaking like a rebellious child."

There was a pause. Bareheaded, still standing, his forehead red, a tear trembling in his eyes, Everard waited. On his side Count Maximilian, whose anger was rising like an oncoming tide, walked up and down, stopping sometimes to stare at him whom, through an effort on his part, he had managed to call his son, and that in his mother's very chamber, in the chamber of Albina, at the same place where, fifteen years before, he had crushed her whom he judged guilty, under the weight of this same wrath that, reawakening, suffocated him still today.

Maximilian felt himself as full of hatred for this boy as for an enemy; he could not forgive him the feelings of remorse he had occasionally felt on his behalf. He could especially not forgive him for that deep terror he had experienced the night he had suffered the dream in which he had seen the dead Albina rocking her baby to sleep. And so he halted suddenly before Everard, his arms crossed on his chest, and as if the boy had been able to follow his tumultuous thoughts, which turned him topsy-turvy and burned his brains, he shouted:

"Well, answer me, then!"

"I thought you told me to be quiet," the boy replied.

"Did I tell you that? So be it. Well, now I order you to speak. Let us see. Where did you come from? Why do you leave this castle for weeks on end? I arrive here five days ago. I ask for you. I inquire about you. They tell me they don't know where you are. That after having attended the funeral of some bumpkin, you left here with God knows what vagabond."

"Sir, it was Gaspard Muden who died, and—"

"And you, Count von Eppstein, you conducted the funeral services of this peasant! That's very fine of you! But after having done this deed, in order to become popular among the peasants, then what became of you? Where did you go then? Answer me. . . . But, bloody murder, answer me at once!"

"Pardon, my lord," Everard replied gently. "But whenever I leave this castle either for several days or even for weeks on end, I know perfectly well that I alarm nobody."

The Count took these quite simple words, powerful in their honesty even, for an embittered reference to the abandonment in which he always left his son, and, in truth, such was the awful position of this father as far as this child was concerned that Everard could not utter a single word that would not wound him. Now, everyone knows what Maximilian's anger was when aroused, and everyone can understand what rage the involuntary irony of him whom he regarded as an intruder in his family must arouse. He walked straight over to Everard and in a voice of thunder cried loudly to him:

"Will you soon cease insulting me? You have nobody to become alarmed about you, you say? Nobody? Eh? By God! Do you deserve that somebody should be alarmed for you? You accursed child! You who shame us by your ignorance and your low life? Are you worthy of your place in our household, in our family, and in a father's heart? Have you earned your share of your inheritance and our love? Who are you, sir? Who are you?"

"They told me I was your son, Count Maximilian von Eppstein, and unfortunately all I know about that is what I have been told."

"They told you! You profane joker! They told you," the Count repeated. All his suspicions reawakened at these words, and all his old anger. "Ah! They told you that you were my son. Are you sure," he continued, leaning his clenched fist on the boy's shoulder, "are you sure that whoever told you that was not lying?"

"Sir," cried the indignant boy. "Sir . . . Oh! By the sainted memory of her who looks down upon the both of us, it you who lie, for you calumniate my mother."

"Wretched bastard!" cried the Count.

At the same time, Count von Eppstein, incapable of resisting the violence of his anger, raised his hand and brought it down across Everard's face. The boy bent under the blow.

Afraid of himself, Maximilian drew back a step immediately afterward. But the boy slowly raised himself up and looked directly at his father.

There was a moment of awful silence. Then Everard,

pale with humiliation, his chest swollen, tears shining in his eyes, his hand on his suffocating heart, then Everard, in a staccato voice, was content to say this simple and yet profound word, which was so naive that it was terrifying, these child's words that are more frightening than any threat made by a man:

"Take care, sir. I am going to tell this to my mother!"

CHAPTER

XIII

Completely distracted, Everard left the room and the castle. For some time he walked straight ahead of him, without knowing where he was going, and could not regain a measure of composure and reason until, bathed in tears, he had thrown himself upon the grass and flowers that surrounded his beloved grotto.

Two hours before this he had felt so proud and so joyous; his new ideas of life had made him feel so grown-up; a friendship and a love had just so happily entered his life of isolation; and now suddenly, one outrage, one alone, had thrown him back again into childhood. Therefore he wept. Caught between his love for Rosamund, whom he feared, and the scorn of his father, of whom he was ashamed, he felt himself alone upon the earth. Both castle and cottage were closed to him; there remained as only asylum his little, lonely valley and as only friend, the protective shadow of Albina: a wilderness and a ghost.

"Oh, Mother, Mother!" he cried as he sobbed. "How we have both of us been insulted! Mother, do you hear me? Do you still hear me? Or are you really going to fail me and reject me, you also? You must know how I have been mistreated. It is not so much the hateful injustice of that slap in the face. But to be humiliated along with your good name, to have been chastised with your memory, to see what I love stigmatized, what I respect soiled, that's where the pain and ignominy are! Mother, tell me what to do. Is my anger unholy? Is my rebellion a sacrilege? Mother, counsel with me, and especially console me, for it is certain that my suffering is truly awful!"

These complaints, these cries, these prayers, rose all at once from Everard's chest, but the tears he was shedding without stopping, for he was crying all the time he complained to his mother, little by little lost their bitterness and their keen anguish, so much so that he finally was able to listen, to look about him, and to question himself with a degree of tranquillity.

The night was calm and clear, the stars twinkled in the sky, the white rays of moonlight broke into crumbling diamonds in the stream, the wild hawthorn cast out into the breeze its penetrating perfume. In the dark thicket a delighted nightingale sang praises of this beautiful and peaceful nature. All was joyous, love, and ecstasy in the forest, and Everard's soul, delivered as if by a superior power from the agonizing thoughts that at first had grieved him, lulled by secret melodies, made drowsy by such discreet beams of light, slowly became peaceful. Soon he raised his head, looked at the gorgeous sky, and under the soft evening breeze, the tears on his cheeks dried away.

"Yes, Mother. Yes, my good mother," he murmured, "you are right. I am the one who did wrong to be so affected. It is I who was wrong to look upon these insults as an offense. The affront to you which he tried to make, my own holy mother, could no more reach you than a hand could catch this impalpable ray of the moon. I was a fool to weep over any reproach or any punishment that did not come from you. As for you, you love me, Mother. Yes, I hear you. Yes, I feel you near me, Mother, in this serene night. It is you who imprints upon it this chaste and suave harmony. It is you who are the hidden soul of night. Thank you. Thank you, Mother. All is becoming peaceful inside me because I sense that you are not disappointed in your son and that you pity him and caress him, on the contrary. The song of the streamlet is your voice. The breeze is your breath. Thank you. One word more, one kiss more, Mother, with the balmy wind, and I will fall asleep calm and happy under the gaze of your angel eyes."

And in fact, as he murmured these words, the boy closed his eyes, and his respiration became so soft and even that it soon proved him to have fallen into a deep sleep.

Now let us see if anyone slept as peacefully in the castle as in the forest.

Count Maximilian had remained unmanned and thunderstruck by those simple words of Everard: "I am going to tell this to my mother." Because of his remorse, always restless and watchful, these words carried a terrifying significance.

Who in the world had taught the boy that prophetic threat *"Mane, Thecel, Phares,"* from the Book of Daniel, that was heard by an earlier uneasy conscience? He stood there, asking himself this, standing rigid, pale with horror, his hands shaking. Staggering, he tried to take a few steps and then violently yanked the bell pull and threw himself down in an armchair.

Several lackeys ran to answer his summons.

"Build up the fire! Bring some more lights!" cried the Count. "Instantly! This very instant!"

The lackeys hastened to obey. Soon the fire burned up in the hearth. Six new candles were lighted in the candelabra on the mantelpiece.

"Light up the chandelier also!" the Count cried. "And you," he told another lackey. "Run and fetch Everard and bring him to me here."

At that moment he could feel at the depth of his being so much terror that he wanted them to bring him back the child; if he took back his insult, the boy, he thought, would withdraw from his side, his threat. But, soon thereafter, the valet returned to the room saying that they might search all they would for the young Count but that they had not been able to find a trace of him anywhere.

"Then," said Maximilian, "have my secretary come up here. I need to work with him."

They called the secretary. Under the pretext of verifying his farmers' accounts, Count Maximilian had him stay up there with him until nine in the evening. At nine the announcement was made that dinner was served. Count Maximilian descended the staircase alone, bidding the secretary await him there and continue working. It seemed to him that the presence of a strange person in the chamber would drive away the ghosts.

Albert awaited his father in the dining room. He was a tall young man, sad, impertinent, boring, and bored. The Count was so pale and so agitated that even Albert looked at him in astonishment, however, asking him, with more affection than was customary with him, if some accident had not happened to him. Maximilian answered him gaily and loudly that no such thing had occurred. Then he sat down at table after having moved the chairs around with loud crashes and then talking, laughing, drinking, and eating a great deal. For an instant it occurred to the Count that he would get drunk in order to fly from his terror by means of intoxication, but then he thought at once that drunkenness itself might spawn more specters than those he feared. He ceased eating at that very instant and fell into so profound a reverie that he did not even hear Albert leave the room. Drawn out of this sort of torpor by a valet who inquired if he was not indisposed, he cast a quick glance around him, noticed that he was alone at table, and asked to know what had happened to his son. Then, learning that he had retired to his own apartment, he made up his mind to return himself to the Red Chamber.

He found his secretary still in front of the desk and still laboring.

"You haven't heard anything, Wilhelm?" the Count asked as he reentered.

"No, Excellency," replied the secretary. "Why?"

"Oh! No reason," said the Count. "I thought I heard a second person walking."

"My lord was mistaken," answered the secretary.

And he turned back again to his work.

The Count walked up and down with large steps inside the chamber, halting from time to time before the secret door and staring at it with an unconquerable terror.

"Wilhelm," the Count inquired, coming back to a place behind the secretary's armchair, "how much longer do you think this job will take you?"

"Why, I have for three or four more hours, Excellency," said the secretary.

"The thing is that I should very much like to have this work in my hands tomorrow morning."

"I can take it to my own chamber and spend the night on it."

"I have a better idea," said Maximilian. "Finish it here."

"But probably then would I not hinder the Count from sleeping?"

"No. On top of that, I feel slightly indisposed. And I would not be at all sorry to have someone near me."

"I shall do as His Lordship wishes."

"Well, then, do as I tell you to do. That's the best thing to do, I think."

The secretary bowed in sign of obedience, and believing that in actual fact the Count was in a hurry to verify the figures he was getting, he went back to his calculations.

As for Maximilian, enchanted to have found a pretext for having somebody stay near him, he called for his personal valet to come and undress him, and then he went to bed.

In spite of all these precautions, Maximilian had at first a great difficulty in falling asleep. The chamber was lighted. Wilhelm was there. He could hear the pen rasping on the paper. But his thoughts acted also like phantoms for him. One thing reassured him, however: the serenity of that beautiful June night, which was so different from that lugubrious Christmas Eve so full of gusts of wind and storm. This time, on the contrary, a deep calm reigned out-of-doors; all nature seemed to have fallen asleep, and across the half-open shutter, the Count, from his bed, could see the stars shining.

Laughing then at his foolish chimeras and reassured, moreover, by the presence of Wilhelm, the Count, in order not to look into the light, drew the curtains of his bed and ended by falling into a feverish sleep.

He could not have been able to calculate for how long a time he had slept when abruptly he awoke with a start and without apparent motive. He sat upright upon his bed, an icy sweat on his forehead. Then what a peculiar thing! He saw, through the separation of the bed curtains, that the candles of the candelabra and of the chandelier were being extinguished one after the other.

As for Wilhelm, overcome with fatigue, no doubt, he had fallen asleep in his armchair. The Count wanted to cry out and awaken him, but his voice was stifled in his gullet. One would have said that an invisible hand was squeezing his throat. He wanted to jump down from the bed, but he felt as if chained to that spot. During these minutes, the candles continued to go out with a fearsome regularity. There remained now only three of them still burning. When they were extinguished in their turn, they would return the chamber to the blackest night.

Almost at the same time, the dull sound of a door rolling back on its hinges could be heard. The Count threw himself back in the bed, his eyes turned toward the wall side and his head wrapped up in the sheets.

Somebody, for absolutely sure, was approaching his bed. He felt it in the air rather than heard it, and despite himself, as if mastered by an invincible power, he raised his head out of the sheets and focused his haggard eyes upon that point whence the thing was coming.

Maximilian shook himself to no avail. He could neither speak nor stand up. He could neither drive the apparition away nor flee from its menace. Finally, the curtains of his bed parted. He stayed there motionless and petrified as he recognized the pale shade of Albina, just as he had already seen her.

The fatal visitor seemed only, this time, more harsh and more indignant than she had been the first time, and when her impassive, stony statue's gaze halted fixedly upon Maximilian, the guilty man stayed colder than the cadaver that was his judge, and his hair stood up on his head from fright.

Then, in the silence of that starry night, just as fourteen years earlier in the midst of the howling storm, the curt, furious voice rang out.

"Maximilian! Maximilian!" this voice said. "Decidedly you wish to forget the protests of your dying wife and the orders of your dead wife? Ah! You strike my child, and you blaspheme me in my tomb! Take care, Maximilian. Take care! This child will condemn you, and the tomb will be your punishment. For the last time, listen to me and try to remember, and try especially to believe what I say. For if you were not to believe in the words from my icy tongue, it is my icy hand which would engage to convince you."

The Count started as if to speak, but with a gesture heavy with authority, Albina imposed silence upon him. She spoke again.

"Listen, Maximilian. Everard is your son just as he is mine, your son as much as Albert is. You love Albert, but you neglect Everard. So be it. I watch over my child and have no need of you to make a man of him. Go away if you wish. Leave this castle if that suits you, without a backward thought for Everard. Return to Vienna and your ambition. I consent to that, and I not only authorize you to do so. I hold you to this engagement. But I forbid you, in the name of God the living, to raise your hand upon my son and to touch a single hair of his head. Abandon him but do not threaten him. Indifferent? Yes. Violent? No. You do not wish to be a father to him, but do not become his executioner. The right to correct him or to chastise him, you do not have at all, and I, I do not want you to touch my Everard. Have you heard me plainly? Now, if you disobey me, Maximilian, pay attention here: In this world you are lost; in the other world you are damned. Yes. Damned and lost! The first time you saw me after my death was upstairs in the baby's nursery. Today it is here, on the intermediary floor, inside your own room, inside the Red Chamber. The next time, and now think about it, it would be down below, inside my bedchamber, in my crypt, inside my tomb."

"Horrors," murmured the Count.

"One word more, Maximilian, and I return to my granite residence. My soul really speaks to your soul, and no illusion during your sleep has abused you; but you could, as you did fourteen years ago, say to yourself upon awakening: 'I dreamed it.' Now, for Everard's sake and for yours also, I do not want to leave you in that mortal error. Maximilian, do you recognize this chain that you clasped, twenty years ago, around the neck of your fresh, young fiancée and which they buried four years later along with the icy remains of that young woman? This chain, Maximilian, which you will discover tomorrow morning on your shoulders, will persuade you that you have no right to believe that this night you suffered a terrible nightmare. You will not be able this time to fall back into your blind and fatal carelessness, for you will see with your own eyes, you will touch with your own fingers, the proof and the token of my presence and of my words, this chain. Receive it from the dead as you gave it to her when she lived."

And, so saying, Albina lifted the chain from her own neck and slid it around Maximilian's neck as he crouched there completely limp with fear.

The Count's lips moved, but without his enunciating a single word.

"And now," continued Albina, "I have said all of it. Farewell, or good-bye for now, one or the other, Maximilian. Remember!"

The Count only half heard these words; he did not even see the ghost move away from him. His eyes were closed; his respiration had stopped. He fell without other motion upon his pillow.

Lying all this time upon a bed of moss, Everard was sleeping the sleep of the just.

The following day, when, at the first rays of sunlight, Maximilian awoke, or rather when he recovered from his fainting spell, his first movement was to take his hand to his neck. He felt the cold, gold chain lying under his cold fingers, and he went whiter than the sheets.

"Wilhelm!" he shouted. "Wilhelm, wake up now, you rascal."

Wilhelm awoke with a jump.

"What is it, Excellency?" the bewildered secretary asked.

"The thing is that I want to speak to the forester Jonathas. Go downstairs and tell a valet to go look him up for me this very instant. I must speak to him."

"And this piece of work," Wilhelm asked timidly. "Must I finish it here?"

"No. Take it off to your own room. I wish to be alone."

Whatever diligence Wilhelm employed in obeying the Count, and the valet in obeying Wilhelm, Jonathas was warned that the master was asking for him. He entered the Red Chamber as Maximilian had just finished dressing and was standing there waiting. His first movement was to draw back in terror as he saw how undone the Count was and how pale. But Maximilian attempted a smile.

"Jonathas," he told him, "draw near and do not deceive me. You were present when they sewed my wife Albina in her shroud, when they laid her in her bier, and when they nailed her coffin closed, were you not?"

"Alas, yes, my lord."

"How had she been dressed?"

"In her white wedding gown; and, despite death, she was still very beautiful, I swear to it before you."

"Jonathas, did you notice, did you see, that she had something around her neck?"

"Yes, my lord, a gold chain which Your Excellency had given her and which she had recommended they leave on her."

"This gold chain. Would you recognize it?"

"Yes, my lord. Yes, if it had not been enclosed under a casket of three layers, of oak, of spruce, and of lead, the whole sealed under a marble slab."

"Look carefully, Jonathas. Is this it?" Maximilian asked him.

"Profanation or miracle, my lord," cried Jonathas. "That is the very same chain!"

The Count grew even paler. He let fall the chain back around his neck and signed for Jonathas to retire.

A quarter of an hour later, the carriages and carts of Count von Eppstein having been made ready in haste, the Count, accompanied by Albert, set off precipitously toward the route to Vienna without asking for Everard again and without looking behind him.

CHAPTER

XIV

Worn out by his walk home of three days and by the cruel upset of the preceding evening, Everard did not awaken until late the following morning. The sun was already high above the horizon, the birds were singing at top voice, all was light and joy. However, in the azure blue of the sky, a black cloud was gathering slowly over the north.

Everard cast a sweeping glance across this beautiful sky; then, from time to time, he looked over at the black cloud.

"That," he told himself, "is the symbol of my destiny—calm and happy today, since my mother holds no grudge against me, but uneasy and troubled tomorrow. Where shall I be tomorrow? I no longer wish to stay at Castle Eppstein, where my father would receive me worse than any beggar. I cannot return to the cottage where Rosamund replaces me and where, through God knows what instinct, I shiver at the thought of meeting her. So what shall I do? What refuge remains possible for me? You alone, you alone, Mother—!"

The boy let his head fall in his hands and dreamed. He no longer wept, but he was serious. A thousand projects and thoughts combatted each other in his mind. Finally, he thought he had made a firm decision, and so he rose to his feet.

"Let's go. That's it. No weakness. The only possible

course that remains open to me is to rejoin my uncle Conrad. How shall I manage to do that, alone as I am and without funds? I don't know, but I shall go. I shall leave behind me this whole country which I left for the first time only eight days ago. Providence, which watches over us all, God, and my special Providence, my mother, will not fail me. With their aid I shall be strong and courageous, I hope; and if, after all, some insurmountable obstacle bars my way, if some unexpected event throws me off course, if I am forced to retrace my steps and even to renounce this plan, it will happen because God and my mother shall have wanted it thus, and I shall submit. I am doing what I think is right, and so let them do with me whatever seems good to them. I will regulate my conduct as I can; let them guide my destiny wherever they wish."

Everard's preparations were not long to make. He was carrying with him all his possessions and all his future hope. All he had to do was to grasp his walking stick and set out for the road. But before departing, before abandoning his beloved forest, his valley, his grotto, he fell down on his knees and recited a devout prayer addressed to his mother.

He rose to his feet, pleased and determined, and without wanting to reason it out too much, without allowing himself too much reflection, he set out bravely up the hill to meet the high road that would lead him back to Mayence. It might have been around noon when he came out on the main road, bordered with elms, that ran along one side of his forest and which on its other side followed the Main River and the route into France. Thus he was going to leave forever his native castle and his nourishing forest. By the first turnoff on the way downhill, he would practically be in a foreign country. One last time before reaching it, he turned around to cast a last glance, to say a final farewell to the houses scattered here and there in the Eppstein domain.

Yes, Everard had been right to allow Providence its part in his plans and not to disturb its sacred role, for as he cast one last glance at the slope that at the end of one more minute he would no longer have in sight, the youth saw at that exact second that Jonathas the forester had just come out of a forest track. He had his gun on his arm, and with the other he held the bridle of his little horse that Rosamund used to ride so proudly. In fact, the pair of them, father and daughter, stood out brightly against the blue sky and green trees.

Our traveler, who had only, as he said, one last look to cast over his homeland, stood motionless contemplating Jonathas and Rosamund as if he were seeing them in a dream, and as if the friends who were coming toward him would never end by seeing him also. He stood still, not budging, looking at them coming from far away. With them there appeared to him a quite different life from the one he had been projecting for himself a minute before that time. Had Everard passed along the road five minutes sooner or five minutes later, his whole future would have been altered.

But before good Jonathas, with his gray hair, and the beautiful Rosamund, with her blond tresses, reach Everard, let us plunge into the young lady's life and let us ask about the sweet secrets enclosed in her heart and in her mind.

The double character of her whole childhood, as it was spent in the Convent of the Holy Linden, had been based on the penetration of the mind and the purity of the soul. Rosamund, like any rare thing, returned to Eppstein very educated in her mind and very innocent in her body. Language, history, and music—she had ardently studied such disciplines, but she knew nothing about evil. In her marvelous aptitude for grasping and conceiving whatever she was taught, she had never got to the point of knowing what vice is. At the age of fifteen, she was a woman in her mental faculties, but at heart she had remained a little child.

In addition, very few events had up until that day filled her existence. Some eager studies and some affectionate girlfriends, that's all. Many emotions and a great many ideas, few experiences. Among all her fellow students—and her fellows were the richest, most noble heiresses in Old Austria—she had always been first by her intelligence, and, which is rare, she had also been the favorite girl. Her sweetness caused her to be forgiven for her superiority. Her girlfriends—and all the students were or wanted to be friends with her—consulted her, respected her, yielded to her ascendancy, and did it without envy. She was the queen, worthy, good, and gracious, a fresh and charming girl of the people, and with that, beloved by her school mistresses, who looked upon Rosamund as one of them. Thus, when she left the school, there was, among the nuns and among the pupils, a veritable wave of despair.

They really had not much else they could teach her there at the Convent of Holy Linden, and so it was she who taught the others. At the age of fifteen, the curiosity that was native to her had pushed her into advanced studies, until each branch had less and less mystery for her. But let us not make a mistake here.

Her grace and her modesty had not been the least altered in the world. It is without affectation and with the most perfect simplicity that she would have been able to give an outline, which makes one realize that she had drawn it from a study in depth, of the history of nations and of great individuals. It is with sincere enthusiasm that she spoke of the French dramatist Corneille or of the German poet Klopstock, of Goethe, or of Shakespeare. As a musician, she entered no less into the genius of Gluck or of Palestrina, of Mozart or of the less well known contemporary Italian opera composer Paisiello. And you can trust this also, that her quick appreciation of poetry, her precocious musical intelligence, did not hinder her in the least from jumping rope and flying a kite to perfection. As many nuns as saw her grave and thoughtful when she was seated on the pupils' benches in study hall, just as many found her later, silly and giggling under the wide-spreading chestnut trees of the garden. It was this charming combination of expansive gaiety and of reflective application to study that made her beloved and respected by all, both at the same time.

Among all her girlfriends, and, we have said, Rosamund's girlfriends went from the first to the last corner in the convent, among all these girlfriends, the one whom Rosamund preferred was the daughter of a former ambassador to the court of England. Her father had retired for some years by then from the intrigues of diplomacy. Lucile von Gansberg's mother was an English woman. As a result, Lucile, for whom English was the native tongue, taught this language, as they played, to her inseparable companion, without counting the fact that more than once this daughter of a great lord brought home as her guest the daughter of the poor forester. Rosamund guessed in this way, by brief glimpses, a little about life in the world. But she always returned to the convent without having the peace of her own noble heart disturbed in any way. She only saw the world and was only herself seen through a veil of purity. Such were the events of her simple and tranquil existence. We are omitting one event, however, that probably preoccupied the two little heads of Rosamund and Lucile more than the insipid compliment of lords at the court of Vienna. This was their reading of *Romeo and Juliet,* which they read on the sly under an arbor of honeysuckle. This burning, pure poetry of love bore these two earthly angels off into an ideal world, which was a thousand times more dangerous for them than the real world. The passion that Shakespeare knew so powerfully how to paint left these two sisters all dreamy and all upset. The innocent foolishness of their fifteen years would probably soon have taken precedence over their hearts' reveries. The chaste and innocent being of Rosamund awoke first from this perilous dreaming, and this vague revelation of what love is remained the only shadow that dampened the bloom of these two goddesses of the dawning day.

When Rosamund had to leave with her father, to withdraw from the convent and lose her friends, when these two inseparable friends were at the moment of separation, their sorrow was poignant. Such regrets, moreover, and it is worth repeating, were shared by all those who knew Rosamund. Everybody made over her, kissed her good-bye, and wept to see her go.

"We will love you forever," they told her from all sides. "We will never stop thinking of you. Alas! Now who will patch up our quarrels? Who will counsel us? Who will go beg pardon for us of the sisters? Our guardian angel is leaving us. Our guide is going away."

And then there were a thousand protestations, a thousand presents, a thousand kisses. They wanted to keep her at least a few more days. They could not accept her leaving so suddenly. This was why Jonathas remained at Vienna longer than he had wanted.

The mother superior and the nuns alike were not less sad than the pupils.

"If, far from us, later, you were not happy," they said to Rosamund as she left them, "come back to Holy Linden. You will always find your place in the dormitory and in the classes, and our motherly love for you in our hearts."

"Thank you, good mothers, thank you!" Rosamund replied, in tears. "Oh, certainly, if my father were not alone, if my dying grandfather were not calling me home, if I did not have a brother who is awaiting me, I would never leave you. It seems to me that I am going to leave here all the calm and all the joy of my life. If one day I were to suffer, or if one day I were no longer necessary to somebody, oh, then certainly, I would return, and something, alas!, tells me, good mothers, that I shall return."

However, they had to leave. The ancestor was dying and

had no time to wait any longer. They had to leave the convent, the nuns, the daily companions. She had to leave Lucile. After having kissed each other a hundred times, after having promised to write, the two friends bade each other a final farewell. As a souvenir of her, Lucile insisted that Rosamund should accept a small bookcase of wild cherry wood filled with their favorite authors, and an English edition of Shakespeare was hidden in a corner of it.

"Whenever you read our great poets," Lucile told her, "you will recall, Rosamund, the days when we read them together and her who read them with you. Farewell, my dearest sister! Farewell! Perhaps, until we meet again."

And the heavy convent door swung shut behind Rosamund.

"Will it ever again open to me?" the young lady said to herself as, thoughtful, on her father's arm she walked away. "Shall I ever again see these peaceful walls, these good sisters, my dear girlfriends . . . ? Oh, I do not dare say: 'May God be willing.' I was happy there because I was young. I would never return except because I had suffered. And when our joys become our consolations, they are almost always painful. When our paradise becomes our refuge, it is almost always sad. Therefore, as for this joyous nest of my childhood, may it please the Lord that I never see it again!"

Soon the displacement of travel, however, and the novelty of all new impressions succeeded in distracting Rosamund a little. At first silent, she soon answered Jonathas. Finally, two days later, along the road she was the one who questioned him about Eppstein, about life as it was lived there and about those people she was going to see.

The good countryman Jonathas asked nothing better than to satisfy his darling girl upon all the points about which she was curious. He had been slightly jealous at the regrets of Rosamund, poor father that he was! He told himself not how happy she was going to be but how beloved she would be. She would first of all be all his personal pride and all his personal happiness, and then she would be at home and mistress of all, like before, when she was little and when her mother spoiled her so. He then spoke to her of their young guest whom she was soon to see again, of Everard, who awaited her with so much impatience and who was so natural, so sad, and so good. That was useless really, even when Rosamund could have forgotten the blond companion of her childhood, his brotherly letters, which she had received from him, would have kept him fresh in her memory. But she stored this memory in her heart, thinking often of Everard, orphaned like herself, born on the same day that she was.

He was her age, had been abandoned, was unhappy. A gentle pity tinged the affection that Rosamund's heart saved for him. She would console him; she would people his solitude. She pressed Jonathas with questions on the young man's life, and all Jonathas's answers showed her our same poetic, charming dreamer. She was in a great hurry to see him, without explaining her impatience to herself. Moreover, even if she had searched herself, the chaste girl would still have thought her impatience to be only natural. Everard was her brother. Everard had been nourished with the same mother's milk as herself. Everard had been raised along with her, treated like her by her mother. Everard was the son of her benefactress, the son of Albina, whose memory was always kept alive at Holy Linden. Finally, by birth, by education doubtless, Everard was going to be the only person who would understand her, with whom she could talk not only heart to heart but, even better, mind to mind. Her father told her that he was plain and excellent. She did not ask at all if he was witty and educated. That went without saying, in her dream. The essential was that he should not be haughty and scornful.

As for the distance that separated them, was not their shared sorrow enough to efface that? And then, I ask you, is that what girls of fifteen think about?

Beautiful and chaste child that she was, Rosamund therefore dreamed without scruples and in all innocence of him whom she named under her breath her brother. She called for that instant with all her heart, when she could hold out her hand to Everard and tell him a thousand things that she had to tell him.

Might one not add that the hope of finding her childhood friend almost, in Rosamund's heart, compensated for the grief that the thought of her grandfather's approaching death awoke in her? In any case, why should we not admit it? This egotistical forgetfulness of youth, which sees only itself in the world and which only loves looking forward, is so natural, we were going to call it so charming, that we have to pardon it and willingly collaborate in it. That she neglects the past, that she cares little for yesterday, stems from the simple reason that her kingdom is tomorrow, is the future!

We know about Rosamund's arrival at Eppstein and her first sight of Everard. Not only was he modest; he was shy. Not only did he not show himself to be overbearing; he was afraid. His gentleness and his embarrassment did not sit badly with Rosamund's serious and decided mentality. What she scorned most were impertinence and haughty airs. But her happiness changed to sadness when she saw Everard go so far as to avoid her. Did he not guess how she felt? When he left with his uncle Conrad, almost without looking at her, she could hardly hold back the tears. She found herself hurt because of all the affection she had felt at once for this tender, melancholy youth. It seemed to Rosamund that she could have helped him, supported him; and she suffered because of having to give up her role as beloved sister, a role she would have filled so well. His coldness, which she had not deserved, broke her heart.

What should she do to bring Everard back, for he seemed to be going farther and farther away from her?

During the whole time of his absence, she had been uneasy and preoccupied. However, her father showered her with care and tenderness and tried to distract her. Every morning, willy-nilly, she had to ride horseback, she had to pay a visit to some part of the forest, of her kingdom. And Jonathas was happy when he could make her smile or draw from her some exclamation of surprise or of joy. He spoke to her all he could of Everard, for he had noticed, all right, that this subject of conversation pleased his daughter and that when they chatted together about the absent lad, then color rose in the girl's cheeks, and a flame sparkled in her eyes.

But now we know enough about Rosamund. And furthermore, she has now had time enought to rejoin Everard, whom we left standing motionless and speechless at the base of a tree, watching the girl draw near, as if she were an apparition of herself. Let us therefore return to them. We shall find them together.

CHAPTER

XV

It was Rosamund who first glimpsed Everard. She cried in surprise when she saw it was he.

"Ah! My brother Everard."

No sooner said than she jumped down from her horse and ran to meet the youth, holding out her hand to him. Just then, she was in a charmer's mood. Her father had just told her how, one day, Everard had thrown himself fully clad into the Main River to rescue the child of a poor woman. The child had fallen into the water while playing.

"Ah! So there you are, Everard? What a long time you have been! We were beginning to be worried, truly. That was naughty of you not to have told us what you were doing. But here you are. So all is forgiven."

During this time Jonathas had come up to the youngsters.

"Finally, here is our dear absent son returned," said the good-hearted forester. "You do not know, Everard, that your father came to Eppstein during your absence and asked for you, my word, with much insistence during several days, which did not stop him from departing without having seen you, either."

"He has left!" cried Everard.

"Eh! My goodness, yes. And this morning, as he left, he did not say much about you, I must admit. After all, he appeared to be upset and in a terrible hurry to get gone.

That's all well and good, but it is peculiar that he should not even have pronounced your name. I was there because he had sent for me to ask for some very strange information, and I told him, seeing that he had already made plans to leave: 'My lord is not waiting until the return of Master Everard?' He imposed silence upon me, in a terrible voice."

"Left!" Everard repeated. "Left!"

"Yes, but in fair return we have you back again," said Rosamund in her pretty voice.

Everard looked at her with a peculiar mixture of tenderness and embarrassment. She lowered her eyes and smiled.

"And since here you are returned," her father continued, "my word, I am going to let you two, if you please, continue this morning promenade together. For the last eight days, Rosamund, while I have been holding my horse by the bridle and telling you stories, my gun was idle, of course, and both wolves and poachers lived off the land. So there, Everard, take my place, my fine cavalier, and lead this child along the prettiest flowered paths. You know them all better yet than I do. You have perhaps not lunched yet? You shall lunch together. She brought everything necessary in her wallet. For dessert you can pick blackberries and wild strawberries, and for water you can drink from any one of the springs. Upon this, my children, I shall leave you until dinner time this evening. I do not need to recommend your sister to your care. Have a good excursion, my dears!"

The forester shouldered his gun, waved good-bye to the youngsters, and, whistling, plunged into the undergrowth.

Rosamund and Everard stayed alone, the one as embarrassed as the other. It was Rosamund who broke this awkward silence first.

"Since we must eat our lunch, Everard, we shall, if you like that idea, take this grassy plot for our table, this tall oak for our shade tree, and we shall have a regal meal here while the birds give us a concert."

No sooner said than done. Everard tied the horse to a

tree while Rosamund spread out their food on the grass. And there they were, two old friends, eating together with the best appetite in the world. Even so, Everard still said not a word. They hardly exchanged, during the quarter of an hour that their meal lasted, more than a few unimportant words. But Rosamund, who was watching him, found his eyes more eloquent than himself. She saw his thoughts in his eyes and understood him just as plainly as if he were to have spoken. Under his ordinary, coarse clothing, such as mountain men and peasants wore, Everard was handsome, handsome precisely with that inner beauty that is sometimes termed physiognomic. Through his external mannerisms, his inner pride of person and the dignity of his being shone clearly. His glance, which was open and kindly, charmed anyone and convinced him immediately. Despite his awkwardness now and his silence, a person would have to be an idiot who thought Everard foolish. Now, Rosamund was also a sharp girl, just as perceptive as any good and sincere young lady has any right to be. And then there is between honest and pure persons a secret understanding that never deceives them.

"As soon as we have finished lunch," Rosamund said, "you must show me the places in the wood that you especially love, Everard. Will you do that? Would you be annoyed to have to be my guide and my companion?"

"Annoyed!" cried Everard.

"Or rather," she continued, "have I interrupted your own excursion and your solitude? For I see now that you love to be alone. And to think that I used to pity you!"

"You pitied me? You, Rosamund?"

"Yes, and I used to say: 'Henceforth, at least, he will have a sister, a friend!' I always thought that we would get along so well. I used to remember our days in the past, and it seemed to me that we could resume and continue, in these lovely woods, which seem as peaceful and as beautiful as paradise, the sweet fraternity of our childhood. Life ought easily to be lived happy and pure. At last, I dreamed a romance like the story of *Paul et Virginie,*" she added with a laugh first at her idea, and then a blush followed.

"What is *Paul et Virginie?*" asked Everard.

"It is a wonderful French novel by Bernardin de Saint-Pierre. Do you not know it? I will lend it to you. I dreamed a vision of happiness. We, too, would have lived unknown to the world, but so happy, in these mountains, in this forest, my good father Jonathas along with the two of us. I thought about it all along the road as I came home. Ask my father if I did not wear him down with questions about you and your doings, and he answered in such a way as to encourage my fancies and my hopes. Meanwhile, I arrived home, and at the very first glance I saw that all my projects were merely illusions. I held out my hand to you as to a brother, and you greeted me as if I were a stranger. It is not pride; I know it. My father assured me that you were as noble in your heart as you are by your birth. So where do your coldness and your indifference come from, then?"

"Oh! It is not coldness on my part," Everard said quickly. "It is not indifference, either, but what do you expect from me? I am a child of the wilderness, a wild son of the forest, and yourself in person intimidated me like the apparition of an angel appearing before me, or some fairy."

"What? Truly, am I majestic and terrible, as bad as that?" the girl asked him, and laughed. "Everard," she began seriously, "let us conduct ourselves in such a way that there is no misunderstanding between us. I tell you frankly, and in the simplicity of my heart, that I am attracted to you. This is because I believe you to be faithful and good, and I offer you my friendship and my company. Since we can be two, why stay alone one by one? The nature of God, in whose universe we live our lives, and the sacred memory of those dead whom we love make our affection sacred, too, in some way. Let no false shame and no misunderstanding arise; in the presence of our two mothers and under these ancient oak trees, I ask you to be my brother. Will you do it?''

"Yes, I will do it. Ah! You have a great and generous soul, Rosamund, and I shall try not to be unworthy of our friendship. I blush now to have shown myself so fearful and so timid. But the frightened fawn can now be tamed, my pretty saint, and the deer, instead of fleeing, will come lick your feet.''

"Just as if I were Geneviève de Brabant," said Rosamund with a laugh.

"Who is Geneviève de Brabant?" asked Everard.

"Ah! You take a great weight off my heart," the girl continued, without having heard his unfortunate question. "So, it is from timidity that you addressed me with those words that first evening. It is through timidity that you avoided meeting me, that you left with your uncle Conrad, almost without saying good-bye to me. . . .''

"And that I was going to leave Eppstein and Germany forever and without seeing you again," Everard confessed, "when Providence and my mother set you upon my road.''

"But now you are staying!" Rosamund said quickly. "Now we are going to understand each other and to love each other. . . . Well, what is it? What are you thinking about?''

"I am thinking," continued Everard dreamily, "that it is not from my lack of human contact alone that I wanted to go far away, to rejoin the French Emperor's army. There is also the fact of my father, who—But he has left for Vienna. There was something else. . . .''

"What was it, then?" asked Rosamund uneasily.

There was a silence. Everard sat staring ahead of him, looking seemingly at the night within his thoughts. He shook his head in a way that showed he was deep in thought.

"Rosamund! Rosamund!" he said very slowly. "A magical charm draws me towards you, and yet a voice cries to me, 'Fly! Fly!' Do you not understand me? The thing is that you must not judge me as you would judge others. I am a being alone and apart, and so of a strange nature. I have not lived life as all others have lived it. You see that I begin to share confidences with you. Yes, I trust you, and . . . I am afraid. A presentiment warns me that our friendship will be disastrous, that there lies between us some misfortune! Some instinct alerts me to the thought that I would do better to leave, and yet I shall not leave. There are predestinations in this world, Rosamund."

"There is God," said the religious girl.

"Yes, God!" continued Everard, going deeper into a reverie. "Well, God," he began as he joined his hands in prayer, as if he were alone, "God, you who lighten me with only dim lights, you who give me this vague desire to go far away without leaving me enough courage and strength, I obey you, Lord Almighty. Do with me what you will. What use for my spirit to stir about since your hand leads me? It is possibly my mother who counsels me to leave, but if your destiny orders me to remain, what can I do against it?"

"Oh, yes. Stay. Do stay. Stay here," said Rosamund with a graceful insistence, "We can be so happy together! You have in these woods—father has told me so—your secret haunts. You shall take me there, and you shall see, dear friend, that it is worth much more, but much more, to be two instead of remaining alone. Oh! Even for me, first of all, without you, far from my father, who spends the entire day in the forest, I admit to you that I would die of loneliness, while we two, we could talk, exchange ideas, feelings, read together, study together. You seem surprised. You think I am an ignorant girl, without doubt? Well, you are mistaken. I have learned a good deal, and I would be able to understand you, answer you, more or less, on every topic. I admit that I have not been able to perfect myself like you, who are a man, in French, Greek, history, and mathematics especially, which I barely like at all."

"Rosamund! Rosamund! But I am ignorant even of the names of all those studies."

"What! What are you telling me?"

"The truth. Your mother taught me to read, and the chaplain taught me to write; but they are dead, and I have remained all alone here, abandoned, as you know very well, having no schoolmaster but the forest, no other education than that taught by nature! Who would have instructed me? Nobody. I have not yet opened any book but the Bible, and even that has not happened often. The trees and birds have not twitted me with my ignorance. I only knew it myself a month ago, at the arrival of my uncle. I blush for it for the first time today."

"Is it possible!" cried Rosamund. "Yes, without doubt. I should have reflected about it. I should have thought . . . Poor friend, I beg your pardon to have involuntarily hurt your feelings, perhaps."

"You have not hurt my feelings, Rosamund; but you can plainly see that my company can neither please nor serve you, that I am not at your level of development, and that frequenting me would tire you, far from distracting you. You can see that it is necessary now for me to be left in my ignorance and in my wearisomeness. You can see that I was right and that the best thing I have to do is to leave, to go enlist in the army."

"My friend," Rosamund answered gravely, "your mind is too lofty for you to listen to a false sense of pride and for you to be influenced by some trifling susceptibility. Stay, and we shall be able to be useful the one to the other. You have a learned heart, Everard, and the fields and the woods, and also the sky, must have offered you some good and healthy lessons. You will share them with me, and so I, too, shall learn; as for me, since I owe whatever training I have to chance, or rather to the protection of Countess Albina, do not refuse me the joy to render something to her son of all the good I own because of his mother. Accept me for your master teacher, will you? That would be charming, truly."

"No. It is too late, Rosamund. Too late!"

"Good heavens! Do you believe that learning is a quite hard and difficult thing to acquire? It is very simple, Everard, to become educated, and most interesting. You wouldn't find anything new in it. You will see nations rise like springs of water, geniuses grow like oaks, revolutions burst like storm clouds. There are books which will gladden your heart like beautiful May evenings. There are periods of history which will sadden you like a rainy day in December. Languages are no more difficult to decipher than are signs in the sky and the directions of the wind, and you will recognize the hand of God in history just as in nature. And then will you not be proud and happy to meet in the annals of Germany the chronicles of your own glorious family, to find at each section of our records the names of your ancestors, which is your name, too, of Eppstein?"

"Am I an Eppstein? I?" interrupted Everard with a bitter sadness. "You are mistaken, Rosamund. I am an abandoned child, rejected by my father. That is all I am. What is the use of teaching me? What is the use of raising me up so that I can better measure my abasement? For what I have to do here, Rosamund, what I know suffices. My mother guides me. That's enough. You do not understand me. If you were to enter more deeply into my confidence and into my life, I would reveal to you things that would strike you with astonishment and with fright even. I repeat it to you, my being and my destiny are strange. God marked me in advance for a future that he alone knows and that I can not avoid. I feel that his breath pushes me onward, and that since he sees for me, what use have I for human knowledge? My instinct suffices for me to obey his will, but I would fear my own reasoning power. The best thing for me to do would be to leave here, or to remain untaught, since I am not going to leave."

We shall not repeat all the pleas of Rosamund, all the rebuttals by Everard, all this struggle between enlightened instinct and blind caution. The role of Little Mother suited the serene face and serious nature of our schoolgirl educated at Holy Linden. She told Everard how nice and delightful her studies were, there in the shade of centenary trees and in the deep quiet of scented forest glades. Everard hesitated, almost yielded, then drew back.

The livelong day was spent in discussing everything as they strolled along, admiring the vast prospects and the scenic lookouts over the countryside. Their deliberations were also, one must admit, interrupted with games and dares, and it often happened that they cut short an apology for learning in order to run after some spotted butterfly. Let us not forget that our oldest hero has not yet quite reached the age of fifteen. In short, in the midst of childish games and grown-up sermons, twilight fell, and Everard had to guide his sister back to the forester's cottage. Even then, he had not entirely made up his mind, not absolutely, and still swore he was really going to leave next day.

He did not tell Rosamund everything. He did not tell her that what chiefly drove him away was a bloody affront dealt him by his father and that he could not return to the castle whence this affront banished him. But, although he kept still upon this score, he thought about it certainly, and each time he thought of it, he felt red flushes streak across his face.

It was in the middle of such hesitations that he returned to Jonathas's house, which he had promised himself that very morning never to see again. The forester was waiting for them.

"What a long time you have spent out-of-doors!" he said. "I was worried. Everard, here is a letter addressed to me from my lord the Count in Frankfort and which a groom has just delivered posthaste. Read it. It has to do with you."

Everard took the paper with a trembling hand and read

it. Maximilian notified Jonathas that henceforth he intended to make his permanent headquarters in Vienna and that from that day onward he would never again visit Eppstein. He added:

> Tell this to my son Everard and notify him that he can dispose of the castle and of a quarter of its revenues. My steward will go down each year to collect the remainder; but tell Everard that he shall not leave Eppstein or attempt to rejoin me. Our two destinies must remain separated, and I forbid him to bring them together. It is upon this condition that I leave him free and master of his life within his own house. He may do as he likes, everything he likes, provided he does not come where I am. I shall not trouble him, but let him not trouble me the more. I shall ask him to give me no account of his actions, but let him never require from me any account of mine. Let us remain strangers the one to the other in order to stay happy. Such is my resolution, express and formal, and misfortune upon him who resists it!

Once he had finished reading the letter, Everard let his head fall on his chest. He was both sad and joyful at once. He seemed lost in thought for a moment.

"Well?" inquired Rosamund anxiously.

"Well, Rosamund," he said with shining eyes but with his chest swollen with a sigh. "Well, God wills it. I shall stay."

CHAPTER

XVI

L ess than a mile from the hamlet of Eppstein, at two hundred paces from the cottage of the forester Jonathas, there lay, at the edge of the forest, a wide village green where the country people from roundabout gathered on Sundays. This fine circle of lawn was the greening hall and thick carpet for the country dances, and near there, a huge grove of centenary linden trees served as a meeting place for the old sages and for the selectmen of the village. Between these trees a spring had been hallowed out into a well in the earth, and one could go down to it by a stone staircase that was all mossy.

Around this spring, benches had been built in front of a retaining wall, all of which was very convenient for drawing water.

Three years after the death of Gaspard, a young man, on a dreary and warmish morning in September, had seated himself on the grass, right where the lindens were thickest, and, cardboard on his knees, was drawing a twisted, knotty old tree trunk that a swarm of bees had chosen for their kingdom. Frequently, the young man interrupted his work to look across at the lawn. Yet it was a weekday, and not a soul appeared there. All one could hear was the continuous gurgle of the spring and the song of the whitethroat warbling in the foliage.

However, after an hour's wait, a girl came out to the edge

of the lawn, and the sketch artist rose to go to meet her. But he halted after a few steps and stayed there looking at her, without being seen by her.

This young man was Everard. The girl was Rosamund.

Always noble and handsome, Everard wore, but with more elegance and distinction than formerly, his same plain and picturesque costume. He had his same look, which was both deeper and sadder. His forehead was still high and serious, but now it was lined more visibly with the reality of a somber destiny and heaven knows what hidden fatality.

Always ravishing and modestly proud, Rosamund wore the customary red tunic and black skirt; the pleated border of a white shirt encircled her sweet face. She was carrying a sandstone bottle on her shoulder and a smaller one in her hand as she headed toward the spring.

When she stepped down the worn stone steps, Everard left the grove of lindens and ran to join her.

"Hello, Everard," she said as she saw him, in a voice that indicated she expected to find him there.

They sat down together on one of the benches.

"Look, Rosamund," said Everard as he opened his drawing pad. I have almost finished my sketch, and, my word!, thanks to your good teaching of yesterday, it has not come out too badly, it seems to me. I have tried to impress it with that horror which our great Albrecht Dürer lent to our forests. You were telling me his simple and sublime story the other day."

And, taking the pencil from his hand, she corrected a fault in a few quick lines.

"Now it's magnificent," said Everard, clapping his hands, "and I am twice as happy with my masterpiece since you have touched it. You must be as good as you are beautiful, Rosamund, to show so much indulgence and to be so patient with your clumsy schoolboy."

"Child that you are," said the girl as he kissed her hands

softly and gazed at her with the admiration of youth, "is there not a charming attraction in our studies? Are our lessons anything else than a series of pleasures? Is my schoolboy not my companion? And then I shall be so vain, Everard, to have returned you, to have almost given to the German nobility, one of its most historic representatives, a nobleman called by his rank to such a high destiny and who otherwise languished in ignorance and weariness! I have done this for you. Ah! I feel so proud when I think of it, of what your mother would have done, of what Count Maximilian should have done. And what progress in three years! How promptly you have grasped everything! How fast you have guessed all of what I only knew by halves! Now what would they be beside you, all those gilded butterflies at the imperial court in Vienna?"

"Alas!" Everard replied sadly. "It is not by learning that you have made me happy, my sister Rosamund. What use is it to enlarge the thoughts of a person when his life is so narrow? What use are wings to a caged eagle? What difference does a renowned name make to an obscure destiny? I never so well understood my isolation as after having studied the world, so that if I did not bless you for your presence, I would be angry with you, I believe, for your lessons. Since I have seen you, I exist; but since I have begun to think, I suffer. We shall perhaps one day, Rosamund, deplore this fatal gift you have given me."

"No," answered Rosamund. "I shall never repent for having returned one of the Eppsteins to himself and to his country."

"Ah! I am an outcast Eppstein and forgotten," Everard said with a sorry shake of his head. "I shall never be an illustrious general like my grandfather Rudolph, whom Frederick the Great feared, nor a deep diplomat like my maternal grandfather, who continued the tradition of the great Austrian statesman Prince von Kaunitz. I shall be at most the hero of some dark and terrible legend, and if I am famous one day, it will be neither in military camps nor in our schools, but perhaps around the bonfires of our country people."

"Everard, dear brother, more of your weird ideas!" interrupted Rosamund.

"Oh! You may say all you like. I feel a crime somewhere connected to my fate. Precisely since you brought me into reality. I have become conscious of the strange life that God willed for me by placing me as a baby near the dead mother. In the light of truth which you have helped me grasp, I realize clearly now that I am, as it were, outside mankind: a shade, a phantom, a threat perhaps, and a means of vengeance. I am all that, except just a man."

"Dear friend!"

"Oh! You can do nothing to stop this. You are before me, Rosamund; but my mother Albina is behind me. You would be a very glowing future, but she is a so formidable past! Wait. Let's speak of something else."

Then followed a pause full of deep thought.

"Have you read *The History of the Thirty Years' War*?" Rosamund asked.

"Yes, and Wallenstein is a great general, as Schiller is a great poet. Thanks to you, Rosamund, who introduced me to the chronicles of bygone days, who have, I might say, added to my own life all these other successful and world-famous lives, I thank you for having taught me to feel enthusiasm. Ah! When I speak bitter words to you, pardon me. Do not listen to me then. I am unjust. I am bad. But in my heart of hearts I love you like my sister, and I also venerate you as I venerate my mother."

"Everard," said Rosamund, and truly her grave and serious attitude made her resemble a young mother exhorting her son. "Everard, I know you are good and gentle! But I blame you, really, for being sad and discouraged. Why do you believe in Fate and not believe in Providence? That's bad of you. Do not God and your mother both watch over you? One single thing was lacking in your case, and that was the education of your mind. I was chosen to bring it to you, and winter at the side of the fire, summer in your grotto, or here on the wall around this little spring, we have talked together, read, and reflected. You soon learned what I knew, and then, exceeding my imperfect teaching, you showed me in your turn what I had not yet learned. Now, whether you are to remain here in this retreat or whether you are to go out into the world at Vienna, at the imperial court, you will cut the figure wherever you are of an enlightened and distinguished man of intelligence. Now you will yourself be able to direct and counsel others. Please do not, with your doubts and your sources of sadness, I beg of you, do not disturb the joy I feel thinking that I have contributed my weak means to making you worthy of the name you bear and of the future which awaits you."

"Well, I will be joyous, if you want me to, Rosamund, joyous all the time you will be near me, as flowers are joyous so long as the sun shines upon them."

"It's about time, my brother!" said Rosamund. "Let me now draw water for my household needs and take it right home, and then, if you wish, we can finish going over together the history of the German imperial family of Hohenstaufen."

"I should say that pleases me!" the youth cried gaily. "Rosamund, I promise you not to think of tomorrow if I can stay near you today."

And the two friends squeezed hands, their smiles full of true affection. Then the girl took her little bottle and leaned down to fill it with water. Everard grasped the larger bottle and also leaned down over the soft, cool water. The sky was a pure blue above their heads, and their adorable faces reflected in this mirror of the spring.

Thus surrounded with azure, their heads came almost to touch in the water, and they laughed at each other and said hello to each other.

When they had lifted their heads:

"Give me a drink," said Everard playfully.

Rosamund held out her bottle to him, and he drank. A sculptor who could have caught their graceful poses would have created the loveliest work imaginable.

"We must look like some biblical tableau of Abraham's servant Eliezer, who brought back Rebecca, for example," the girl said with a laugh.

Lightly she tripped up the stone steps and walked away from the spring, bearing her smaller bottle on her shoulder. With the other bottle in his hand and his drawing board under his arm, he was not slow to catch up to her.

As they walked along, they looked at each other often. Everard's eyes were full of admiration and tenderness, but in Rosamund's glances there was less an expression of love than one of discretion and kindliness.

CHAPTER

XVII

The recital of a single morning can make us understand what had been, for these long years, the pleasant life of Everard and of Rosamund. The tender dreamer from the Taunus Mountain slopes and the sober pupil from Holy Linden had developed the one and the other in the direction of their characters and of their destiny. Rosamund had taught Everard; Everard had fallen in love with Rosamund. The solitary walker was henceforth no longer alone. He had someone to whom he could open his soul, to whom he could consecrate those parts of his heart and his life that his mother left unoccupied. He made it his happiness to obey Rosamund. Whatever she gave him to do, he made short work of it, and effortlessly. She held over his wild spirit a sovereign jurisdiction. All was for her in his untaught and devoted nature.

The only thing that Everard kept for himself was his cult for the shade of Albina. Rosamund was his confidant for all the rest, but he opened only with reserve, even to her, his visions of the night and of the day. The secrets of these apparitions and the counseling of his dear ghost were revealed only by half. Like true love, Everard's filial respect had its reticence, which forbade him to betray this sealed tomb, sealed for all except him.

Everard had from this time a double existence and a double love, and yet his mother seemed not annoyed at the division. When Rosamund was there, he worked with her, happy to hear her and to follow her thought. When she had left, he plunged into the forest and into his reverie when it was his mother whom he summoned, his mother who came, who resumed over him her ancient authority, and who spoke to him in the wind or in the breeze, always to instruct him and to improve him.

Now, concerning these sessions, he said nothing of their details or purpose, like a respectful lover who does not speak of his mistress's favors. The cold rays of the moon or the pale brilliance of the stars were the only witnesses and the only confidants; only, one must believe that his mother pitied him, if she did not blame him, and that if he did not incur reproach on her part, he was troubled by her apprehensions and by her pity. Generally, he returned from his grotto most often depressed and even gloomy, and when Rosamund asked him about it, he gently refused to answer her. Then he wept bitterly and spoke in vague terms about a dreadful future. She was not able on those days to comfort him.

Aside from this one area, he belonged entirely to Rosamund and underwent from day to day, always charmed extremely, the sway of the girl.

We must say that she used her power with infinite wisdom and gentleness, as if maternal instincts within her were, alas!, to find no other occasion for use. She had undertaken with joy and carried through to the end with love the instruction of the young and undisciplined mind of Everard. She had gone back with him over the difficult, ungrateful paths of science. With patience and good humor she had shown her student all she knew: history, geography, sketching, music. She had familiarized him with the French and English languages without mentioning their national literatures. In several areas he had outdone her; in others, she had maintained superiority. But to tell the truth, it had been a charming and touching spectacle to see this child teaching another young person. And it was a strange mystery, this transformation made by a girl, of a rough and almost illiterate peasant into an elegant, lettered man.

For anyone to recount all the events of these three years at Eppstein would be impossible. Nothing was simpler than the existence that Rosamund and Everard lived, an existence barren of deeds, fertile in ideas. In two words, one could tell it all. To follow them through one day would be to know them for the past three years.

First thing in the morning, Everard would leave the castle, where he had claimed a bedroom permanently, and after having said his prayers at length over the tomb of his mother, come knocking at the door of good Jonathas. While Rosamund, who was the best and most exacting housewife, finished putting everything away and setting her house in order, he studied alone, reviewing all his lessons of the previous day and preparing those of that day. They breakfasted together, simply and pleasantly. Hours of work then followed, animated and intense, in the house when the weather threatened, in the woods, on the meadow, at the spring, when it was fine. The studies were none the worse for having been done beside a wheat field. The readings were no less well grasped for having been accompanied by birdsong. Because flowers picked along the roadside marked the pages of the books, perfumed books advanced their readers just as well.

Evenings were reserved for rest and for conversation. In winter, they would sit before the flaming hearth, in summer on the bench at the front door, under the honeysuckle and the jasmine. In winter, they listened to the rain falling or to the snow; in summer they watched the sun set and the stars rise in the east.

Then, like a good fellow, Jonathas had to tell some marvelous tale, or Rosamund would, or some charming legend. The forester especially, who was the best storyteller in that country, had never run out of memories, among which he did not omit, in the purity and sincerity of his heart, all sorts of love stories, which were perhaps dangerous for auditors as young as his, if he had not softened their effect just by his own chaste candor and reverent innocence.

When no stories were being told, Rosamund would sit at her harpsichord and play the prettiest pieces from Gluck, Haydn, Mozart, and even Beethoven, who was just beginning to cast his spell. Nobody could possibly describe the effect that these immortal melodies cast over Everard's being. The lad was at once as vague and as deep as ocean water, or like music itself. While Rosamund's small fingers ran nimbly over her keyboard, the youth's reveries wandered rapid and wild through the limitless fields of the imagination.

We have already said how he felt himself surrounded by an eternal harmony and what heavenly voices he heard at all hours in total silence. Now, he sometimes recognized, in the sublime inspirations of the masters, the scattered notes of the concerts played by his own ecstasy. Rosamund also, in those moments, appeared to him, like Albina formerly, preceded by the sounds of seraphic harping, and all shrouded like her with a veil of melody. He would then willingly have adored her as a saint is worshiped, and it took Jonathas's voice to awaken him so that he would not believe himself transported into paradise.

Then, although events in his solitary life were rare, the beautiful is so truly universal that in such a sonata or such a symphony he often believed that he was finding the story of his own humble lot. Yes, this sustained bass was so majestic and so grave that it seemed the sad and gloomy basis of his own existence, the eternally present thought of his dead mother, the dull, grumbling threat of an unknown future, while the sparkling and vivacious fantasies, delicate arabesques of sound embroidered over sustained chords, recalled for him his life in sunshine, Rosamund smiling and

the meadows and the crimson woods and his studies inter-
spersed with play. Everard smiled and rested, rocked by the
caprices of harmony; but suddenly a thunderous note
brought him back, a bolt of lightning in the clear blue, the
formidable precursor of some sinister deed.

When stories were not being told, when music was not
being made, Rosamund and Everard read aloud. These
readings could pass for the true, the only, events of their
retreat. That is how one evening Rosamund read *Hamlet*.
Everard listened to the somber drama in silence, stood up
without a word when it was finished, and left bowed down
by the weight of his thoughts.

The next day he confided to Rosamund the impressions
that the terrible heroical drama of doubt had made upon
his mind. Did there not exist a strange conformity, a sort
of moral parentage, between himself and the hero of skep-
ticism? Both saw without ceasing a ghost by their sides.
They were both young, sad, and weak. They felt, both the
one and the other, that they had something horrible to do
and that Fate had selected them for its instrument. What
Everard dared not add was that, like Hamlet, he hesitated
before life. The fact is that he feared to hope, feared to
believe, feared especially to love. The truth is that in his
bitter discouragement he would willingly have said to his
Ophelia: "To a convent! Go to a convent!"

"There is even so one point where we differ," said Everard pensively, "this Prince of Denmark and myself, poor
exile that I am. That awful mission with which Destiny has
loaded him, Hamlet knows. And I do not know what my
mission is. He sees the goal towards which he walks and the
dagger with which he must strike, and he is fortified. What
would it be were he to go, like me, towards his crime in
darkness, if he knew himself as the executioner, but a blind
executioner?

"Yes, Rosamund, I horrify you and solicit your pity, do
I not? But I am not insane; my revelations do not deceive

me. Hamlet is the instrument of a vengeance. I must be the occasion of a chastisement. My mother is sad because of it and weeps much from her dried-up eyes. I shall perhaps not strike, but I shall be the cause for whom God will strike. I have not come on earth to do anything else, Rosamund. There are men who are great, who accomplish great works, and who renew the face of the earth. As for me, I was not destined to do any of these memorable deeds. Alas for me! I am not free like my fellows. I shall serve in the hand of our Lord God or in that of the devil only to have someone punished. A pebble thrown upon the edge of the road, I am good only to cause one soul to fall into hell. That is where my life leads, this life that you are trying to make intelligent and useful, Rosamund. Ah! You are wrong! What's the use, my God? That a palace should be lighted, I grant it. But the lamp in a dungeon serves only to illumine misery."

Such were sometimes the bitter complaints of this lost soul, and Rosamund's smile had great difficulty in bringing him back to hope and to resignation. The generous girl succeeded, however, by means of caring, courage, and goodness. She corrected *Hamlet* by teaching him *The Imitation of Jesus Christ,* and *Werther* with the *Life of Saint Theresa.*

Who would win this struggle between love and fate? Which would prevail, the hopes of Rosamund or the terrors of Albina, the living or the dead? God alone knew.

Now we know the touching or fearsome details, the childish or weird ideas of these three years in the lives of Everard and of Rosamund. Let us add that if we have often pronounced the word "love," the two youngsters had themselves never let it pass their lips. Everard was too sad, and Rosamund too pure, for that. They were the classical lovers Daphnis and Chloe, but they were different because Christian. They loved each other without knowing it, without having been betrothed the one to the other. A revelation from the outside could by chance enlighten them. In and of themselves nothing certainly would warn them of it.

They went on, however. They lived innocent and alone under a blue sky, in a rustic house, in the shade of great trees, always and everywhere together, hand in hand, their foreheads touching when they read in the same book. And, seeing them thus, in some graceful or relaxed pose, one would often have taken them for some antique group of white marble sculpture.

CHAPTER

XVIII

Jonathas was a good fellow, with an honest and open heart; but his mind lacked foresight entirely, so that he was hardly capable of ferreting out a hidden passion or of anticipating it or of halting its inroads. With Everard now a young man and Rosamund quite the young lady, he still saw them as his two children. On the other hand, he was not totally mistaken, for their innocence, as we have seen, justified his blindness. Had they really been brother and sister, according to the baby names they still gave themselves, a more sincere purity could not have been present at their meetings or in their games. Had anyone asked them if they loved each other, they would have replied in all candor: "Yes." However, as in the case of Dante's lovers Paolo and Francesca, all that was needed was one word uttered by chance to reveal to them what was unconsciously taking place in their hearts.

This chance God sent at the appointed hour to precipitate the finale of this simple story. One day the forester, as he came home from a reconnaissance around his woods, found a letter at the cottage. This letter was from Conrad. This companion of the Emperor Napoleon, who for the last three years had given no news of himself to his relatives at Eppstein, still said very little about himself but wanted to wish well the people in the cottage and ask them not to forget him. He hoped, moreover, to drop in and surprise them some morning. He still thought frequently, even during his glorious military victories across Europe, of the little family sheltered in a fold of the Taunus Mountains. He sent greetings to all. They were the only relatives he had left in the world now. At bivouac, and equally when the trumpets sounded their call to battle, his memories of home at Eppstein flashed before his eyes. Did they, for their part, think occasionally of him who had been so long absent? Did Jonathas mention his name sometimes during long winter evenings before the fire? Did the children recommend him in their prayers to the Heavenly Father? His young nephew Everard, once his host and companion, who, after having done the honors of Castle Eppstein, had escorted him to Mayence—was he still as untutored, as lonely, and as much a dreamer? Or else, had he finally been tamed like the youth Hippolyte in Racine's play *Phèdre?*

Those were Conrad's questions.

"Oh! Yes. Certainly, he has remained in our memories and in our hearts!" Jonathas cried, all emotional. "Worthy Conrad! How good and kind it is of him not to have forgotten us! Let us sit down to dinner, children, and we will drink to his health."

The strapping Jonathas drank, in fact, a few more glasses than usual at dinner that night in order to toast Conrad's memory, and after having drained two or three Sunday goblets, he felt his heart expand and his tongue loosen.

It was toward the end of December. Darkness had fallen during the meal. Outside, the snow was drifting down in large flakes, but a roaring fire burned in the cottage, and as one knows, sitting at the corners of the hearth in dead of winter, when the wind whistles out of doors, encourages everyone to gossip almost as much as wine does.

As soon as the dinner was finished and the table folded back in place, Jonathas sat down in his huge armchair of polished leather and folded his hands. The two youngsters sat down side by side, opposite him, on a bench backed up against the cupboard bed, and they all prepared to chat.

Of course, Conrad was the subject of the conversation. Jonathas was about the same age as his brother-in-law and had known him since his earliest childhood. He spoke now of Conrad's lonely trips through the forest, of his serious bent, and little by little he came to tell how Conrad, who was in his own right a Count von Eppstein, which is to say, one of the great lords of all Germany, became first a guest in the forester Gaspard's cottage and eventually, the suitor of the peasant girl Naomi.

This was a story that bore too close an analogy to their own story for Everard and Rosamund not to listen to Jonathas with the closest attention. The family room where they sat was lighted only by the fire in the hearth, so much so that the forester, sprawled out luxuriously under the high mantel over the fireplace, sat alone in the full circle of red light. Huddled in the other corner, the two youngsters remained hidden and lost from sight in the shadows. Without knowing why, they held their breath and felt the same anticipation they would feel when faced by some shattering catastrophe.

"Do you know," said Jonathas with a sly look, "when and how I began to realize that Master Conrad loved Naomi? It was from noticing by what obstinate accidents they kept meeting each other. Naomi had a pet white goat that she used to take out herself to let it browse along the forest border. Well, would you believe it? No matter what time of day she chose and which path she took, you can be sure that my Lord Conrad, who, without seeming to be doing anything, was walking there, gun in hand—or book. Neglectfully, he half greeted Naomi, and, thus, he got the conversation started. When it wasn't the goat that needed air, it was a visit that had to be paid. When it wasn't a visit, it was Sunday services that drew Naomi out-of-doors. And it was always love that drew Conrad in the footsteps of Naomi. And in those days, when I was just as young as they were, my word, it was not very remarkable on my part to have observed that all these walks were only lovers' rendezvous."

Everard and Rosamund exchanged a quick glance, although the darkness prevented them from seeing each other plainly or face-to-face. The thing is that they, too, drawn by an invisible magnet, had often come across each other in the same forest path without being too sure of how that had come about. They had not set a place and time to meet, they had thought they were alone, each had been thinking of the other one, and suddenly, where the detour left the path, at the break in the hedge, they came across each other so joyfully, but still quite surprised at the same time at this invisible connection, at this secret attraction that brought them together without their conscious will having had to arrange it.

"I still remember," Jonathas continued. "I remember a certain day when Father Gaspard's dog bit Naomi's pet warbler and killed it. The little girl began to cry hot tears. She loved her little bird so dearly, and it used to go back and forth into the woods like an untamed bird, but at first call of its mistress, it would come perch on her finger and sing its musical song. Conrad said nothing but ran off through the bushes. He came back that evening, his clothes all torn and his hands all bloody. He had gone to search out, all the way to the bottom of a thicket, where even my dog Castor had not thrust his nose, a nest of singing whitethroats. He brought the whole nest back to Naomi. So it was five nestlings for one and the future replacing the present. The little one's sobs pretty soon changed to jumps of joy. But this exploit on Conrad's part was so out of character for him that truly, if Gaspard had been less blind . . ."

Rosamund and Everard did not hear the end of his sentence. Their hands had met and were held tightly together, for Rosamund at that very moment had suddenly thought of a surprise that, for his part, Everard had made for her.

One day she had traced for him on a scrap of paper the exact plan of the little garden that she herself once cultivated at the convent and which she missed a good deal. It was a garden some ten feet square at least and contained a rose bush of white roses, a currant bush, strawberries in abundance, and a countless number of annuals for all seasons. The next day, as she walked up and down Jonathas's garden, Rosamund cried from joy and surprise. A little plot of land just like the one she had left behind her at Holy Linden was in bloom in a delightful corner of the yard. When she raised her head, she saw Everard, who had waited to spy out her discovery. She was all the more grateful for his thoughtfulness because this was probably the first time that Everard had held a spade or a rake in his hands.

Now, the story of the warbler bore, one must admit, a strong analogy to the story of the little garden, so that the two youngsters were both delighted and troubled. Rosamund had squeezed Everard's hand as if to thank him again for the pleasure that he had brought her that very day. Their burning hands had remained joined. Carried away into another life, they believed they were involved in a dream as they heard what Jonathas was telling them, and he took up the thread of it again, swept backward in time by the powers of his early memories.

"Those were noble natures truly," he continued. "They were pure like children of God, and it was, after all, not their fault if they were young and handsome and loved each other. I, too, was about their age more or less, and I sought in marriage my good Wilhelmina, so that I understood them better than they understood each other. It happened that Naomi fell ill, not dangerously, thank God. However, the doctor declared that she should not go out for a few days, or even leave her room. Conrad had no reason to worry, but there he was, forced to be alone. So he fell into a bit of black melancholy out of which nobody could stir him. I used then to replace Gaspard sometimes in his duties as forester. Well, at each one of my rounds I would meet this poor Conrad, who was so brokenhearted, so disconsolate, that he made me feel bad, too. He hid his tears when he caught sight of me and tried to hide his grief from everybody, including himself.

"So I used to ask him about this, keeping my distance and the due respect which his rank required of me but all the time influenced by the fatherly affection I had for him. He would reply: 'What do you want from me, my good Jonathas? I don't know what's the matter with me. I can't understand myself what sort of peculiar sickness I have. Everything hurts me, everything irritates me, and for no good reason. And if I shed tears, I swear to you, Jonathas, it's also for no reason.' "

"That's what he used to tell me, and I pretended to believe him, but in truth, the fact is that I understood the cause of this sadness he had, all right. And I would have been able to diagnose it for him. I had it too. I loved Wilhelmina just the way he loved Naomi, and I had been separated from Wilhelmina."

If the shadow where they sat sheltered had not been so deep, Everard and Rosamund, who were already very embarrassed, would have suffered much more. At the father's words, they felt themselves twenty times a minute blush and grow pale by turns. In fact, a month earlier, Rosamund had gone to spend a few days at Spires with her father's cousin, and upon her return, Everard had told her all about his lonesomeness and with what despondency the long days spent far from her had been filled. He assured the girl that she had taken his soul away with her and that he had cried for hours on end, not knowing why.

"Good Lord! Good Lord!" each told himself. "When we are so attracted to each other all the time, when we would each of us give his life to satisfy a wish expressed by the other, when we only feel alive and breathing under the eyes of the other, is not that being in love? Good Lord! Good Lord! The name of the enigma that we have been trying to solve, is it really 'love'?"

And an entire unknown world opened before these two dazzled, wildly happy youngsters. They burned and shivered at the same time. Their bodies touched, their hands did not release each other; they would have heard the beating of their hearts had they been able to listen to anything else except their tumultuous thoughts.

The night outside, however, was peaceful and serene. The breeze, which had whipped their cottage, had stopped blowing. The moon shone from a sky swept clear of clouds and darted some of its rays through the slits in the shutters. The forest seemed asleep. The silence that surrounded Rosamund and Everard grew until it almost frightened them.

"And how did Conrad and Naomi finally come to an understanding?" asked Everard in a voice that trembled so much that Rosamund understood he was as disturbed as she was.

"They understood each other without words. Go on," said the good Jonathas, "lovers don't need words in order to speak to each other. When I say 'lovers,' I am wrong, however. With certain persons you should not use the same terms as for everybody else. What I say is true. They were so pure and so respectful that they seemed already married when they were not yet so, and I have always held that the Good Lord had united them before the priest did. And then they suffered so much since that both grief and death have once more purified all these sacred memories of them. The story of their innocent and beautiful affection appears to me as respectable as the lives of martyrs and saints, and when I think of it, their story makes a sort of second religion.

"I venerated them more even perhaps than I loved them, and that is not saying nothing. They knew very well that I was devoted to them, and regarding me already as one of the family, they chose me as their confidant. Oh! How tenderly and sweetly they talked to me, the one and the other! Now, Naomi told her sister Wilhelmina, who told me herself when she became my wife, that one day they were seated alone on the same bench, holding hands. They were reading, I believe, a book, but the only book that they read for real was that of their hearts, so well that without knowing how that came to pass, their pure breaths met, then their lips, their soft lips drew towards each other's, and, my word, they thus told each other, without a spoken word, what, as far as that goes, neither the one nor the other had yet to learn, and that for a long time by then, which is to say, that they loved each other."

And while Jonathas kept talking from the candor of his own soul and from the purity of his thought, Everard and Rosamund, hands pressed tightly, souls melted together, hugged up against each other, intoxicated, breathless, hidden by the darkness. Nobody saw them. They did not even see themselves. The young man had put his arm around his girlfriend's shivering body, and Rosamund, Rosamund herself, drawn by an irresistible fascination, had no longer either strength nor thought in her. Their hair at that moment touched, their breaths flowed together, their lips drew near the other's trembling, their mouths melted into one. But this kiss, their first taste of happiness, lasted only as long as one flash of lightning. Frightened themselves, they drew back in haste. Then, as if he had been waiting for this moment, Jonathas called them.

"Let's go, let's go, children. The fire is dying. Let us part for the night. It is time for you, Sir Count, to return to the castle. And for you, Rosamund, to go up to your chamber."

The forester's voice awoke the two youngsters from their ecstasy and sent them headlong out of paradise on earth.

All three rose. Everard and Rosamund were so upset and so shaken that they were obliged, in order not to fall, to lean the one against the other. After a few words and an exchange of handshakes, they all parted, Jonathas very calm and still dreaming of the past, Rosamund and Everard very emotional and dreaming of the future.

How each heart beat, of our two youngsters, our hero and our heroine! How their breaths came fast, so that they seemed to have just come from running fast and over a long distance! And, truly, had they not traveled fast down a very long road, all in quick descents, called youth and love?

That is how Everard and Rosamund learned what was transpiring in their souls. Destiny seemed to want to use the fragmentary story of Conrad and Naomi to continue in their niece and nephew the history of their great love affair. Toward what terrible unraveling of the plot was their story destined?

We have said it: God alone knew.

CHAPTER

XIX

The next day the two lovers, for we can henceforth give them this name, met for their morning lesson in the grotto carpeted with moss and warm even in the winter. Everard's joy showed through his heart into his eyes; Rosamund seemed more reflective and more serious than ever.

It is needless to say that they had not slept, neither the one nor the other.

After the first moment of surprise, the young man had spent the night in a sort of delirium and drunkenness. Beloved! He was beloved! And he also was in love! What had filled their two thoughts and their two existences, this turmoil, these languors, these involuntary surges, were then what is called 'love'? A second life was revealed to Everard. A thousand sweet memories were lighted now with a new daylight; a thousand streaming hopes shone in his future. Oh! He would not be sad, not now. If his destiny was to be somber, what difference? Had he not now near him another in whom he could take refuge?

As for Rosamund, her wakefulness had been full of anguish and fright. Not that her courageous soul repented having yielded to an irresistible attraction, but she did not forgive herself for having brought Everard a new subject for misfortune, for having given to Maximilian's injustice a new pretext for wrath. Is this the way she should repay her benefactress Albina for so many kindnesses? For finally her love, pure in the eyes of God, was reprehensible in the eyes of the world. The example of Conrad and Naomi, which the preceding evening had fascinated Rosamund, terrified her the next morning. Where had their holy passion led them? To exile, to despair, and to death. And even so, Count Rudolph did not hate his son as Count Maximilian hated Everard, and Naomi did not owe Conrad his education, that life of the soul!

That is why, as she arrived at the grotto, Rosamund was grave and why Everard was joyous.

As soon as the young man noticed Rosamund, whom, shivering with impatience, he had been awaiting for a long time, he ran toward her.

"Oh!" he cried. "Rosamund, it's you! Oh! Words fail me, fail my lips, but listen, but let me tell you one word only, one word which contains the world: I love you! And one more word which contains the heavens: Rosamund, you love me!"

And the young man fell on his knees before her, his hands clasped, looking at her with rapture.

"Everard, my dear, my brother," said Rosamund with an accent and a gesture imprinted with the dignity that never deserted her. "Everard, please rise and let us talk as brother and sister, according to our custom. I shall never go back on the tacit avowal which escaped during our ecstasy. Yes, I love you as you love me, Everard."

"Heavenly angels, do you hear her!" cried the impetuous youth.

"Yes," continued Rosamund pensively. "Yes. I repeat it, for these words have heaven knows what magic where the soul dwells. I love you as Naomi loved Conrad, but think of Conrad and think of Naomi. I give you my life. I cannot, alas, accept yours. You say occasionally that you perceive a great disaster upon your horizon. This disaster, if it was through me that it should come, Everard! Ah, I would die first. I can accept to be unfortunate, as for me. But to suffer in you would be above my strength, I warn you. The best would be to forget, then, this dangerous dream which we dreamed last evening."

"I should forget to live," answered Everard, "for this dream is my breath. It is my being. It is my existence. This dream is me. Henceforth nothing can ever separate us again, Rosamund. And you are mine as I am yours."

"Who is talking about separating?" Rosamund asked, her soul strong but her heart ignorant, because it obeyed, without becoming suspicious, the subtle counsels of an imperious passion. "We can stay together, Everard, but on condition that we live as in the past, that we erase both of us this feverish evening from our memory, that we regain the calm and purity of our relationship of other days. We can stay on condition, Everard, that my brother serves me as a safeguard and as support and that our mothers, those two saints, remain present between us. If you want it thus, we shall have many more happy days; for I confess that it would cost me too much truly to renounce right now our sweet intimacy. But if we do our duty with courage and resignation, God will sustain us and cherish us, and we must consider how the future lies in his hand."

"The future . . . ! That's it," said Everard bitterly. "Let us adjourn our happiness as we adjourn our creditor whom we are unable to pay."

"Everard, my dear friend, my dear brother!" said Rosamund as she looked at him sadly. "Why this irony and this injustice? The pure and peaceful joys which sufficed yesterday seem beneath contempt to you today? Do you no longer wish to have just a friend, just a sister, who is sacred to you and honored by everyone else?"

"Yes, Rosamund, yes. The world must honor you and venerate you, and that is why we must not at all limit ourselves, where our future is concerned, to uncertain words. Listen to me. My abandonment, which, as God and my mother know, has made me shed so many bitter tears, pleases me today and becomes useful to me. My father decided, on condition that he be nothing to me henceforth, that I should be nothing to him: I am therefore free and master of my love. Well, my life is yours. I do not give it to you. God gives it to you, since when he made me an orphan, he remitted to me my right to dispose of my life. Accept it merely, I plead with you to do so, Rosamund. Accept it. Be my wife."

"Alas! Alas! Everard, that is what Conrad must have said to Naomi . . . And Naomi . . . Remember, Everard."

"Naomi died on the scaffold, did she not . . . ? But in my case, it is not a secret marriage that I propose to you, Rosamund. No. It is a marriage in broad daylight, in the chapel of Castle Eppstein, a marriage recognized by men and by God, a marriage that I shall not hide, even from my father. The books you had me read taught a little about the world, and I have guessed more or less, I believe, the designs and the opinions of Count Maximilian. If I sought to rise, to appear in public life, if I sought a share in his glory and in the renown of his name, if I clamored for my place in the sun of imperial favor, he would curse me and destroy me. But that I should cloister myself in obscurity, that I should close the doors of the court and of fame, that according to his bigoted notions I should make a poor marriage, that will not offend him at all, I promise you. And far from turning me away from such routes, he would drive me into them if he could. I embarrass him over there in Vienna in his ambition and in his vanity, and he will be happy, believe me truly, Rosamund, to be rid of me by my own actions. From the moment when I shall have raised between us this barrier and when he shall not have to give an account of me to anyone in front of whom he would have to blush, from the moment when he will be able to accuse me alone and complain, then he has the good role. Then secretly he will be grateful to me for having yielded it to him. He then will be able in all tranquillity to think about his own fortune in the present and of my older brother's in the future. Albert will henceforth be really his only son. I shall not be able to come, like an importunate third party, to cast myself in front of their sublime projects! I shall be a rebellious child, like Conrad von Eppstein, who shall have married a simple peasant girl, whom his father has legitimately disowned! Like Conrad, the world will forget me today and will forget me tomorrow. However, unlike Conrad, we shall not have to run away. Nothing will force us to change our style of life or displace our happiness. Count von Eppstein lives and resides in Vienna, and according even to the letter he wrote me, he shall never depart from it. So we, Rosamund, can remain here, in your father's house, alone and unknown, which is to say, peaceful and happy. Come now, Rosamund. Come now. You can accept this all right. It is not the wealthy heir of Eppstein who offers you his hand. It is a poor person who has been proscribed, who is truly wretched and truly humble. To him you, generous girl, will bring the serenity of your person, the joy in your eyes, the treasure of your love. Let me ask you if the devotion I claim from you does not make you smile? Will not our union be paradise, and this paradise, when I, Everard, am your brother and your friend, will you have the courage to refuse it?"

"Everard! Everard! Do not tempt me." Rosamund said in a troubled voice, but all the while pushing the young man back with firm hands. "Yes, you are offering me heaven. But we are on earth, and you are a child and a crazy one to hope for absolute happiness. And similarly, you were a blasphemer and sacrilegious when you foretold such a wretched future. Alas! Poor maker of dreams that you are, do you not know that the best here below is not to dream but to wait?"

"Rosamund! Rosamund!" Everard cried. "Do not reject me in this anguish about my destiny. This misfortune which my instincts foresee, it seems to me that you would have the power to turn it away from me and the power like that of a good fairy to change with one sign from you all my doubts and illusions. If you drive me away, on the contrary, I shall think that you are afraid to share the dowry of my suffering that destiny holds in store for me."

"Oh! Do not say that. Do not believe that," Rosamund quickly replied. "I am only afraid of provoking your pains. But to associate myself with them, I swear it, would be a veritable joy for me."

"Very well. It is agreed, then. You are mine, Rosamund. You are my wife. Let grief come after that! Let death come! One day of paradise with you on earth, and let it continue here below or up in heaven. Who cares?"

And the young man spoke with so much force and so much eloquence, there was so much fire in him, that Rosamund felt fascinated, like during the evening before, and carried forward. She had fallen back upon a large boulder, but he had at once and as if by enchantment fallen upon his knees before her. Vaguely she looked about her at the grotto, at the banks of moss, at these places that had witnessed so many calm, delightful hours spent together. In her heart she felt the bliss of angels and let herself go, she, the immaculate, the noble child, into perilous emotions, into the strange prestige of this happiness. Then even the silence around her was filled with trouble and seduction.

It was precisely the vivacity and novelty of these sensations that awakened the chaste, proud maiden. Passing her hand over her white forehead as if to erase even the reflections of such thoughts, which made her heart race, she stood up suddenly and with a gesture commanded Everard also to do likewise.

Then, standing tall before her subjugated lover, she spoke to him in a voice full of force and decisiveness.

"Brother, no weakness and no dangerous dreams. Are we in one minute, without reflection and just like giddy children, to engage, I will not say our souls, alas, for our souls have been engaged for a long time, but are we to engage our existences? Brother, take courage. Keep a level head. Let us envisage with tranquillity the future which God has prepared for us and the route which we should now follow."

"Ah! You are stopping to think!" cried Everard. "Therefore you do not love me."

"I love you in a holy way, Everard. God is my witness. There is in my heart, when I think of you, something so soft and delirious, but there is also something exalted and, I might say, something maternal."

"You do not love me. You do not love me," Everard repeated.

"Listen, Everard," answered Rosamund, and she was both sincere and strong. "It seems to me, really, that if I love you, it is not with a love similar to yours. I love you according to my nature, probably. Nevertheless, I can certify one thing, for once my excitement had subsided, I was able to do a great deal of thinking last night. I plumbed my soul, deeply. Now, listen. I promise you and I swear it, Everard, that if I do not belong to you, I will never belong to anyone else in this world, except to God. The idea that I should unite my destiny with another than you, Everard, is intolerable to me! If that could console you a little and appease you, I would be very happy."

"That delights me today, Rosamund. But is it enough for tomorrow?"

"Tomorrow, like today, my existence is yours, Everard. But believe me, let us not remove our love from the sanction of suffering and of time. Let us reserve for ourselves the right to misfortune. I imagine that were we to accept our joy without submitting to any test, fate would be revenged upon us. And anyway, I have been taught in all things to give up his share to God. What am I asking from you? Patience. I am perhaps wrong to leave you a probably chimerical hope, not to be reasonable except by halves, and for the present only. However, although you say I do not love you, the effort is above my courage, and I cannot renounce, like that, all the happiness I glimpse. . . . May God pardon me for it! Dear God! Oh, Mother! Oh, Albina, pardon me for it!"

"Oh! My mother, Rosamund, my mother not only pardons you, but thanks you for her son, for you are going to make his life, from the somber, sad existence it was, into a beautiful and shining life. And wait. Rosamund, and in her name, and may this hallowed name sanctify my thought and my deed, in her values, accept this ring which she wore as a girl. Take it for the love of her and of me, and since you do not deign to close off my future for me, may this talisman affiance you to me, my adored saint!"

"Everard. Everard. Do you wish it?"

"I beg you and implore you," he said.

"Then hear my conditions," Rosamund replied.

"Oh! I am listening. I am listening."

"First of all, if I become engaged to you, and I do it with all my heart, I intend that you shall stay free, entirely free."

"Ah, Rosamund!"

"I wish it, Everard. In addition, while guarding in our souls the memory of this solemn morning, we shall never speak of it again. We shall again become what we were yesterday, brother and sister. We shall undertake our lessons and our peaceful conversations. Never the word 'love' shall be pronounced between us, and so we shall await, calm and confident, the changes that will be brought by time and by providence."

"But, good Lord, shall this painful test never have an ending limit?"

"In two years, the day when we shall both reach our twentieth birthday, Everard, you shall declare your intention to your father, and we shall see."

"Two years! In two years!"

"Yes, brother. Do you accept my express desire, which is irrevocable?"

"I am resigned to it, Rosamund."

"Put your ring upon my finger, Everard. Thank you, dear. From this day I am your fiancée in my heart. But from this moment I become again, in all my speech, your sister."

"Dear Rosamund."

"Show me the end of your translation of *Hamlet*, Everard."

We can understand that despite the heroic resolution of the youngsters, the lesson that day was brief and disturbed by a few distractions. Even so, they did not weaken, and when they said good-bye afterward, they had remained faithful to their promise and to themselves.

CHAPTER

XX

Rosamund was happy with a calm joyfulness. She believed, the poor child, that she had won by gaining time, and because she had steered a course between her love and her duty, because she had negotiated with passion and still kept her conscience clear, she was pleased with herself and kept telling herself that God and Albina must be pleased, too.

"Two years is so long!" she kept saying. "From here to there, alas, Everard will probably not love me anymore. I shall anyway have saved him from all remorse. Meanwhile, I can keep him close to me, and if in two years he still loves me— But you are my witness, dear God, that I am certain he will no longer love me."

As for Everard, when he left Rosamund, he was drunk with love and crazy with joy.

"Two years," he told himself, "is very short, since I will see her all the time. I shall use these two years of novitiate in persuading her of my love and of my tender care. I do not believe I am mistaken concerning my father's disposition. I will test him, moreover, I hope, by means of a ruse that God will pardon. I shall try to alarm him about my future projects and make him think I am ambitious. Then he will be happy to find, instead of a legitimate exigency which would frighten him, a love which will reassure him. He will let me do all I want while loading me down with reproach, and Rosamund, too proud to accept me when noble and powerful, is too devoted to drive me away when I am lone and abandoned. Yes, that's it. Beginning today, I will write my father and worry him with a few ambiguous sentences. Let's reread first of all, as a guide, the note he sent Jonathas some time ago, and where he renounced his authority, if I wish to renounce my right."

Everard had preciously put away that letter in his bedroom, at Castle Eppstein. He set off then with slow steps and lowered head toward the high towers of the family domain, all the while rehearsing the phrasing of this letter he wanted to write the Count. He had it all fairly well drawn up when he arrived at the castle portals.

"Yes, that's how I must take him," he said. "That's the right chord to pluck. My success is almost certain, and I must have recourse to a letter, by all means, since my father swore not ever to return to Eppstein."

Talking that way to himself, his heart joyous, Everard was slowly crossing the threshold of the great doors when, raising his head, he saw standing before him, glowering and haughty, Count Maximilian clad all in black mourning. The same shudder ran in the veins of both father and son.

Count Maximilian von Eppstein belonged to that race of politicians, tortuous and wily men, who regard a straight line as the longest distance between two points. Any stranger who had observed the attitude and the accent that he assumed while receiving Everard would have suspected that the sly diplomat, through the thousand detours and periphrases of speech, had a hidden purpose that he did not lose sight of. One could see that this deep and clever man wanted to sound out his son and study him before pronouncing a mysterious word that he held back on his lips and worked up to as a dramatist works up to his hero's reversal of fortune.

"My lord von Eppstein!" Everard finally murmured. He was stupefied.

"Say your father, Everard, and come embrace me, my son," answered the Count.

Everard hesitated.

"I was in a hurry to see you again," continued Maximilian, "and that's why, to see you, I have come from Vienna in four days."

"To see me, sir?" stammered Everard. "You came back to see me?"

"Just think of it, my son. It has been three years since I have seen you, three years of the odious cares of politics which detained me far from you, at Vienna. But allow me to compliment you, Everard. I had left a child, and now I find a man. You have a manly and charming air which delights me, and seeing you so different from what you were, my father's heart fills with happiness, with pride, and with joy."

"My lord," said Everard, "if I could believe you, you would also make me very proud and very happy."

Everard could hardly contain his surprise. Was this really Count Maximilian, formerly so harsh and so cruel, who spoke to him now with this gentleness and goodness? Thus, despite the candor of his soul, Everard, who was enlightened by the intuition of love, suspected a trap and kept up his guard. On his side the Count spied out on Everard's face his impressions and his thoughts.

What a singular spectacle was this interview, after an absence of three years, between this father and this son, both suspecting each other as they embraced, playing the one against the other as close as possible with a thousand protestations to the contrary, as if, players or duelists, they had cards or swords in their hands, scrutinizing their looks and their movements in the midst of polite fatherly and filial formulas.

"Yes, Everard," the Count continued in his same carefully enunciated speech but with the same questioning looks, "you could not imagine with what satisfaction I drew near to Eppstein and what rejoicing I anticipated for myself at the sight once more of a son a little disregarded and too much neglected perhaps but who will pardon me, I hope, for this apparent forgetfulness by taking into account the cares that obsess me. In your isolation, Everard, and I deplore it today, the science of books and the acquaintance with the world have not reached to you. However, with a generous nature such as yours, certainly, education can never come too late. Here," the Count continued, "is the learned Dr. Blazius whom I present to you and whom I brought from Vienna to see where you are in your studies and to raise you to a level of instruction which is necessary for you."

At that moment, Everard saw advancing through a door from the vestibule a tall man, dry and black. This man, when his name was pronounced, bowed deeply before Everard and mumbled a few words among which his future student caught only the words "My Lord" and "devotion."

"That's it," thought Everard, "and the respects paid me by my teacher, like the caresses of my father, both enlighten me. They want to know if by chance I have not become dangerous and if I have remained the ignorant and inoffensive boy I was formerly. The moment has come to spread some alarm in their suspicious hearts and to demonstrate that I am able, when needed, to recognize and see through their projects."

"Father," answered the young man with a bow, "I am very grateful to you, as well as to this gentleman, for wishing to bring to a poor recluse the learning for which truly I am all the more avid since up until now I have only been able to gather such a really paltry part."

"No doubt about it, my lord. No doubt about it," answered the qualified teacher, "and I like a thousand times over to speak to an unformed mind, like a clean slate, or a blank sheet of paper, where no writing has as yet been traced, than to an intelligence already perverted by false doctrines. We shall have everything to do but nothing to undo, and that's a great deal."

"I thank you for hoping so," said the Count.

"And I for not despairing," said Everard, who because of his solid, honest nature was becoming indignant at this comedy he also had to play in and who took a queer, bitter pleasure at mingling his irony with their falseness.

"We are then going," said the doctor, "and I applaud myself here, we are then going, I repeat it, to take these things back to their elementary states: history, languages, sciences, philosophy."

"In order not to lose time," said Everard, watching upon his father's face the effect of his words, "we shall do well, my dear doctor, to leave the results, which I believe I possess fairly well, and go back immediately together to basic principles. Thus, to confine ourselves to history, I think you will not have much to teach me about facts, but I shall be happy to chat with a man as enlightened as you concerning the philosophy underlying the events. Are you like me for our German Herder against the French ecclesiastic Bossuet?"

The Count and the doctor exchanged astonished glances.

"As for languages," continued Everard, "I know enough French and enough English to interpret Molière for you and Shakespeare, with my book open before me. However, if you desire to make me descend further into the thoughts of the great geniuses, to study with me the spirit of their works after the letter, I promise you that you will find in me, Doctor, a schoolboy who, if not very intelligent, at least will be very attentive and zealous."

Maximilian and Blazius could not get over their surprise.

"Everard," cried the Count, "who then made you so learned in your solitude?"

"My solitude itself," said Everard, who felt that here he should double his caution. "Yes, I carried books out into the woods from the library: grammars, chronicles, treatises on mathematics. I only left them after having understood each one. I deepened my readings by reflection. I had some trouble, doubtless. The exact sciences presented a great deal of difficulty, but by dint of patience and courage, I overcame difficulties, and I have had the joy of seeing one day, finding at hand the curriculum of studies required by the government's schools, that I could present myself at the examinations at military schools as at those of the universities, and that, if I even followed you to court, Father, far from giving you occasion to blush for me, I would perhaps do you some honor."

"Is it possible!" cried the Count. "But this is a miracle, Doctor, a veritable miracle! Look to questioning him, for I can not believe it. Let us go in. Let us go in quickly, Doctor. I am in such a hurry to be reassured. And you, Everard, my dear son, come, come!"

And the Count drew Everard into the dining room, which was on his way.

There Dr. Blazius sat the pretended schoolboy down to an examination, but he saw soon enough that he would do well not to venture too far himself with the young master, for in many areas the apprentice was, if not more advanced, at least better taught than the doctor. Everard's remarkable aptitude had, in truth, upon many points of academic debate, surpassed the somewhat superficial knowledge of Rosamund, and he had fun, despite his accustomed modesty, astonishing by his assurance the classical pedantry of the credentialed Dr. Blazius.

"It's a miracle!" the dumbfounded teacher finally declared, "A miracle that you owe heaven, my lord Count, not certainly by way of damages but at least by way of consolation."

"Also," continued Maximilian, "have I felt such a joy that in an instant I have almost forgotten the grief of my soul and my black clothes. Alas, yes, dear Everard, learn the funereal news which I wanted to announce to you only after having made trial if you were worthy of your ancestors and of yourself. Your elder brother, my poor Albert . . ."

"Well?" Everard asked with anxiety.

"He is dead, Everard. . . . Killed, killed as if by a stroke of lightning, in three days, by cerebral fever, at the age of twenty-one! When such a splendid future opened before him, prepared by my care and by his talents; for, poor young man, he had already so much finesse, so many resources of wit, he knew so well how to stand on the slippery terrain of the court, he handled so cleverly the most complicated intrigues, he uncovered in the flash of an eye our enemies' tricks and gave them so skillfully blow for blow! And God took him from me, Everard! Do you understand? But he only struck me with one hand, since he returns another son to me, one as worthy as Albert of my affection and of the favors of His Imperial Majesty. You will continue your brother, my child. Here you are now the eldest and only heir of the Eppsteins, and you know to what such an honor engages you. A new life will begin for you. Let us forget the past and look only at the future, shall we? Count henceforth upon all the tenderness and all the protection of your father. I have formulated projects which are going to make us regain immediately what time and terrain we have lost. Don't worry, my son, don't worry!"

Everard grew pale and felt his knees buckle under him. At a glance he had just envisaged all the change that the event his father announced was going to bring into his existence. However, since his face, despite his inner combat, remained impassive, the Count continued.

"Everard, you are as of today an officer in the service of Austria, do you understand? Here is your commission, and that is not all."

The Count went to a chair upon which a sword had been laid and presented the weapon to his son.

"And here is your sword," he continued. "I was not

supposed to give you the one and the other for six months, but since you deserve them as of now, receive the one and the other from my hand. And now, Everard, believe it truly, the favors of the Emperor will not stop there. But we shall speak of all that another time. For the moment the memories which the sight of you have awakened in me, the memory of my dear Albert evoked by my regrets, the happiness felt in seeing you just as I could have wished you to be, all these emotions, good or painful, have worn me out. I leave you to chat with Dr. Blazius. Before the end of this day I shall see you again, dear Everard. I shall tell you of the great plans with which I want to associate you and which you will understand, I am sure of it. Be joyful meanwhile, dream wonderful dreams, my boy. Your dreams will never be too high for the destiny that awaits you at the court in Vienna, where you will follow me in a few days."

Then the Count left after having embraced Everard, who was crushed under the blow, and after giving a nod to Dr. Blazius, who bowed down almost to the floor.

"In a few days at the court of Vienna!" repeated Everard as aghast he looked sadly at his commission and his sword; "In a few days . . . Oh, my God! My God! What is she going to say when she learns that?"

And he darted out of the castle despite the cries from Dr. Blazius, who, making no pretense of following, shouted after him.

"My lord von Eppstein, do not forget that we dine in an hour and that the Count, your father, awaits you for dinner."

Everard made only one bound from the castle to the cottage. He found Rosamund walking in the garden that he had laid out for her. Pale and out of breath, he appeared suddenly before her, still holding his commission and his sword.

"What is the matter, Everard?" Rosamund inquired.

"What the matter is," he said, "is, what is the matter,

Rosamund? The Count has arrived, and, as always, he brings misfortune along with him."

"What do you mean, Everard?"

"See. See," cried the youth.

And he presented Rosamund with the commission and the sword.

"What is that?" she asked.

"Do you not guess, Rosamund?"

"No."

"My brother Albert is dead, so here I am eldest of the family, and my father, who brings me this commission and this sword, has come to fetch me, to take me to Vienna."

The girl became as pale as death, and nevertheless a melancholy smile flickered on her lips.

"Give me your arm, Everard," she said, "and let us go in."

The two youngsters entered the cottage, and while Rosamund let herself fall in Joanthas's armchair, Everard placed the sword in a corner and tossed the commission on the table.

"Well, Everard," said Rosamund, "did I not tell you this morning that it was necessary to take misfortune into account? Only, he came to claim you sooner than I thought."

"What difference, Rosamund!" Everard replied. "Do you for a moment think that I shall leave?"

"Without a doubt. I do believe it."

"Rosamund, I shall never leave you. I have sworn it."

"You did not swear that, Everard, for you would then have sworn to disobey your father. And you have no such right."

"The Count abandoned me. He wrote it to me himself. I am not his son. He is not my father."

"A bad thought had driven him away from you, Everard, and a good one brought him back to you. It is God himself who has not wanted that division between son and father. You will obey, Everard, and you will go to Vienna."

"I told you, Rosamund, never."

"Then it is I who will return to the convent of Holy Linden, for certainly, Everard, I will not be the accomplice of your disobedience."

"Rosamund, you do not love me."

"On the contrary, Everard, it is because I love you that I desire to see you accept what your father proposes. There are duties imposed upon men the very day of their birth and from which they can not extricate themselves. So long as you had an elder brother, so long as the glory and the name of Eppstein rested upon another head than yours, you could be happy and unknown. Now, for you to refuse to accept the heritage made illustrious and also painful which heaven sends you would be a crime at once against your ancestors and your descendants. The career of arms which your father proposes to you is a beautiful and honorable one. You will therefore leave, Everard."

"Rosamund! Rosamund! You are surely cruel!"

"No, Everard. Only I speak to you as if I did not exist, because before such interests, the existence of a poor girl like me must—"

"Well, then, Rosamund, swear me one oath," said Everard.

"Which one?"

"It is that if I can not turn my father away from his resolution to go to Vienna and if I am forced to embrace the career of arms, where I will bring nothing but disgust of life and scorn for death; finally, if by this career I manage to get free, become master of myself, lone and unique arbiter of my will, Rosamund, then you will fulfill the promise pledged this morning. You will be mine."

"I have sworn, Everard, to be only yours or God's. I swear it a second time. Count on me to keep this promise."

"And I," said Everard. "Listen well, Rosamund. I swear by the tomb of my mother never to have any wife but you."

"Everard! Everard!" cried Rosamund, who was horrified.

"The vow is made, Rosamund, and I will not retract it. To me or to God. To you or to nobody."

"Oaths are terrible things, Everard."

"For perjurers, yes. But not for those who wish to keep them."

"Remember one thing, Everard. It is that you will not need to come find me in order to release you from your oath, for from this moment, I release you."

"That is well, Rosamund. Here is the dinner bell ringing. Until tomorrow."

Everard left behind him a girl frightened by her lover's cold resolve.

CHAPTER

XXI

A fter supper, where the Count had shown himself even more sprightly and affectionate toward his son than during the day, Maximilian soberly invited Everard to follow him into his own apartment. With his spirits low and his heart pounding, the youth obeyed this order from his father.

When they were both together in the Red Chamber, Maximilian motioned his son toward an armchair, where the youth sat down in silence. As for the Count, he began to walk with large strides from the window to the secret door, observing under his brows this Everard, for whom, up until then, he had shown so little of a father's affection. Almost intimidated by the boy's unwrinkled forehead and innocent gaze, he evidently was at some loss for words to open his business. Finally, he decided to stun him by putting on those overbearing and pompous airs that he used successfully in diplomatic negotiations.

"Everard," he said as he sat down facing his son, "allow your father, kindly, to disappear temporarily and let him turn over his role to the statesman, to one of those men responsible for the destiny of a vast empire. You have been summoned to fill by my side, Everard, the role which your brother's death leaves open. You also will govern, one day, at your rank, whole peoples and ideas also, my son. But you ought to feel, as you accept a so glorious and so perilous mission, what rude duties this destiny imposes upon you. You must strip off your passions and your personality. You must say that you will no longer live for yourself but for the common good. You must, in your sublime abnegation, renounce your own desires, your own inclinations, even your own personal pride, and put yourself above social conventions, above good and evil, systems and prejudices, above all human concerns, in a word, in order to lead impartially, just like God, if I may dare make this comparison, just as God leads the world and the universe, the great nation for which you will be responsible in that administrative area which will have been relegated to your care."

Pleased with his majestic preamble, the Count paused to catch the effect of his words upon his listener. Everard seemed attentive but not particularly impressed, and his attitude could just as well have come from boredom as from respect.

"You must have meditated previously upon such grave topics, and you doubtless share my opinion on this score, Everard?" Maximilian asked, somewhat uneasy before this obstinate silence.

"I am, in fact, of your opinion, Father," the young man answered with a bow, "and I admire with all my heart persons who so clearly grasp their own importance; but I think, and you think like me, very certainly, that while sacrificing one's inclinations, one's preferences, one's happiness even, a man ought to maintain inviolable the rights of his conscience, so that in abnegating his vanity, he safeguards his honor."

"Empty words all that, young man," the Count replied with a scornful sneer, "distinctions so subtle that you will shortly appreciate their nothingness. Have a stouter heart and a stronger soul."

"I do not know, Father," answered Everard, "whether or not the words 'virtue' and 'probity' are for some people at a certain rank empty words. For me, however, in my humble retreat, they are both sentiments and instincts to which I cling as I cling to my life, and I will even say more than to my life. Now, allow me to tell you here, Excellency, I fear that you may have falsely conceived too flattering hopes where I am concerned. You should realize that, after all, I am only an educated peasant, a wild being raised in these woods and mountains, and that I would have great difficulty making myself over according to the theories and usages of society. I could probably, without too much disadvantage, show myself once in high society, but for me to live there habitually and conduct myself according to that world, it would be, I believe, an impossibility. I know myself, and since morning today, I have reflected deeply. Accustomed to the air of my forests, I would suffocate inside city walls. Grown in truth and freedom, I would soon die amidst intrigues and dependencies. I would feel such indignation and such rebellion as would ruin me and compromise you probably, Father. I beg of you, my Lord, renounce therefore all these so very brilliant prospects for me, and since you have in view only my happiness, return alone to the court and leave me in my meadows."

"I do not exactly have your happiness in view only, Everard," replied the Count in a voice already tinged with severity, but not yet allowing himself the luxury of the anger that he could feel stirring deep inside him. "I also have in view the glory and the good fortune of our house, of which, unfortunately, you are at this hour the last heir. Eh, well, my God. Me, too, once upon a time, I should have preferred to run and hunt over my domains rather than saddle myself to the yoke of public affairs, but a man is not with impunity called Eppstein. My father constrained me to the sacrifice of my own tastes, and at this hour I thank him for it, as you will one day thank me. I tamed both my leaning towards idleness and my violent pastimes, for I once was as choleric and savage as you see me today moderate and patient, my son. You must not, however, fight me too hard, Everard, and it would be dangerous to push me to the limit, especially where I am, inside my own family, a head and a supreme judge. An old man awakens sometimes. You may as well know that my wrath is something awful."

The storm rumbled. The Count's words became dull and clipped. Nevertheless, he managed to resume more moderately.

"It is not with you, Everard, that I have to fall back upon threats. I hope not. You will yield to my fatherly exhortations, and, to make you see reason, I shall have only one word to say: Everard, my child, I need you."

"What! Father," cried Everard, who was swept off his feet by the innocence of his heart. Touched by the naive, appealing voice of the professional courtier, Everard cried again: "What! You could have need of me?"

This expression of sincere devotion was not wasted on Maximilian. He resolved to profit from it.

"That is to say," he continued, and he placed his hand on his son's hand. "That is to say, Everard, that you are necessary to me. You have no idea what a slippery terrain a court really is and what eternal intrigues push us off the slopes. Well, two months ago, one of these plots put me two inches from my own ruin. The devotion of your brother was about to save me when God took him from me. So, Everard, I who had forgotten you, my poor boy, I thought of you, and I came back to you."

"Tell me, Father, tell me!" cried Everard with an outpouring of love, "and I will do what my brother would have done."

"Oh, you will do it, Everard," Maximilian replied, "for you will understand that men called by birth to the supreme offices of the state are to pay for this glory with a complete abnegation and to obtain their grievous dignities only through many a sacrifice and many a trial. The novitiate of high honors is hard and painful, Everard. Titles are bought by many excessive concerns for others, by many disgusting transactions, by many sleepless nights, by many days without recreation. Princes and their ministers, sometimes through caprice, I must admit, more often to test us, impose difficult conditions upon us. But the goal is so luminous, so fine, so vast," the Count resumed with enthusiasm, "that we forget the obstructions sown along our route."

This time the diplomat had missed his target. At such a painting of raw ambition, Everard had regained his aplomb. He was thinking of a way to elude his father's hideous offers.

The latter mistook his reverie for attentiveness and continued speaking.

"Well, my son, while numerous obstacles confront anyone who wants to succeed, you, while playing, you, while asleep, find yourself transported to a degree that twenty others could not attain after twenty years of drudgery! Everything depends, for you, upon a formality, upon a nothing, upon an insignificant piece of paper. There is the question of your marriage."

"Me to be married? Me?" cried Everard. "Me get married? What are you saying there, Father?"

"Yes, I understand that you are a little young, but that makes no difference. Look here. Listen to me all the way," replied the Count, who was reacting to a start of fright from Everard. "You can get astonished afterwards if you want to. However, this will be for your happiness. I guarantee it. The marriage I propose to you, Everard, your poor brother was on the point of concluding when I lost him. So I thought of you, for, you see, this marriage, it is a magnificent future, it is an unexpected good fortune, it is a level high road which leads you right up to the throne, and I shall say even more, Everard, to the throne itself if the reality of power has as much value as its appearances. Well, you can be still. And what! Such a future, does it not blind you?"

"Father, I tell you, this is no way my dream."

"What the devil!" But where was he? "Well, Everard, this dream you scorn has been the dream of the whole court. The most noble Lords have fought each other for the glory of becoming the husband of the Duchess of B. . . . but all understood that they had to step aside and yield to the name of Eppstein. All have stepped aside."

"And what is this Duchess of B. . . . whose name I never even heard pronounced?" said Everard. "She must be the heir of one of the oldest houses of Germany, you say?"

"The Duchess of B . . . , Everard, is all and it is nothing. She is a simple woman without a name. Yes, since they had to create a duchy for her. But she is veritably our Empress. Do you understand, Everard, what he can do for himself and for his family, the man fortunate enough to become the husband of that woman?"

"No, Father. No," Everard replied. "I do not clearly understand."

"How so! You can't understand that this woman is free and that to maintain appearances this woman must be married! Well, the husband of this woman will be able to want everything and to grant everything. His grandeur and that of his family will become a necessity of state. Look at things from this social summit, Everard, and answer me if your head does not turn."

"About what, my lord, must I answer?" asked Everard.

"Why, my proposition, probably."

"What proposition?"

"Eh, for God's sake. On my proposition of marriage. Is this affectation on your part or imbecility?"

"Neither one nor the other, my lord. It is stupefaction. What! You, a Count von Eppstein, you propose what to your son . . . ? Oh! Excuse me, Father. You are testing me or teasing me. You were not speaking seriously, were you?"

"Everard! Everard!" the Count replied between clenched teeth.

"No, my lord," continued Everard without hearing him.

"I don't believe you. You love titles, honors, more than glory. That seems strange to me. Even so, I can conceive of it. But to speculate upon your ancestors, to sell the name your descendants will bear, is more ignominy than I can understand. And it can not be you, Maximilian von Eppstein, who asks me to do such a thing! That you should have stimulated me to become ambitious, maybe! But that you should want me to become infamous, you would really not wish."

"Wretch!" cried the Count, pale with fury.

"Not wretched, but crazy to have been so long deceived as to your intentions, my noble father. Oh! Pardon me. What do you want? You must not rely too much upon my penetration. I take everything idiotically, at its face value, and so I commit strange blunders. I was telling you, my lord, that you would do better to leave me here, in my corner, and to pursue alone your grand plans. You see plainly enough that I am good for nothing. Because I understand two or three languages does not mean I would know how to speak at court. Abandon me, my lord. Return to Vienna without me and do not force me, I beg of you, to leave this poor village where I have enclosed my ambition and my vows."

For the last few moments, the Count, in the midst of his anger, was still observing his son. He was struck with a sudden idea as he watched his face. Finally, he appeared to have taken a resolve.

"If, however, you had not been mistaken, Everard," he said. "What if this marriage project was not a simple proposition but a fact? Would you resist it then?"

"Yes, my lord," the young man replied with firmness. "Only I should begin by calling solemnly upon you, and by saying to you: 'Father, in the name of heaven (and he had on his lips: 'In the name of my Mother!' but, without knowing why, he had not dared remind him of this memory), do not constrain me to my own shame! This abjection of your only son cannot make you as happy as it can make me miserable.' Father, take my life if you need it, but spare my conscience. And if you persist in having your own way, my lord, I should raise my head and say to you: 'Count von Eppstein, by what right do you come asking me for my honor? My life belongs to you perhaps; but my virtue, not. And just because I bear one of the proudest and noblest names of all Germany, you will not put me, if you please, below the last of our artisans to whom at least a wife gives herself wholly.' I should disobey you, my lord."

Everard also spoke with the heat of passion. The Count held him fixed under his cold and penetrating eyes and smiled.

When the young man had finished, he took his hand, and with a contentment that appeared sincere, so well played was it, he gave him his reaction.

"Well done, Everard. Very well done. Come on over here, my dear son, let me embrace you. And forgive me for having doubted you, loyal heart that you are. But I know you only from today, after all. You make me the happiest of fathers, my noble child; for I see at present that you are worthy of her whom I have really destined for you. She is the purest and most charming girl in Vienna. She will be yours, my Everard. Yes, she is one of the richest and noblest heiresses of Austria, a treasure of chastity and beauty. Lucile von Gansberg will be your bride."

Count Maximilian had just named to Everard the girl of whom Rosamund had spoken to him a hundred times.

"What! Father!" cried the young man who was stunned. "What! Lucile von Gansberg, this beautiful and chaste girl—"

"The thing is all arranged. You are to be wed within the month. Your honor has no objection to make against this union, I presume."

"Even in my solitude," said Everard, with lowered eyes, "I knew that Lucile von Gansberg is the most desirable partner and the most preferred match in all Germany."

"Well, Everard," the Count said, "I await your thanks. A pure woman, a spotless sword, these are fine presents which are certainly worth a thanks."

"Yes, Father, I thank you," Everard said as he kissed the hand that Maximilian extended to him. "Yes, you are the best and most provident of fathers. I do not know what terms to use to express all my gratitude, of which I am suffused; but I can not . . . I dare not . . . I could not love nor wed Lucile von Gansberg."

"Aha! Now I've got you, my young master," cried Count Maximilian in a terrible voice, rising from his chair. His eyes flamed. "Oh! Ah! You consummate hypocrite, you! You have finally fallen into my trap! I find you truly adorable. It was therefore not honor which hindered you from marrying the woman I destined for you, eh? It was not the woman but just the marriage which was repugnant to you. What is this great love affair you have been hiding beneath all this, if you please?"

What had been played as comedy was now turning toward drama.

Pale and trembling, Everard had not the strength to utter a single syllable. The Count laid a hand on his shoulder, a hand that seemed as heavy as lead, and in a sharp, imperious tone of voice said to him between his teeth:

"Listen, beloved son. Now I am not asking you. I am ordering you. I do not say: 'Wilt thou?' I say: 'I want.' The Prince has my word on it. The marriage has been announced. Were it not for my fifty years, I would do without you, stupid rebel. But I need somebody young. You are my son, so I take you. Oh! Not a word from you. For if I get to the bottom of your refusal and that very suspicion puts me into a fury, you had better take care! I am a man to fear when you push me to the limit.

"You want, I believe, to babble something. Shut up, I advise you, and keep your eyes lowered. Believe me, there are memories which exasperate me more than they frighten me. But truly I end up pitying you and fearing myself. Leave, and I will give you until tomorrow to think about it. Leave, I tell you, on the double. Tomorrow, please God that the night stands in as a good adviser to you; for, think about it, your injured father will be an implacable judge."

Pale and trembling, the Count pointed with his finger toward the door Everard should leave by. This man's wrath was truly hideous. He tapped with his feet. He shook with rage. Foam spurted from his open mouth.

Troubled by the sight of this terrible, towering rage, vanquished by the absolute power of paternity, and moreover convinced that he would gain nothing by a dumb and blind stubbornness, Everard left the room, staggering.

All that took place on Christmas Eve.

CHAPTER

XXII

Everard darted out of the castle and plunged into the forest. The night was cold but fine; the sky all blue, the wind very bitter. It had snowed each of the preceding days, and the earth seemed covered with a vast shroud. The pines alone detached their dark greenery from the sinister whiteness of the fields. Bareheaded, his hair all tangled, Everard plunged forward, panting, without purpose, without thought, feeling neither cold nor winter breeze. His instinct, rather than his reason, led him straight to the cottage; but it was going on midnight, and all was closed, all lights were out. Five or six times he made the rounds of it; but seeing that all seemed asleep, he ran to his grotto, and falling on his knees upon the threshold, he burst into tears, calling his mother.

"Mother," he cried as he wrung his hands in despair. "Mother, where are you? Do you know what they want to do with your son? Tell me. Do you know into what shame they want to drag him? Do you know what threats surround him? Will you let them work this dishonor or his ruination? You were here this morning, at this very place where I am crying, and you saw me drunk with joy. Do you disapprove of my happiness? It seemed not so to me, and yet never once have you spoken to me all the day long. It is true that, lost in my ecstasy or in my grief, I have not once called upon you; but I am calling you to come now, and so forgive me and reply to me."

Everard listened. All he heard was the thin whistling and the cracking of spruce branches in the cold; he stayed a few minutes without uttering a single word. One would have said that he was afraid to hear his own voice.

"Mother!" he began again softly, "you still say nothing, or if you are speaking in this mournful complaining of the winter wind, I don't hear you anymore, I don't understand you anymore. Are you disappointed with me because of my love? Are you turning away from me? Or else would it be that you have some terrible things to reveal to me, and would you prefer to be still? My God! My God! Could it be that the event of my life draws near?

"Are you not going to counsel me, then? I should perhaps do well to flee? What do you say? But perhaps it is already too late? Ah! Nothing! Nothing . . . ! Mother of mine, you are not answering me, not a word! And always with that this weeping wind! It is frightening. Alas! Have you withdrawn your love for the first time in my life? I feel that I am alone, and I tremble; is it God who has taken you far distant from me in order that I may be handed over to my fate or to my evil angel? Would you have died, you shade of my mother?"

And all continued to be silent except the glacial breath of the north wind, which ran bellowing from the hilltops down into the valleys. Everard began to shiver with cold and fright.

"Mercy from heaven!" he murmured in dejection, in a voice suffocating with sobs, "I am certain that my guardian angel is no longer at my side. What will happen tomorrow, then? What will the Count do? What shall I myself do? Ah! I should have left three years ago! But is there not still time for it? Yes, that's it. Let's go. Let's go rejoin Uncle Conrad: he is my only, he is my last, support.

He was your friend, my mother! Let us go. Let me fly from before my destiny."

And, completely disoriented, he stood up, starting to move as in flight.

"And Rosamund! Rosamund!" he cried. "I must see Rosamund again. In last analysis, she is my fiancée, she is my wife. Leave, leave without her . . . ! Oh! That is very cruel of you, Mother, to chastise me and to leave me alone here like this. . . . How I suffer! You used to pity me at the thought that I was to be the executioner; but, up until now, I am only the victim."

A more violent gust of wind, stronger than the others, so violent that it uprooted one of the old oak trees that towered with its shade over the grotto, seemed to respond to Everard's sobs and ended by striking him with terror. He spent the rest of the night alternating between fright and collapse, resignation and revolt. Sometimes he walked forward precipitously, then fell down sobbing; sometimes he threw himself down in despair, hiding his face on the ground, his teeth on the moss of the grotto. When the pale and late glow of dawn gilded the Taunus Mountain tops, he was whiter than the ground buried in snow, colder than the rocks clothed in ice. Whoever could have seen him then would have taken him for a ghost, so pale and icy cold was he. The fact is that all night long, despite his prayers, despite his pleas, despite his sobs, Albina had stayed mute.

The sun, a mournful December sun, a sun that was dying, cast across the dried trees its wan rays, and Everard, who was worn out, began to walk in the direction of the cottage. The only resolution he had taken was to see Rosamund and to ask her advice. He told himself, all right, that the best was to escape far from his father, out of Germany altogether, but he wanted to see Rosamund again.

As he walked, plunged deep in thought, he raised his head suddenly at the sound of the hunting horn and the barking of dogs; then, through the undergrowth, he made out the grooms, the pack, and last of all Maximilian on horseback and hunting. He had only time enough to jump a ditch and throw himself into a heavily forested area. As he continued his route, he thought he could make out, on several occasions, at the crossing of paths, one of the Count's valets, who seemed to be following him. But perhaps it was only a new illusion due to his delirium. It is certain that he was feverish.

He arrived at the forester's house in a state of exhausted panic. Alerted earlier in the morning, Jonathas had gone out, as was his duty, to accompany his master on the hunt. Everard found only Rosamund at home. The girl cried out when she saw her lover enter, so pale and near collapse. Then Everard told her all that had transpired at his second interview with his father. His recital was long, for twenty times he was unable even to speak and twenty other times he was choked with tears. Rosamund was, as always, sublime in her clear reasoning and in her devotion.

"Dear one," she told Everard, "if really Lucile von Gansberg were to have become your wife, I would say to you: 'Everard, Lucile is a noble girl. Obey your father, marry Lucile, and if you are not happy, at least you will remain noble and honored.' But this union with the Duchess of B. . . . is monstrous, Everard, and I have the duty to dissuade you, for it is not you and me alone whom Count von Eppstein wrongs here. He offends justice and God. He is your father, Everard. However, he has a soul full of violence, it is said, and tyranny. It would be wrong and dangerous to fight him. So the best course to take is assuredly for you to go far away. Do not trouble about me, Everard. I knew perfectly well that our dreams were only fancies and that unless the world were to crumble, I could never be your wife. No matter! I am yours and will never belong to anyone else. I shall stay here or elsewhere praying for you and loving you without hope. Without hope, for look at yourself. You are wealthy now. Now you are a Count, and your father, even if he would consent to a union between us, which is impossible, would find that I would refuse. I repeat to you, nevertheless, that all my life I shall be faithful to you as if I were your wife. As for you, Everard, go, be free. Remain great and good. Appease Count von Eppstein from a safe distance. Force him, by your good deeds, to pardon you, to name you his son, and, after that, forget, if you so desire, the poor girl who will never forget you."

"Rosamund, angel on earth, you are not abandoning me also! Not you!" cried Everard with tears in his eyes. "Speak. Oh! Keep speaking. May sweet, clement thought sink into my spirit with your words. Yes, I shall obey you, dear guide of my heart, and your last lesson will be no more lost than the others. I shall leave not to save myself but to save my father; for you see, Rosamund, you have recalled me to wisdom and clemency. My mother did not answer me last night. It is today the anniversary of Christmas, and I am afraid. I am afraid for him.

"I shall therefore run away before his danger, perhaps before his damnation."

"Everard, what do you mean?" asked Rosamund, worried at the alteration of the features of the young visionary.

"Nothing. Nothing," murmured Everard. "The dead *know.* The living remain *unknowing.* Let me leave quickly, Rosamund. Only one last kiss. Oh! Fear nothing. A sister's kiss. A kiss on the forehead. A kiss which I shall receive kneeling."

Everard knelt, and Rosamund, as was her custom after each lesson, placed a kiss on his forehead, a kiss as soft and chaste as her heart, a kiss accompanied by a sigh.

At that instant, behind the two lovely, pure youngsters, a sardonic chuckle could be heard. They turned around with a start and saw Count Maximilian standing on the doorsill, wearing his hunting costume, a whip in his hand, his gun in the other.

"Good. Very good," he said, saluting them ironically.

And after having tossed his whip and cap on the table, he stood his gun against the wall. Growing red in the face but standing motionless, Rosamund lowered her eyes and dared not take a step. As for Everard, he had thrown himself in front of her and with a proud and decisive look on his face, he defied the insolent, jeering sneer on the Count's face.

Slowly, Maximilian stripped off his gloves, whistling a hunting tune and rolling his mocking eyes over one and the other lover. Then he threw himself down in a chair and, nonchalantly crossing one leg over the other, began to talk.

"Here lies the clue to our enigma," he said, "and a very charming word it is, in truth. Here lies the reason for this spartan virtue. A perfectly darling and appetizing reason, too, I must admit!"

"My Lord," said Everard, "if your anger—"

"My anger?" the Count interrupted vivaciously. "Eh! Good Lord! Who's talking about my anger? It is truly a question of that. I am a gentleman, my Everard, and, in addition, a son of the eighteenth century. I have not yet even taken vows of celibacy, thank God! And a good dog has hunting in his blood. No, my children, no. I do not begrudge you. If I had you followed, Everard, it is because that was to my interest and not because I was trying to embarrass you, believe me. I have sent your father into town, on one pretext or another, my beauty, for he is not in the secret, I like to think it, and he could have spoiled your friendly interview. You see that I am not a tyrant. Only, I do not wish to be a dupe, and I do not understand that your little love affair—"

"Pardon, my lord, if I interrupt your words," said Everard firmly, "but there is a misunderstanding here which it is my duty to set straight. Condescend to grant me a minute of your attention, I beg you.

"You abandoned me in old Castle Eppstein, alone, without a guide, without a tutor, without support. I had to grow up as I could, like a forest tree. Were you my father? Was I your son? One would not have said so by your indifference, and I was going to say 'by your hatred.' One day you wrote me that I would have to renounce all pretensions to your love, as you renounced your rights over my obedience. Then, faithful to your resolve, you no more concerned yourself with me from then on than as if I were already dead or unworthy of you.

"A peasant teaches his son to read so he can learn the word of God. You never even inquired if I knew how to read. You left me idle, ignorant, a vagabond, and you went far away with your son Albert, the only son you loved, to win appointment, titles, and honors.

"Now, it has happened that your beloved son had been taken away from you by God, whose justice is often terrible. You then remembered the abandoned, because for your projects you needed an associate who was your son. You expected to find a loutish soul, a wild fellow, and you were to put him in shape to serve your schemes. You were surprised to see that a liberal education left you nothing to do, and you rejoiced not for me but because that advanced by a year or two the success of your manipulation. Well, do you know who taught me science, life, and God, who formed my heart and my mind, who replaced my absent father by lessons, my dead mother by counsel? Do you know, my lord?"

"My word, no," replied the Count. "You explained your solitude, but your master's name remained vague."

"Well, my lord, it is Rosamund right here. It is Rosamund, whom you almost insulted just now. It is this noble and pious girl who granted to your son the blessing of education which she received from my mother and who, day by day, hour by hour, patiently reviewed with me the rudiments of these studies. She made a man of your son, of whom you made something less that a cur. She raised me to dignity, to hope, to love. She prepared me for the rudest misfortune as for the highest destinies. Now insult her. Now!"

"You are eloquent, Everard," Maximilian said. "I perceive it with pleasure. However," he added with a snicker, "what results most clearly from the marvelous discourse you just poured out with so much fire is quite simply what I had conjectured myself from the first, which is to say, that this dear child instructed you. Eh! But that's very fine of her, and I could not be more grateful to her. However, I trust that in exchange for her lessons you gave her back some others. You are not untaught. So be it. But is she also inexperienced?"

Straight and stiff, Rosamund tried to answer, but her lips moved without articulating a single word. She stayed motionless and as pale as a statue.

"Heaven and earth! You persevere in your error," cried Everard indignantly.

Still mute, Rosamund raised her arms to heaven, in a sublime gesture.

"My lord, take care," Everard continued, and he was staggering with fury. "You have so long forgotten that you were my father that in my turn, God forgive me, I might, too, forget that I am your son."

"Oh, yessir, sir, shall we come to that?" said Maximilian, leaving off his insulting laugh to become suddenly lofty and serious. "That would be curious to see, in truth. Young man. Young man. Calm yourself, I advise you. Your boy's temper would blunt itself fast against my own. Contain your fury. That's more prudent of you. And let me finish with your Dulcinea, who, while not being a Duchess, still gives a close imitation of the same career, from what it appears to me, that you refused this morning."

"God in heaven!" cried Rosamund, who fell in a faint upon the tile floor.

"By all hell!" cried Everard, grabbing his sword, which he had left the evening before in the angle of the fireplace.

Then, half drawing it, he advanced upon the Count; but when he was two steps away from him, he halted and thrust his sword back into its scabbard:

"You gave me my life," he said. "We are quits."

On his side, Maximilian had thrown himself upon his gun, which he had cocked.

The father and son, at that hour, looked at each other with eyes aflame with rage, seeming not two men but two demons.

"I gave you your life, do you say? You are mistaken, wretch, for I gave you nothing, and you owe me nothing. Draw your sword, then. Our two rages have suffocated us, even mastered us. Let us go out in the fresh air, swords and angers . . . ! Ah! You retreat . . . ! Well, as for me, I shall not retreat."

He went toward the door and hailed four or five valets whom he had brought along with him.

"Seize that girl," he said, "fainted or not. Seize her and throw her off my property."

Everard placed himself in front of her and drew his sword.

"If one of you touches her, he is a dead man," he said.

Intimidated, the servants hesitated.

"Cowards! Advance, will you?" cried Maximilian, raising his whip.

They took a step forward, but Everard stopped them at the point of his sword.

"My lord," he said, "I declare to you that I, Everard von Eppstein, I shall follow this child wherever she goes, whether by choice or by force. Do you understand me?"

"Suit yourself," replied Maximilian. "Do what I commanded, you dunces," he continued, motioning to his servants.

"My lord," said Everard, placing the point of his sword on his fiancée's heart. She was still unconscious. "Rather than allow one of these men to touch Rosamund, I protest that I will kill her right before your eyes."

"Do it if the point is sharp enough," said the Count. "Ah! Ah! Are you still afraid? Take this woman away, or I myself will take care of her."

"My lord," cried Everard, "take care. I will defend her against the whole world."

"Even against your father?" said the Count as he advanced upon Everard, gun in hand.

"Even against the assassin of my mother," cried Everard, blinded by God knows what frenzy.

Carried away by the vertigo of anger, Maximilian picked up his rifle, took aim at his son, and fired.

"Mother, mother, take pity on him!" cried Everard as he fell.

Count Maximilian remained standing, his eyes fixed, cold and pale, as if thunderstruck; for he seemed to see, near the unconscious Rosamund and Everard, Albina and Conrad alive.

It was Conrad, indeed, who saw Maximilian in his strange hallucination. It was Conrad who, according to his promise, had come to visit the Eppstein family. He had entered just in time to push the gun away in his brother's hand and to save his nephew's life, making what would have been a fatal wound only a slight injury.

Coming to his senses, the Count saw him by his side. He first thought himself the pawn in a hideous dream and swept his unfocused eyes madly around him. He found he was in the same room, but alone with Conrad, all the others having withdrawn and the floor spotted with blood.

"Where is Everard?" said Maximilian with a shudder.

"Upstairs. Be reassured. Wounded only in the shoulder, and not seriously," replied Conrad.

"And Rosamund?"

"She has regained consciousness. She is taking care of Everard."

"But you . . . are you Conrad, Conrad changed and grown old like me? How do you happen to be there? What is that uniform of a French officer?"

"Yes, it is I who was Conrad! I am at present one of Napoleon's generals. I will tell you all about it when you are feeling better."

"And so you are alive! I wasn't dreaming! But the other one! The other!"

"Of whom do you speak, Maximilian?"

"Of her who was standing there beside Everard, one hand stretched out towards him as if to defend, one hand stretched out towards me as if to threaten."

"Who are you talking about?" Conrad repeated. He was worried.

"Oh! I recognized her," Maximilian continued, his eyes rolling in his head, a fierce expression on his face, his gaze implacable. "I recognized her, all right. I am condemned. Everard can say what he wants: 'Take pity on him, Mother!' I can expect no grace now."

"I don't know what your talk means," said Conrad. "Only Everard asked me to tell you that, for his part, he forgave you and would pray for you."

"What's the use? What's the use?" the Count repeated anxiously. "She was there, I tell you."

"Who? She?"

"She, the punishment, she, the expiation. She, Albina! But come, brother, come, and let us go out of here. Do you not hear this blood speaking and screaming for vengeance? Do you not see that I am drunk, drunk with murder and fright? Come! The air, it seems to me, will be good for me, the great, pure air of the fields! But perhaps my breath will corrupt it? Oh! I am damned!"

"Do you not wish to see Everard and give him back pardon for pardon?"

"No. No. I wish to see nobody. I am no longer a father, I am no more a man. I no longer belong to the earth but to hell. . . . And then, what difference would my pardon make? The pardon of a person accursed is an anathema! Come, Conrad. Let us go out-of-doors, I tell you."

Maximilian left the room and the house of Jonathas with his brother, who had difficulty keeping up with him.

He went bumping against stones and rough spots on the road, and, to see him run thus, his hair streaming in the wind, his eyes wild, you would have said that he fled before someone. He fled, in reality, before remorse, which always catches up with and outruns its target.

The two brothers soon arrived at Castle Eppstein, and Maximilian, always as if pursued, went to take refuge in the Red Chamber after having made the sign to Conrad to follow him. With a terrified look, he double-locked the door and drew the bolts shut.

"Now, here I am safely," he said as he fell into a chair. "Let's see, I am wide awake now. I can recognize who I am and recall myself to reason. But everything that has just happened to me, is it a terrible reality or else a vision in a feverish state?"

"Alas! All of it is only too certain," said Conrad.

"But you yourself bear witness for me. You are not a ghost, are you? Say."

"My life is a secret, but I am alive," said Conrad. "I was passing through Eppstein to keep a promise I made to Everard and to Jonathas. Luck or rather Providence brought me precisely on time to push away the barrel of your gun and spare you a crime. And what a crime? The murder of your own son!"

"Is it possible? Is it possible?" Maximilian babbled, back in his delirium again.

"Yes, and in order to save you from madness, brother, in order to bring you back to some notion of the truth, I will tell you willingly my dark story. We find each other again, moreover in so strange a moment, so terrible that all rules are confounded, and that I do not even believe I need to have you promise on your honor an inviolable silence. This mystery, without being an absolute necessity, has become a habit for me and like a need I have. I have lived so much outside accepted conventions that the motives which have directed my actions would be so badly understood and very falsely interpreted. The judgment of the people as a mass could so easily slander me and condemn me, from legitimate semblances of my conduct, that I prefer having only God as my judge, God, who sees inside my conscience the purity of my intent. And then I like this shadow where I hide because, having dissembled from others the first part of my life, I sometimes cannot myself even remember all these disguises."

Conrad launched into the recital of his stormy and sinister existence. He began soberly but ended it weeping. Maximilian lent him his rapt attention. Little by little, his face became serene and calm once more. From a cabinet he took a pitcher of water and spirits and drank two or three glasses, from time to time.

"Thanks, Conrad," he told his brother when the latter had ceased speaking. "Thanks to have brought me back to reality. Yes, although your story is very strange, although the man whom you chose as associate is miraculous, at least I found myself back once more, listening to you, among beings whom I know, who live and breathe. I was out of my mind a while ago, Conrad. I had some sort of mad visions, what sort I couldn't say, and some recurrence of childhood terrors, too. I think it must have been my anger which made me drunk. I spoke to you of Albina, of ghosts, of vengeance, did I not?"

"Actually, you did," said Conrad, who was surprised by this sudden return backward on Maximilian's part.

"My God," Maximilian resumed with his bitter smile on

his face, "can it be that the strongest minds sometimes have such moments of weakness and of error? To think that I, Maximilian von Eppstein, admitted to the council of the heir of Caesar, that I should have been able even for an instant to collapse under some old wives' tale! I must have amused you, brother."

"You made me sad, and I pitied you," said Conrad. "Your fury and your horror frightened me and threw me into consternation as much as your savage irony and your egotistical cold-bloodedness hurt and scandalize me even now."

"Oh, come on!" continued Maximilian, shaking his head, which was still loaded with dark thoughts and doubts. "Come on! One has to be a man and not get caught by visions. I was wrong to let myself get out of control with this anger, which was terrible, I admit, and I thank God and you, Conrad, for having saved me from murder. But, in truth, I was no longer master of myself. That insolent youth had heated my blood too hot. As a result, he got off cheap with a minor wound, did you say? That will serve him as a lesson and will better dispose him to obedience where I am concerned, I hope. As for the threats from a dead woman, as for my dreams where she has appeared to me, I am not so young nor so silly as to persist in believing such phantasms. And you, Conrad, who are a superior man, are of Napoleon's soldiers, you believe, like me, that these nightmares are vain and untrue, isn't that a fact?"

"Who knows?" said Conrad, deep in thought.

"How's that?" replied Maximilian. "Would you lend credence to ghosts and phantoms?"

"Jesus," said Conrad, "handed down a law to the living that they should pray for the dead. Why should the Bible of the departed not order them to watch over the living?"

"Be quiet. Be quiet," the Count cut in on him, all pale and shaking once more. "No! That can not be. All links are broken between death and life, I am sure of it. I want it to be so! Brother, brother, do not cast me back again into my panic and fear."

In one second and for one word, that man, who so recently bragged about having such a strong sense of logic, had become all over again more timorous and more shaken than a child or a woman. Even so, he made an effort, and raising his head, he managed to speak.

"And even if that should be," he said, "that when God chose the elect for Paradise, and guardian angels to stay on earth, would he have granted this marvelous gift to the damned? And I believe, I know, Conrad, I am certain, in spite of everything, that Albina is not worthy of heaven and that an adulterous woman would not be fit to protect anybody, not even a child, from her crime."

"Albina!" cried Conrad. "Is it of the pious, the chaste, the noble Albina that you dare speak in this manner?"

"Did you know her?" asked Maximilian.

"I was told . . . ," answered Conrad, embarrassed.

"Ah! You were told! Yes, she had a fine exterior of holiness, and she knew how to deceive people, the hypocrite! But to you, my brother, I am willing, I ought, to reveal her shamefulness. . . . Yes," pursued Maximilian, who grew heated and soon tended to rave. "Yes, finally I have a need now to justify myself by condemning her. And you are going to agree with me that I have been and am right, that I must face her threats, that she is a slut, that my tortured spirit has alone produced all my terrors, that my remorse was unjustified. Oh! I was just and I was not guilty; if my words killed her like a knife blade, then that's good for her. This Everard is not my son. He is the son of a Captain Jacques, may God damn him to hell!"

"Of a Captain Jacques!" cried Conrad, drawing back.

"Yes, a Frenchman, who was full of sweet, chivalrous affection for her, some mysterious adventurer whose real name she never wished to tell me, nor his history, either; some stranger she used in public to call her 'friend' and her 'brother.' "

"And who was really her brother and her friend, you miserable wretch!" said Conrad in a voice of thunder. "For this adventurer, this Frenchman, Captain Jacques, that was me. That was myself, Conrad von Eppstein, your brother and hers."

Maximilian rose as if shot out of his chair by a spring. He stayed on his feet, standing, stiff, and growing paler all the time.

"It was I," Conrad insisted, "who foolishly requested her to promise me discretion and silence, both of which that generous soul granted me all the way to the death. I therefore, along with you and like you, but at least involuntarily on my part, am her murderer. I am the one who also remained silent, even recently, about my first and fatal return here twenty years ago in order not to awaken your terrors. It is I who now cry to you at this present time that you killed an innocent woman. Brother, you will answer for this before God!"

Conrad stopped, for truly the collapse of Maximilian, of this man so energetic and so haughty, was terrible and pitiful. The Count was as pale as a corpse. You would have said that the hand of God weighed angrily upon his shoulders. It is only barely that he dared raise his eyes, which were filled with an inexpressible terror. He thought he could distinctly see at his side the avenging angel, sword in hand.

A long silence followed the last spoken words. Conrad did not feel enough strength in him to curse anymore. Maximilian kept whispering: "I am lost." Over and over he repeated these words, in hollow and lugubrious tones.

It was already 4:00 P.M., and darkness was falling fast. Huge black clouds, chased by the wind, were running across the sky, the pines cracked, the crows in cawing bands overhead circled the keeps of Castle Eppstein. Abruptly, Maximilian roused from his stupor.

"Get somebody! Let some people come . . . ! Why are we alone?" he yelled. "Conrad, order all the people in the castle to assemble in the grand hall downstairs. Have them light the torches and all the candles. Tell them to make music and a lot of noise. Make them stop me from seeing and from hearing!"

"You are saved and you repent," Conrad told him gently, because he was struck with commiseration, despite himself, for the other's frenzy.

"Do I repent . . . ? I am afraid," said Maximilian. "You understand, don't you, Conrad? Light! Noise . . . ! Can I stay here inside this chamber, inside the Red Chamber, underneath the nursery with its cradle, beside the staircase leading to the caves? Do you see nothing sinister in these red curtains that sway in the trembling flame of this lamp, in this fire that crackles, in this air even, and in this silence? Do you not see that there, upon my neck, lies the golden chain, last and fatal warning from my icy cold creditor? Do you forget that we are on Christmas Eve? Quick, then, some carols, some torches, a crowd . . . ! Or rather, let them order my vehicles and let my servants mount up. I want to leave this very instant for Vienna."

"Brother," said Conrad. "Why run away? Why surround yourself with valets? The best thing for you to do is to repent, since you do feel a salutary fear."

"Who says I feel fear?" cried Maximilian, straightening himself up suddenly. "Whoever does lies."

He fell back in his armchair, his fists clenched, his teeth pressed tight.

A strange struggle was being waged in him between shame and fright. The pride of Satan carried the day.

"The Eppsteins are not afraid!" he began again, laughing his head off, and his laughter resembled a loud hissing.

Conrad shook his head in pity, and it was his speechless pity that pushed Maximilian into rebellion.

"The Eppsteins are not afraid!" he continued, even more forcefully. "When alive, that woman trembled before me, and now that she is dead, do you suppose she could make me tremble? Not one bit. I defy her, her and her vengeance, and her rebellious son also!"

"Blasphemies . . . ?" cried Conrad in horror.

"Eh! No. Common sense. I believe in God. That's indispensable at the imperial Austrian court, but I do not believe in ghosts, by the devil! And the legend of this castle has always made me shrug my shoulders. Leave me. I wish to be alone. It is your reveries which made me so wild. One night when my nerves were irritated, I had a nightmare. That's not worth troubling about, for heaven's sake!"

"Ah! Maximilian," said Conrad. "I should prefer to see in you the terror which you now refuse to face rather than this sacrilegious gaiety."

"But what terror are you talking about? Are you the same idle dreamer you always were? It's you yourself, your sudden apparition, your humbug and your pity for my victim, that have addled your brain. But I fear nothing, do you understand, neither ghosts, nor the devil, and I am going to prove it to you. You shall go and leave me alone, and you shall go away, if you please, and, quick time, alert my Everard that he has to leave his Infanta here and that he is to prepare to follow me to Vienna to wait upon the Duchess."

"Brother, what are you thinking of? I am not going to leave you," said Conrad.

"Yes, you are, by hell! You will leave me because you exasperate me, finally. I am not a child which trembles and crouches down, and I intend to remain alone to send my instructions to Vienna and my acceptance in Everard's name."

"Take care, Maximilian," Conrad told him again.

"Take care yourself!" answered the Count as he

thumped his feet on the floor, "You ought to know that I have very little patience. I wish to stay alone," he repeated with the obstinacy of a madman. "I wish to remain alone!"

"Must we let God's justice be done?" Conrad asked himself.

"Will you get out!" Maximilian shouted.

"Yes, poor wretch! For were you to escape this night her who can go quickly, she, who goes slowly because she has all the patience of eternity, would recover you tomorrow."

"Hell!" Maximilian yelled again as he advanced upon his brother, his eyes flaming and his fists doubled.

But Conrad stopped him short by the calm and imposing stare of an honorable man who masters the irreverent.

"Farewell," he told him, shaking his hand with a bitter pity.

Slowly he went toward the door, opened it, and left.

"Good night!" Maximilian shouted as noisily he shot home the bolts on the door. "You see that I am offering the ghost a fair game because I am shutting myself up with it. Ah! Ah! Ah! Say there, if tomorrow I am not downstairs at eight, have the goodness to have my door burst in! Good night! And may the devil, who makes you shake with such a craven fear, accompany you, coward!"

Maximilian lacked the strength to utter another word. He fell to his knees, trembling, exhausted, livid.

Conrad, who was listening in the corridor, heard nothing more. He wanted to send one last farewell to his brother, but the words froze on his lips, too. He thought of mounting watch there on the threshold, but a greater power than his will drove him away. And he sensed the will of the Almighty pushing him outside. He made his way down the great staircase with tottering steps and went out to rejoin Everard at Jonathas's house.

CHAPTER

XXIII

Conrad, Everard, Rosamund, and Jonathas, all together, spent in the forester's house a sad night of insomnia, terrors, and tears.

Once the preliminary bandage had been applied to his wound, Everard wanted to get up. He was half lying on a chaise longue. Seated by his side, Conrad held his hand. Rosamund came and went, preparing a drink for the injured youth. Now and then, in a burst of thankfulness, she would fall on her knees and say a fervent prayer.

As for the good fellow Jonathas, whom these events, which he should have been able to foresee, at least in part, struck like a bolt of lightning, all he did was weep and choke back sobs during the whole of that wintry night of watching.

Among these four persons, united by the same anguishing thought, there were, during this endless night, silences that lasted hours. All they could hear was Jonathas crying, the regular striking of the wooden clock, and the wind that was raging outside, threatening to rip off the fragile roof of the house. Then exclamations, prayers, invocations to God, fell in the stillness of this mournful waiting and made it even more awful.

"Let us pray for him," said Conrad.

"Lord Jesus, have pity on him," responded Rosamund.

"Mother, pardon him," whispered Everard.

Midnight sounded. Conrad's question made them all shiver.

"Is he still living?" he asked.

"Alas! He is lost," replied Everard after a pause. "My mother always told me so, he must perish, if not by my hand, at least, because of me. I have not been his hangman. I am the ax. And yet my poor mother pitied him, but destiny has proved stronger than her. Everything has run together towards this predicted event, everything. Not only that which was impure and evil, like the Count's ambition and my brother's vices, which killed him, but what was good and holy, like Jonathas's trust and our consecrated love. Fate so ordained it. The terrible passions with which my father was possessed demanded their victim: He is lost!"

An hour later, Everard had more to say.

"What at this present time is taking place over there? What awful calamity awaits us? Dear God! We were so happy yesterday morning. We were enjoying such delightful dreams! And now what hope remains to us, and what is our life to be henceforth?"

"Let us pray," said Conrad and Rosamund, both at the same time.

The dawn, that sad December dawn, darker than a May night, was very slow to appear that particular day.

As soon as the palest glow gleamed on the windows of the bedroom, Conrad arose.

"I'm going up there," he said.

"We will all go," replied Everard.

No one made an objection. Everard leaned on his Uncle Conrad. Rosamund and Jonathas walked together, behind them. And all four took the path toward the castle.

Eight o'clock was ringing at the moment when they arrived in front of the great portal. The valets inside were just beginning to stir.

"Some one of you has seen Count von Eppstein since last night?" Conrad asked them.

"No," they replied. "The Count locked himself in his bedroom, forbidding anyone to disturb him."

"Has he rung for you this morning?" Conrad asked them. "I am Count Conrad, your master's brother, and here is his son Everard, whom you know. Follow us."

Followed by two or three servants, Conrad and Everard climbed the stairs to Maximilian's chamber. Rosamund and Jonathas remained downstairs. Having arrived before the bedroom door, Conrad and Everard exchanged a look that sent fear into the one and the other, so pale was each one.

Conrad rapped. No one answered. He rapped harder. Same silence. He called out in a soft voice first, then in a loud voice, then with despair. Everard and the Count's servants joined in. All fell into silence once more.

"Someone bring some crowbars," said Conrad.

The door was pried open.

The chamber was empty.

"We shall enter alone, Everard and I," said Conrad.

They entered, closed the door behind them, and looked about.

The bed was not undone. Nothing seemed disturbed. Only the secret door stood open.

Conrad took from the mantel a candle that was still burning. Then uncle and nephew plunged into the narrow passageway and descended the funereal staircase with slow steps. The gate to the crypt was open. So Everard, taking the light from his uncle's hand, led Conrad to his mother's tomb. The marble slab had been raised. The skeleton's hand extended from the sarcophagus, holding Count Maximilian strangled to death by two turns of the gold chain around his neck.

The next morning, after having performed the last honors to Count von Eppstein, Conrad, Rosamund, and Everard stood in a group, facing each other.

"Farewell," said Conrad. "I am going to go get myself killed for my Emperor."

"Farewell," said Rosamund. "I promised to be the bride of Our Lord or young Everard. I cannot be yours. I am returning to Holy Linden."

"Farewell," said Everard. "I will stay here and suffer."

Struck by a bullet in the heart, Conrad fell on the battlefield of Waterloo.

Rosamund, one year later, took holy vows in Vienna.

Everard lived alone at Eppstein, continuing to dwell in the Red Chamber where the terrible events we have been recounting took place.

The death of the soldier, the prayers of the virgin, the tears of the solitary man—were they sufficient to obtain grace for the murderer?

Afterword

1. Alexandre Dumas
2. *Castle Eppstein* and Gothic Fiction

Alexandre Dumas

A lexandre Dumas the Elder was born July 24, 1802, in the small lumber town of Villers-Cotterêts, which lies northeast of Paris, on an ancient invasion route between Germany and France. His hometown boasted a grand castle inhabited until the French Revolution by the Dukes of Orleans. Alexandre Dumas was the son of a Napoleonic general of the same name and the grandson of a black woman from Santo Domingo. The popular author was a very tall, very large man with brown skin, very curly black hair, and sparkling black eyes. He exuded charm, joviality, physical strength, generosity, and so much goodwill that he was known familiarly far beyond the frontiers of France. He was therefore one of the most photographed of writers, more widely represented by French artists probably than any other celebrity of his generation. He lies interred and respected in his hometown, which loudly claimed him and whose townspeople erected a splendid monument in his honor.

General Dumas had died when his son was only four years old, leaving his widow and son impoverished. From an early age the future author worked an eight-hour day, in an office. His penmanship supported his mother and himself, and he studied each night from 7:00 to 10:00 P.M. He and his mother removed to Paris in 1832 with fifty-three francs as entire fortune. Through the good offices of another Napoleonic general Maximilien Foy, Dumas was hired by the Duke of Orleans, the same "bourgeois" who was to become King of France Louis-Philippe. Dumas's boast was remembered: "I am going to live by my handwriting; but I promise you that I shall one day live by my pen." He purchased reams of sky-blue paper and became, perhaps, the world's most prolific author. Each evening he continued his studies, believing, as he says in *Castle Eppstein*, that education is the life of the soul. It cannot come too late into anyone's life.

Commencing in 1825, where he could find work as a writer, in the vaudeville, Dumas quickly transferred to the theater. Thus, he first discovered what was probably his own distinguishing talent: a genius for dialogue. Four years later, on February 11, he was to see produced his historical tragedy of Henry III. Dumas begged his patron the Duke of Orleans to attend the opening night, and he had them hold the curtain until 8:00 P.M., at which hour the Duke and his aristocratic friends finally entered their box. Dumas later told how in an hour or two he emerged from obscurity to become one of the most celebrated authors in all France. By himself he also had launched what was later to be recognized as a new and revolutionary school of literature: Romanticism. "From the third-act curtain my play was no longer a success," he recalled. "It was delirium." That he had copied his first masterpiece almost verbatim from Schiller's *Don Carlos* troubled him not at all.

Dumas also remembered the final inspiration that had launched his literary career. He used to study every night, he said, without really knowing why. Then one night he attended a presentation of Shakespeare's *Hamlet,* given by players from London:

Imagine a blind man whose sight was restored . . . discovering an entire world of which he had no idea; suppose Adam awakening after his creation. . . . Oh! That was what I was hunting for!

The influence of Shakespeare on the famous French Romantics is well-known, and his influence on writers of Gothic fiction is similarly well documented. The reader will see in Dumas's *Castle Eppstein* another, deeper influence also. Dumas's hero, Everard, compares himself personally to Hamlet, and in such psychic detail that one can justify transferring this identification to Dumas himself. He also had a ghostly father.

The Romantics came into power in 1830, following Dumas's initial triumph in the theater the year before, and that same year Dumas's Duke of Orleans became the bourgeois King Louis-Philippe. His July Monarchy (1830–48) rested upon principles that Dumas himself seems personally to have realized: education as a means of rising from the proletariat to the middle class, real estate as a second method for joining the wealthy middle class, violent revolution discarded as a means of progress, superior intuition recognized as a God-given sign of genius (i.e., Napoleon Bonaparte), laissez-faire economics hailed as the most perfect liberalism, and industrialization advocated as the most perfect form of production. Dumas personified some of these same middle-class beliefs: hard work, unremitting toil, the morality of success, worldly wisdom, antirevolutionary politics, mass production, the manipulation of public opinion, and the amassing of money.

Dumas turned to Germany and to German literature for his first tragedy and for *Castle Eppstein,* which is either his first or one of his three first prose romances. Madame de Staël in her works on literature from 1800 had championed the superiority of the "moderns" and specifically of such German moderns as Goethe and Schiller. Her extravagant praise of German culture established this image in the French mind, where it remained until France lay defeated by Germany in 1870. Significantly, that terrible French defeat in the Franco-Prussian War also marked the death year of Alexandre Dumas.

Castle Eppstein could reasonably stand as a textbook or classical example of Social Romanticism as inaugurated in French letters in 1829–30. The book lacks unity of genre, being at once Gothic, pastoral, developmental, and/or psychological. Individual scenes diverge also from the tragical to the historical to the anecdotal to the melodramatic and to the horrible. The language of the book is not learned but familiar. The syntax is loose rather than tightly structured, or periodic. The reader is conveyed from present time backward to the Middle Ages, then returned to the Napoleonic Wars of fictional time, where he is finally abandoned. A character from the proletariat intermarries with a member of the most ancient German nobility. Everywhere Dumas emphasizes the individual, seen as complicated, unique, worthy of attention, and dignified. Most characteristically, Dumas continually extends the domain of reason to other areas of knowing, preferring for his part the cloudy areas for which he lacks a complete ready-made vocabulary but even so perceived as dream states, hypnagogic reveries, the unconscious, quasi-divine intuition, and extrasensory perception.

Everyone has always recorded his amazement at the literary production of Balzac, who, like Sir Walter Scott, died largely from overwork: forty-five volumes. His productivity was easily surpassed by Victor Hugo, who lived to walk home into France with the starving, defeated survivors of the Franco-Prussian War: forty-eight volumes. The lady Aurore Dupin, Baroness Dudevant, who called herself George Sand, outdid Balzac and Hugo: 120 volumes. Their hard labor gives an idea of Alexandre Dumas's tireless, Herculean physique: 257 volumes. Older French critics had always looked down upon Dumas with great distaste. He was in no way an ordinary man. Gustave Lanson said he had the energy of a butcher, or of a cannibal.

Those were unkind words for a man who earned millions largely so he could spend them offering Lucullan banquets to all his friends and acquaintances. His son, who is the famous dramatist Alexandre Dumas *fils,* acknowledged for us the fact that his father really suffered acutely from racial discrimination. "My father," said the son, "was this big kid I had when I was a little boy. My father," he also tellingly revealed, "was the kind of man who would get up on the back of his own carriage and ride through the fashionable streets of Paris so people would exclaim: 'Oh! Look! Alexandre Dumas has his own Negro!' "

There were middle-class virtues Dumas scandalized the French by repudiating in his own lifetime: economy and thrift. Thus, he earned millions year after year, which he religiously spent on food, entertainment, travel, and the construction of his own, personal medieval castle. Not to be outdone by Horace Walpole or by Sir Walter Scott, from whom his *Castle Eppstein* to a marked degree derives, Dumas also personally felt the castle to be the symbolic center of his own life. That literary man who continued the often pseudomedieval adventure story according to his favorites, Scott and Dumas, was Robert Louis Stevenson, whose *Master of Ballantrae* also plumbs the depths of this significant symbol.

Another great admirer of Dumas was the English librarian of the British Museum, Richard Garnett, who compared Dumas to the great god Pan dining at the table of the Greek gods or to the Titans blasted from their mountain peaks by Zeus himself. Since literary admirers of Dumas are otherwise as scarce as hens' teeth, we should recall Garnett's expert assessment made in 1902. Here was this Dumas, said Garnett, a simple man with neither moral nor intellectual pretensions, self-educated, never classed by French critics as even a good author, mocked by British pundits, who could not believe he was being translated, and yet almost a hundred years after his death, still in possession of his old charm, power, and popularity—still a best-selling author. That galls.

His genius resided in his originality, in his innovations, decided Garnett. First he launched the Romantic revolution in the theater. Then first of the Romantics, he discovered not the novel but the romance of epic proportions. Imagine an author publishing simultaneously: *Castle Eppstein, The Count of Monte Cristo,* and *The Three Musketeers.* Then he followed by another couple hundred romances known or as unknown today as *Castle Eppstein.* To prose melodrama he added indiscrimately, as he wished, history, religion, panoramic landscapes, foreign lands and cultures, picturesque men and women characters, natural and logical plots of colossal proportions, the whole made real, gripping, and memorable. How many generations of breathless children have learned to read, heart in mouth, in order to discover the well-deserved fates of the Count of Monte Cristo's enemies and to see over and over again the "truncated mass" of the evil Lady de Winter fall into the mud of the riverbank. How many generations of youngsters have learned the French language because they secretly worshiped the fire, the vehemence, the exuberance, the passion, and the vigor of a French author who was, unbeknownst to them, also an American black man and whom the academic French, Professor Bédé excepted, held in such sovereign contempt.

Several other grudges put Dumas into his critics's black books—that he commercialized, industrialized his literary production, that he plagiarized, and that he maintained a novelistic workshop where he employed hack or ghost writers to assist him. The newspaper and the periodical came into prominence during Dumas's day, and he seized these means of selling his work serially and, incidentally, of reaching a wider public. Because of him, to no small degree, the prose romance and prose novel became the most successful literary form of the century. In this field nobody alive could hold a candle to Alexandre Dumas, who ranged around the world for his plots and characters.

Dumas took as his motto and subject everything he had, all he had read, seen, and learned. Opening his arms to the new reading public from the lower classes, he offered them everything: his scholarship, his money, his stories, his travels, his love of history, his hatred of evil men and women, his recipes for cooking, his travels, and his joy in living. His much admired travel books were translated by Alma Elizabeth Murch for Chilton Books in New York by 1962: *Adventures in Spain, Adventures in Algeria, Adventures in Switzerland, Adventures in Czarist Russia,* and *Adventures in Caucasia.* Eric Swenson had included a short story by Dumas in his *Pocket Book of Famous French Short Stories* (New York, 1947), Jean-Paul Sartre adapted Dumas's famous play *Kean* for the twentieth-century theater.

The last accusation against Dumas, that he showed little artistic conscience, must remain as a generally valid allegation. Most collaborators he hired produced little or nothing of and by themselves, however, it has been offered in his excuse. The two most famous, Gérard de Nerval and Théophile Gautier, pursued distinguished careers independently of whatever writing Dumas paid them to do. As readers will see in *Castle Eppstein,* Dumas is careless about such details as proper names, routes, and distances. Otherwise, his stamp remains clearly upon this work, which must have meant a great deal to him personally. The great compilator and specialist of Gothic fiction, Montague Summers recorded *Castle Eppstein* in his *A Gothic Bibliography* (London, undated), which Summers eventually had to have printed at his own expense.

Otherwise, *Castle Eppstein* has remained a lost book among several hundreds of Dumas's lost books. Several reasons come to mind to explain this cold shouldering of a wonderfully entertaining Gothic novel. First of all, the French Gothic novel was born in the unhealthy hands of the Marquis de Sade, of whose cruel sexuality Dumas is entirely innocent but tarnished by association. Second, the descriptive phrase "Gothic fiction," which tells us more or less what a book is about, does not exist in French. The French phrase is "black novel," *roman noir*. Those guilty of racial discrimination probably veered away from any *Castle* work by Dumas, admittedly a black man. Most of all, Dumas's *Castle Eppstein* was probably damned because its author confessed to all his borrowings, real and imaginary, after having been so roundly chastised for not having admitted plagiarizing Schiller and others. That Dumas cataloged so many of his sources shows weakness on his part and the timorousness of an unsure author inventing the new field of popular prose fiction.

The joke is that Dumas especially admitted the influence of Hoffmann and Bernardin de Saint-Pierre, whom he particularly had the good taste not to borrow from.

Most importantly, it would seem, French critics boycotted *Castle Eppstein* because, like all good Gothic fiction, it was about religion, an actual religious heresy of the Middle Ages, when aristocratic heretics shut themselves up in their castles, were beseiged, conquered, robbed, and put to death en masse. Religion was tabooed by Boileau in the seventeenth century, or henceforth in French letters reserved for theologians alone.

Castle Eppstein
and Gothic Fiction

C*astle Eppstein* is a full-length Gothic novel, as its title announces. Most of the action takes place, or rather unfolds sporadically through various centuries, at the castle itself, so that it becomes the central, authentic metaphor. This castle is haunted. In this castle crimes were once committed, and especially one murder, which remains unsolved and unavenged. The thirst for knowledge concerning this crime, but especially the thirst for revenge, may concern those who dare to enter its dark precincts. The central personage in all Gothic fiction is a young woman dressed in white, understood to be a White Goddess, or heretical priestess, symbolized in Dumas by her name Albina, which means ancient, white-robed officiant, and by white hawthorn blossoms. In Dumas she is doubled so that there are two such goddesses, called guardian angels, the one and the other: Albina and Rosamund. The young neophyte, or hero, of such fiction arms himself usually to avenge the ancient, unresolved crime perpetrated against his family at some earlier time. Here the young hero is Albina's son, Everard, he who sees himself as Hamlet, hesitant and undecided, haunted by an angelic ghost and a deadly mission.

Aside from the goddess herself, the chief character of Gothic novels is always the demon lover, the dark devil from the underworld who threatens, personifies evil, and who was once worshiped in the Far East, say some critics, as a vampire and bat god. His name here is Maximilian, and he is beset by anger, one of the seven deadly sins. He cannot understand why his victim has not sought revenge against him. By the end of Dumas's century Bram Stoker will have named this demon lover, or Don Juan from hell, by his most familiar name today, Dracula.

As often happens, the demonic hero symbolizes also the terrible modern times in which he lives, especially favored by authors being the Napoleonic Era. Dumas, too, chooses this period dominated by the bloodthirsty Napoleon, who was perhaps a genius at attracting followers but was most of all a murdering genius of predominant evil. His plague spread east from the western countries of Europe like cholera in Naples, nihilism in Russia, piracy in Denmark, and slaughter everywhere else.

Dumas recalls for us, and largely through the words of Napoleon's officer Conrad, how Napoleon managed from 1769 to 1821 his lifetime and his Wars of the First Empire, from his Egyptian campaign of 1798–99 to his crowning in 1804 to his series of victories: Austerlitz (1805), Iéna (1806), Eylau (1807), Friedland (1807), Eckmühl (1809), and Wagram (1809). By the end of his book, Dumas has skipped the disastrous Russian invasion of 1812 and told us how his character Conrad died at Waterloo (1815).

As frequently in other authors of Gothic fiction, the evil age of Napoleon is represented both directly, as here, and also symbolically. The thunder sounds like distant cannon fire, and the lightning flashes like artillery fire. Horses galloping though the dark forests recall not only the Hounds of Hell, or *maisnée hellequin,* of the Middle Ages, but also the hideous cavalry charges on all Napoleon's battlefields. The Gothic novel thus rings historically true, for men and women of those days of revolutions and wars lived through such terrors and monstrous cataclysms.

Quite fittingly, against this red world of men seen as bloodthirsty hunters and warriors, the central figure of the superior woman clad in white stands out prominently. The battle of the sexes is generally thought to have been engaged during the first French Revolution, which was led in some large part by women demanding equal rights. What they soon got was the horribly restrictive, highly punitive Napoleonic Code, still in force in France and which so shocked Balzac that he saw in it almost the end of any happy family life or any peaceful world to come. When Gothic fiction makes its Albinas, Amys, Emilys, and Lilys central to its structure, it acknowledges that women are the powder keg of this same Napoleonic and modern world.

The Gothic world of prose fiction revolves around such convolutions, the White Goddess herself having evolved from the Egyptian moon goddess Isis and from the Egyptian cult of the dead, which brings us back to Napoleon's Egyptian campaign. Dumas, too, employs ideas of cyclical time proceeding from the nineteenth century to the Enlightenment of the eighteenth, which brought about revolution by its close, and then moving backward again to the fourteenth century, when the Puritan (Catharist) heresy was stamped out in France by wholesale murder so that by 1330 it had gone underground. Who can say how it survived to resurface again fully clad as Gothic fiction?

Medieval also is October's Halloween, when ghosts return among the living by permission of the god of the dead and his bride Persephone. The castle then figures again as a mythological flat surface of the world, facing the four cardinal points: East=knowledge, West=land of the dead, North=hell and winter, and South=civilization. The medieval tetragonal castle can only be entered from the east, through its major portals. All heroic attempts to penetrate it from the other three sides end in disaster. Too far from the living and somewhat too near the dead, as Sir Walter Scott remarked of Glamis Castle in Scotland, the symbolic castle also serves metaphorically as an entrance into the underworld. It is meant to recall to mind the Albigensian Castle of Salvation after the terrible wholesale

murders of entire populations, called the Albigensian crusade of 1208. Thus, Edgar Allan Poe, who was Dumas's
contemporary and one of the world's acknowledged masters of the Gothic mode, said the terror within these por-
tentous black castles were not the terrors of Germany alone
but of the soul. It is no wonder that these ancient and
medieval accumulations of history and mythology resur-
faced after the Reign of Terror in France. Long before
Alexandre Dumas's nineteenth century, early pioneers in
the Gothic mode had known that daily life had again
become a hell on earth.

Renewed speculation concerning the Albigensian, or
Catharist, or Gnostic, heresy coincided in Paris with
Dumas's *Castle Eppstein.* He may even have known personally the authors of new books probing into secrets sup-
posedly lost to knowledge in 1330. The impetus to
uncover lost knowledge and to know arose surely from
that Napoleon made mad, like Dracula, with the blood of
millions.

According to arcane Gnostic imagery, the castle (or Poe's
House of Usher) represents the human body where the soul
is a stranger lost in a labyrinth, or lost in darkness, storm,
and cold in the dark forest of the world. To this lost
stranger a messenger, that is, the white priestess herself,
comes to awaken the sleeping soul. The messenger's name
in Greek is "angel," and she says (for here angels are female) that the soul has a maximum of three lifetimes during
which to learn to resist evil. This lesson in Dumas is explicit: Maximilian is the Satan or demonic lover from hell,
Albina and Rosamund are the angel messengers, and Everard is the soul lost in castle and forest. The soul awakens
in moonlight, or in the rays along which Albina has been
beamed into the castle, to be transported out of this hostile
world, or dark labyrinth. His long lapses into sleep and
silence periodically announce the messenger's arrival, silence being construed as the female principle. Thus, Albina

as the "Elect," silence as worship, the messenger's arrival, the various degrees to "Perfection," the laying on of hands, and the castle as holy center of the earth, all recall actual religious services outlawed by the Albigensian crusade of 1208.

Both Guillaume de Lorris and Jean de Meung, medieval authors of *The Romance of the Rose,* understood this symbolism, having been taught that great literature should be read on four descending levels: literal, allegorical, moral, and anagogical (mystical, spiritual). Both told us centuries ago that the castle was a square measuring 600 feet on each side: "foursquare in shape it stood" (Jean de Meung, vv. 3797–4508). It was surrounded by a curtain wall and a moat, rose into turrets and battlements, four corner towers, contained four portals and a massive round bailey or keep. War watched at the West gate, as in Dumas; Fear guarded the North, Shame barred the South gate; and Danger (Dracula, Satan) bore the key to the only accessible, or East, gate. Guillaume de Lorris (vv. 1279–1438) said the castle "enclosure was a perfect measured square" where "foreign trees" grew as in their native soil. His internal view specified lawns with deer browsing, brooks flowing, flowers, fruits, and Oriental spices perfuming the air, and the fountain of the suicidal Narcissus at the center of this demesnial park. In his elemental universe, air (wind, thunder) means the spirit, earth means labyrinth or path to salvation, fire means poetic energy and enthusiasm and faith, and rain, pool, river, and water generally point to death, or to the fate of Hamlet's Ophelia.

Amazingly, Dumas has incorporated much of this Gnostic symbolism into his novel, where he begins with a traveler lost in the dark forest, passing the flowers and cottage, which are signposts, and acceding to the dark castle within which lies his gnosis, or knowledge. As Robert Graves said so poetically in his *The White Goddess,* our traveler will know the castle as "a royal purgatory" where souls await resurrection. Here meet the three colors of ancient religion: black, red, and white.

Most interestingly, Dumas seems to have felt consciously that in writing *Castle Eppstein* he was treading upon such dangerous ground that he should resort to various stratagems in order to distance himself. His frequent citings of sources and his name droppings of famous authors constitute one way to relegate responsibility to them. More often than not, his references are invalid, such as his attempt to compare his young lovers, Everard and Rosamund, in their innocence, to the hole-in-corner, sick sexuality of *Paul et Virginie,* written by Rousseau's chum Bernardin de Saint-Pierre. On the other hand, Dumas fails to mention his own competition, writers of his decade such as Poe and Hawthorne. And yet the great poet Baudelaire was even then preparing, by translating Poe, to give him a second immortality. Dumas's most successful camouflage was the placing between himself and his text two secondary narrators. Thus, Count Elim, a tall, slender, blond nobleman (a man completely opposite to Dumas) wrote or narrated the introduction to *Castle Eppstein.* The body of the book, volumes I and II, chapters 1–23, was told to Count Elim by an unnamed German university professor, or tutor, from the city of Frankfort. Both primary and secondary narrators resemble Dumas not at all, except in his dreams, quite possibly.

Thus, by its complex structure, a frame within a frame, twice removed from the author, *Castle Eppstein* joins *The Count of Monte Cristo* as Dumas's most carefully designed, most literary fiction. As Albert Thibaudet pointed out first, this latter novel represents a new literary form, the "urban" novel analyzing three great commercial centers: Marseilles, Paris, and Rome. The actual movement of the story lies sandwiched between the deaths by drowning symbolized in the Mediterranean Sea:

Water—Mediterranean Sea—Island—Cave—Marseilles
↓
Paris
↓
Rome
↓
Paris
↓
Normandie
↓
Paris
↓
Marseilles—Cave—Island—Mediterranean Sea—Water.

The major themes of *The Count of Monte Cristo*, crime > revenge, and the major character of the demonic individual who stands above morality, are identical to those of *Castle Eppstein*. Both books keep as their background the career of Napoleon Bonaparte, since *The Count of Monte Cristo* starts in chapter 1 from February 24, 1815, or the Hundred Days from Elba to Waterloo. In both works, justice is a mockery, as seen by the high incidence of crime. In both works, society is in flux: (1) The proletariat moves upward into the bourgeoisie and aristocracy, (2) the new criterion is money, (3) fine people are ruined, (4) diplomats in positions of power are utterly corrupt (Villefort and Count von Eppstein), and (5) the "people" or proletariat are more or less bestial, particularly so in *The Count of Monte Cristo*. *Castle Eppstein* looks at the world more benignly than what probably was the later book. It is true that one cannot understand the abandonment of the Viennese heiress Albina to her murderous husband, Count Maximilian von Eppstein. But the oppression of women, and their degradation in a revolutionary society, strikes the reader more forcefully because it is made more explicit in the cases in *Monte Cristo:*

Valentine de Villefort (poisoned), Mercédès (sent to a convent, like Hamlet's Ophelia and Everard's Rosamund), Eugénie (a transvestite), Baroness Danglars (an illegitimate baby), and Haydee the Pasha's daughter (a slave). After his escape from prison and his symbolic death in the sea, Edmond Dantès, the heroic Count of Monte Cristo, over the next fourteen years becomes Providence itself, meting out death sentences to the guilty. Here Dumas has retold the Faust legend, or hero's bargain with Satan, but also the story of "Sinbad the Sailor" from *Arabian Nights,* a book he also claims in *Castle Eppstein.* Both novels demonstrate, in the person of the satanic or demon hero, Count Maximilian von Eppstein and the Count of Monte Cristo, the doctrine of a modern man's superabundant energy, of his personal power used to amass honor and wealth according to the tenets of laissez-faire economics. Dumas personally kept no money and distanced himself from such greedy men (crocodiles). Both books chronicle the rise of an unscrupulous man via education, money, and power to absolute power. It is Napoleon's "career open to talents" all over again.

The Gothic, whether in medieval architecture or in modern prose fiction, has been called by Rudolf Otto the most numinous of all types of art. Why? Because of its reach toward sublimity, its revival of primitive magic, its closeness to primeval experience, and its negative methods (darkness, voids, silence, vaults, forests, empty spaces, horizontal distances). The figure of the ghost also constitutes something numinous, something that does not exist, something that is other and beyond. It is a striking and memorable moment in *Castle Eppstein* when Everard's mother is seen with her *black* hair streaming over her shoulders.

A reconsideration of such extraordinary experiences in *Castle Eppstein* leads toward the conclusion that the book is, in final evaluation, both Gothic and largely autobiographical. Consciously and subconsciously, then, Dumas sets about distancing himself modestly. Young Everard's vision of his parents is the author's vision: a demon and a black-haired ghost. The self is seen as humble and exalted before such eternal parental power, a young child's view. The father is considered a veritable god of wrath and fury. The beloved mother is predestined to be elect, while Providence is understood as God's guidance, prescience, loving care, and direct intervention to protect the self.

The religious or prereligious facets of *Castle Eppstein* become obvious because clothed in auras of holiness, of dread, of nonrational, primal, and psychical emotions. *Castle Eppstein* is a magically holy place (like Roman sacred groves, like India, says Dumas). With an eerie shudder of the German Gothic *(Schauerromane),* the reader suspects some archaic worship of the dead. Ghosts here possess murderous power in defense of their sons. Mountains, clouds, the moon, the storm, and the howling winds are alive and instrumental in animating doom. Fairy tales sweep readers back to the Middle Ages, tales of the dead and the undead. The demonic dread of Dumas's last chapter is linked to ancient Arabia. The idea of the *pure* and *elect* and of the *impure* is numinous—and key words in Dumas. What was implicit became explicit: This place is haunted. "It spooks" in the Red Chamber.

Most critics of Dumas have quoted blindly the first person who blindly decided that this author knew nothing of, never used, psychology in his fiction. But even a quick glance uncovers the autobiographical basis for *Castle Eppstein.* The Dukes of Orleans in Dumas's native town became the Counts von Eppstein. The lumbermen Everard hides from in Eppstein Forest were more presumably those from whom the impoverished black child hid near Villers-Cotterêts. The Main River in Germany translates the French Aisne River. That castles lay in either case upon invasion routes from Germany to France remains established. In his personal myth the young Dumas was probably the fatherless youth Everard in his personal nobleman's grotto and domain. As the psychoanalyst Erik H. Erikson told us: ". . . imaginative fiction is to life what the sketch is to the picture as the conception to the statue."

Castle Eppstein deals on a personal level with adolescence, that last stage of childhood when the individual is faced with choices and a commitment to life. Everard, who is young Dumas, struggles to acquire a freedom of choice. He finally does not choose a military career. Despite his sorrow at "father-absence," despite lack of funds and a minimal education, he repudiated the world's evil image of himself. He chose to go to Vienna (Paris) and to retain or build his own castle. Once he had successfully negotiated his identity crisis, he was able to sit back and watch his unleashed mental energies fill up the blank pages of sky-blue paper.

The necessary vocabulary required by authors of "Gothic castle" fiction had already been collected between 1764 and 1844, and Dumas seems, like Sir Walter Scott writing *Kenilworth* (1821), to have drawn up a word list, although, as in Scott's case, he did not trouble with the abstruse technical terms of medieval castle building. The one key word that Dumas notably failed to apply to his Castle Eppstein was "ivy clad." Aside from this one omission, he had remembered more or less all those used by the most celebrated founders and continuators of "castle" fiction:

Horace Walpole	*The Castle of Otranto*	1764
Ann Ward Radcliffe	*The Mysteries of Udolpho*	1794

Mathew Gregory Lewis ("Monk" Lewis)	*The Monk* (Castle Lindenberg in Germany)	1795–96.
Jane Austen	*Northanger Abbey*	1818 (written 1797–98)
Sir Walter Scott	*Kenilworth*	1821
Edgar Allan Poe	*The Fall of the House of Usher*	1839
Alexandre Dumas	*Castle Eppstein*	1844
Jules Verne	*Le Château des Carpathes*	1892
Franz Kafka	*Das Schloss*	1926
Julien Gracq	*Au château d'Argol*	1938
Louis-Ferdinand Céline	*D'un château l'autre*	1957
	(Castle to Castle)	1968

Even had Dumas read Poe's *Fall of the House of Usher,* he might not have wanted to use such a poetic and archaic word as "tarn" in his castle-approach scene. He also avoided any trace of sexual symbolism such as that employed so effectively by Radcliffe in her long approach scene to Castle Udolpho. Compared to such French Romantics as Victor Hugo and Balzac, Dumas seems in this book to get by with a minimal vocabulary, which is at no spot either specialized or technical. Nor does he use any accumulations such as Hugo and Balzac dazzle the reader with, by a hundred botanical names appearing on an otherwise ordinary page and average day, for example. Dumas, in other words, wants to be read by young and old alike. Those who assign an author an IQ according to the size of his vocabulary are those who gave Dumas his no more than average score.

Dumas had read and had carefully studied either the masters we have listed or their many French disciples; he knew on every page, at each step along the celebrated morphology, exactly what he was doing. He had not read the very distinguished author and aesthetician Clara Reeve, whose *The Old English Baron* of 1777–78 had added an innovation much imitated by many subsequent practitioners: the first penetration into the castle by the hero, before whom alone the castle portals swing open, all by themselves. Unlike Jules Verne, Dumas also forgot to mention the east portal, or eastern approach by the hero. Otherwise, he comes close to Poe's "Fall of the House of Usher": his cosmopolitan touch, his French Revolution (Poe's epigraph from Béranger), the fall or winter season, the three colors (black, red, white), the tapestries, the vault, the music by Carl Maria von Weber, the books, the noble lady, the body in the coffin, the white robes, the storm at night, the male demon or vampire, the moonlight, the whirlwind, the iron grille or doors, and death by the lady's agency. Poe himself is the hero-observer and narrator, and so is Everard-Dumas.

Dumas's peculiar key word throughout this text is the adjective *sombre* (the English *somber,* the Spanish *sombrío*), which occurs with a maddening frequency because the word has no exact meaning but announces only a Romantic preoccupation with Chateaubriand's *clair-obscur,* the artist's *chiaroscuro.* In French, *sombre* may mean: not lighted (like the Red Chamber), or dark, brown, gray, obscure, shadowy, melancholy, taciturn, mournful, depressed, gloomy, or unsatisfactory. In English, the word was a notorious favorite with such "graveyard" poets as Shakespeare, Milton, Gray, Collins, Dyer, and Thomson, who set the mood for and inspired the first Gothic fiction. Fortunately, the vocabulary of English is by several millions of words so much larger than modern French, which has only a minuscule vocabulary, that the translator of adjectives particularly trips only over the embarrassment of riches.

Dumas himself wrote *Castle Eppstein,* in which his grammar, or disregard of classical French syntax, presents his translator with the one, serious problem. How to vary his serial sentences and clauses that commence *"C'est que . . . ,"* or *"Seulement . . ."*?

Such a difficulty is more than compensated for by his interpolated stories, such as Count Maximilian narrating the tale about Christmas Eve and the Countess von Eppstein. Compensation, too, comes from his wonderfully antithetical structure: dark-light, angel-demon, France-Germany, youth-age, cottage-castle, life-death, war-peace, physical injury-sleep, snow-stone, day-night. His principal theme of education, where Dumas becomes very defensive on the subject of Rosamund's accomplishments, is most interesting, and Flaubert doubtless took several lessons from it.

The most strikingly original scene in the book is the cruel Count Maximilian hunting and torturing animals. Dumas's stance is both humanitarian and antiaristocratic. Flaubert borrowed from him here also, and so did Turgenev for his *Hunting Sketches* (1852).

N. L. Goodric

Alexandre Dumas required only six years in Paris to become the most popular author in that capital, and the loudest champion of Romanticism. From 1829 he published a series of successful dramas and novels which swept him to fame and fortune. For most of his life he was the man of the hour.

Dumas particularly loved history, such as the newly discovered history of Gaul, medieval France, England, and Germany. For this reason, because all this was new and enchanting, he wrote *Castle Eppstein.* Riding the wave of his successes, he made of it another masterpiece.

He also wrote history and the historical novels which he adapted for the theater. His plays too were all hits. Even in his Gothic novel he keeps the reader informed about history, making it the back-drop before which his characters play out their lives. Because he was a genius in literature, Dumas also added something new: *tenderness* for the sad and gallant heroine.

After years have passed and the book is forgotten, the haunting picture of the girl–bride–mother remains fixed in the memory. The crime of her death casts the longest and darkest shadow over this Gothic castle.